the
far-off
land

Also by Rebecca Caudill

BARRIE & DAUGHTER

TREE OF FREEDOM

SUSAN CORNISH

DRAWINGS BY BRINTON TURKLE

the
far-off
land

BY REBECCA CAUDILL

NEW YORK · THE VIKING PRESS

JUV.
FICTION
CAU

Fic   1. US—History
       2. Kentucky

For

Burton and Mary Rogers

of Pine Mountain

Map based on the "Map of the Southern States of America

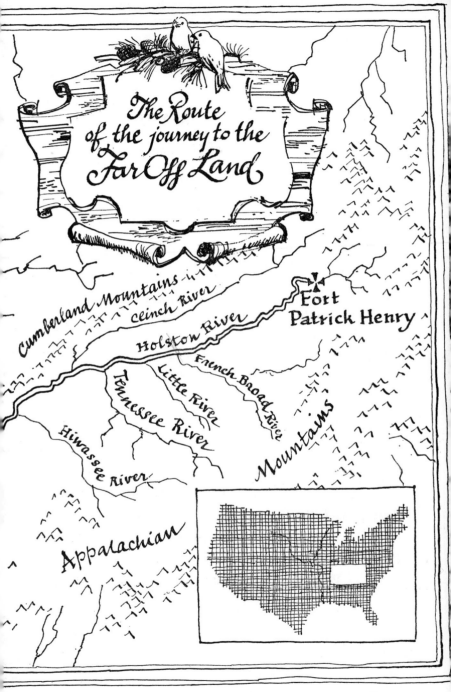

The Route
of the journey to the
Far Off Land

Cumberland Mountains

Clinch River

Holston River

Fort
Patrick Henry

French Broad River

Little River

Tennessee River

Hiwassee River

Mountains

Appalachian

published as the Act directs, London, January 10, 1795."

glossary

of German words

and phrases

Singstunde — song period, or hour of song

Saal — assembly room

Wenn ich mich fürchte, so hoffe ich auf dich. Ich will Gottes Wort rühmen; auf Gott will ich hoffen, und mich nicht fürchten; was sollte mir Fleisch thun?
What time I am afraid, I will trust in thee. In God I will praise his word, in God I have put my trust; I will not fear what flesh can do unto me. (PSALM 56: 3-4)

Gemeinhaus — village hall

Haube — bonnet

Holdselig Kindlein in Kripp und Windlein
"Sweet little child in cradle and breeze"

O Haupt, voll Blut und Wunden
O bleeding Head, so wounded (from hymn)

Was ist denn für den Kinder das Beste auf Erden?
What, then, is the best thing on earth for children?

I have learnt from experience that the established Authority of any government in America, and the policy of Government at home, are both insufficient to restrain the Americans. . . . They acquire no attachment to Place; But wandering about Seems engrafted in their Nature; and it is a weakness incident to it, that they Should for ever immagine the Lands further off, are Still better than those upon which they are already settled.

—*Lord Dunmore, Governor of Virginia, to the Earl of Dartmouth, Secretary of State for the Colonies Williamsburg, December 24, 1774.*

the
far-off
land

chapter 1

B Y THE light of honey-scented beeswax candles, Ketty Petrie redded up the kitchen of the Tavern in the Moravian town of Salem in North Carolina. Usually Sister Meyer waited about to see that kettles and long-handled skillets and wooden kneading bowls were in place and that the stone floor was swept clean; but that night, the twenty-fourth of February, 1780, a Thursday, Ketty worked alone.

The day in the Tavern had been hard, with all manner of folks coming and going from sunup to owl light. Militia-men, stopping at the Tavern in the early evening, had drunk and eaten like woods varmints. They were Tory-hunting, they had told Brother Meyer. Charge their meals to the public expense, they had told him. Then they had fallen to brawling over their spirits. When they had begun hurling their cups at one another's heads, Sister Meyer had taken to bed with a headache.

Ketty, having looked a last time about the kitchen to see that all was in readiness for the morning, was reaching to snuff a candle when a knocking at the front door of the Tavern startled her.

"Not more militiamen!" she said, and groaned.

She turned toward the door separating the kitchen from the publick room, where Brother Meyer was sweeping up pieces of broken redware. As she listened, a stillness settled on the publick room. Brother Meyer, she guessed, hoped the noise was a ghost of the night wind that would go riding away on the next blustery gust.

The knocking came again, louder, longer, saying bad-humoredly to whoever was inside, "Open up and be quick about it!" Ketty heard Brother Meyer prop his broom in a corner, scuff to the door, and open it. What she heard next made her glad. There were two voices and no more, Brother Meyer's and a traveler's. A body could always scrape together victuals to satisfy one empty-crawed traveler.

"It iss late for de supper," she heard Brother Meyer saying. He was tired and his voice was edgy.

"I don't want supper," the traveler said. "I want—"

"You vant lodging?"

"And fodder for my horse," said the traveler.

Ketty heard the click of the latch as the heavy door closed.

"But, first," said the traveler, "I want to know something. One solitary thing."

Ketty stooped and squinted through the keyhole. In the dimly lit publick room she could see a tall man wearing a linsey-woolsey hunting shirt, buckskin breeches, and stout shoepacks such as menfolk out of the West wore.

"Von ting? Vot iss dat?"

"I'm a-looking for somebody. For a girl named Ketturn Petrie. Is she here?"

Ketty clutched the doorjamb. For a second the room, like

14

the earth in Holy Writ, was void and without form. Not a sound was there, nor substance of anything, and the kitchen went as black as pitch.

"Vy you vant to know?" Ketty heard Brother Meyer asking as her senses came slowly to her.

"She's my sister."

"Your sister!" Brother Meyer scoffed. "Humph! Vot's your name?"

"Anson Petrie."

Ketty caught her breath. Goosebumps broke out on her arms.

"Vere you come from?" demanded Brother Meyer.

"The Back Country. Wataugy."

"I nefer hear Ketty Petrie say she has bruder," said Brother Meyer.

"Then she is here! I want to see her. Now."

Hastily Ketty tiptoed away from the door.

"Now? It iss late. Vy you hurry so?" asked Brother Meyer.

"Because I've wasted too much time already," said the traveler. "Snow piled so deep in the passes, couldn't no manner of critter get through till it melted down. And to crown that, I got sick in the lungs and had to lay up at a feller's house for a month."

"Vy you come here?" Brother Meyer demanded. Ketty knew he wore on his face the crafty look he wore when talking with the militia or with all manner of ruffians who had come to the Tavern lately asking for this and that and the best of both.

"To see my sister," said the traveler curtly, "on business that concerns nobody but me and her."

15

"So? Your business, vatefer it iss, vill vait till morning. Bring your horse to de stable. I feed him. Den I show you your bet."

Ketty waited until Brother Meyer had shown the traveler to the only empty bed, above the publick room.

"Brother Meyer, how—what—" she hurried toward him as he entered the kitchen, trying to ask in one question all the questions churning in her mind.

"You heard?" asked Brother Meyer.

Ketty nodded.

"Dis iss true? You haf bruder?"

"Yes," said Ketty. "And his name is Anson. But he went away fourteen years ago, when I was two. And nobody ever heard of him after that. What—what business do you suppose he wants with me, Brother Meyer?"

"De Elders vill hear his business," Brother Meyer told her. "Go to bet now."

On her cot in the room over the kitchen, Ketty lay in the dark, her mind a ferment of wonderings and rememberings and anxieties. She was awake at midnight when Brother Herbst's roosters routed the stillness of Salem with their shrill crowing. She was awake at two in the morning when Brother Nissen, the nightwatchman, trudging along Salem's streets, blew on his conch shell that all was well.

All was well, when uncertain dealings waited at the sunrise? The sound of the conch shell dimmed as Brother Nissen made his rounds on the other side of the square. All was well? Up and down the streets of Salem folk slept in peace, trusting in the Lord and Brother Nissen. The dangers of yesterday were past. With the sunrise would come together the dangers of the new day and the wisdom

16

to meet them. One need never fear, said the Moravians.

In latter years when war and burnings and pillaging went on all around them as if such were the natural way of life, and when every day they were threatened with high taxes and the taking of hated oaths, and the service of their young men in the army, a thing which they had vowed never to submit to, the Moravians said, over and over:

Wenn ich mich fürchte, so hoffe ich auf dich. Ich will Gottes Wort rühmen; auf Gott will ich hoffen, und mich nicht fürchten; was sollte mir Fleisch thun?

In the evening *Singstunde,* when the congregation, gathered in the *Saal,* chanted the words together in an affirmation of their faith, a body could feel fear crumbling under their rolling weight like the mighty walls of Jericho seven times encircled.

"What time I am afraid, I will trust in thee."

Once, twice, over and over, Ketty whispered the words. As cold spring water to a weary, dusty traveler, so were the words to her, slaking her fears and refreshing with confidence her anxious spirit. She pulled the covers about her shoulders and slept.

The shrill crowing of Brother Herbst's roosters and the urgent calling of Sister Meyer awakened her. Remembering that the day held uncertainties, she got up from her cot and dressed quickly.

She found Brother and Sister Meyer already in the kitchen.

"Brother Meyer," she began, "when—"

"Ven vill you see your bruder? Not till he talk mit de Elders."

During the busy early-morning hours Sister Meyer and

Ketty prepared victuals and Brother Meyer served them, waiting on the important guests in the gentlemen's room and the common folk in the publick room. As Ketty turned the corn cakes to be served with wild honey, she strained her ears for the sound of the voice she had heard the night before. But she could not single out one voice from the many voices mingling in the publick room. Nor could she peep through the keyhole. A body didn't peep through keyholes when Sister Meyer was in charge.

It was nine o'clock when finally Brother Meyer pushed open the door and called to Ketty in the kitchen, "De Elders talk mit your bruder. Dey talk mit you now."

Forgetting to ask leave of Sister Meyer, Ketty hastily drew her shawl about her shoulders, slipped out the back door, and hurried across the square to the big *Gemeinhaus*. There the Elders waited for her—Brother Bagge, Brother Marshall, and Brother Graff. As Ketty sat down in the chair Brother Bagge pointed out to her, facing the three most important personages in Salem, she felt as if the Judgment Day had come. She wanted to ask questions of them quickly, but a body would sooner ask questions of the angel Gabriel than of the Elders. The Elders spoke, and a body listened.

But the Elders were slow to speak, and Ketty's awe of them dwindled before her curiosity.

"You have—talked with my brother?" she asked, leaning forward in her chair.

"We only want to make sure that this man is your brother," said Brother Bagge kindly.

Ketty recollected that Brother Bagge had always been kind to her from the day, eight years before, when he had

18

found her and brought her to Salem. The tone of his voice dulled the sharp edges of her uneasiness.

"What do you know about such a brother?" asked Brother Marshall.

Ketty told them as much as she had told Brother Meyer the evening before. "What does he want with me?" she asked impatiently.

"How many children were in your family?" asked Brother Marshall.

"Seven," said Ketty, resigned to the fact that one did not hurry the Moravians. "Anson was the oldest and I was the baby."

"Where did you live before you came to Carolina?"

"Pennsylvania."

"Same story," said Brother Bagge. Brother Graff and Brother Marshall nodded their heads. "Do you recollect anything about the journey from Pennsylvania to Carolina?"

"Anson carried me on his back," Ketty said, rummaging through her memories. "That's what my mother told me."

"And Anson?" said Brother Marshall. "What happened to him?"

"I never heard what happened to him," said Ketty, "the beginning and the end of it, like you hear a story told."

The Elders waited.

"Sometimes," continued Ketty, "Mother let drop some little word of remembrance, or she norated some scrap of Anson's doings, and once in a great while Father did, but grudgingly, as if it hurt him mightily. One day I added up everything they'd said, the way you add a column of numbers, and the answer I got was what I think Anson did.

19

But I never knew if I had got the exact answer, and it was a thing you didn't ask Mother to add up for you to see if you had it right."

"Tell us your answer," said Brother Bagge.

Not only did the Moravians take their time, Ketty remembered. They were also thorough.

"In those days"—she spoke thoughtfully—"folks were hurrying West, just as they are now. One day three men heading West came by our house at sundown and asked Father for lodging. After Mother had fed them, they talked till their heads nodded, about the West and what they would find there—black, level land, and buffaloes, and thick canebrakes for their cattle, and wild game so plentiful a body'd never kill the last of it, and furs enough to make them as rich as the King of Spain. At sunup the next morning they left. That night Anson slipped off and followed them. He'd been moonstruck by their fair talk, Father said. And he was never heard from again."

The Elders nodded their heads solemnly.

"The same story," said Brother Graff.

"Do you know what your brother looks like?" asked Brother Marshall.

Ketty thought for a moment. "No," she said. "I do remember hearing Mother say the Petries had a mark and no one of us could desert without being found. We all had eyes alike."

The Elders looked at Ketty's eyes. "True enough," said Brother Marshall.

"True enough," said Brother Bagge and Brother Graff.

"One thing more," said Brother Marshall. "Your name—Ketturn. Where did you get your strange name?"

"That I know well from my Mother," said Ketty. "I was born on shipboard when the Petries were crossing the ocean sea to America from Scotland. Life had been hard in Scotland. But even so, my mother was homesick for Scottish lochs and glens, and the heather on the moors, and the rivers and the bens—even for the poor rocky earth that wouldn't yield up a decent living no matter how hard a body coaxed it. And she thought to herself, she'd keep a bit of Scotland with her as long as she lived. So she named me for the comeliest piece of all Scotland, Loch Ketturn. Loch Katrine folks call it nowadays. But Loch Ketturn was its old, old name. And Mother always liked old things."

The Elders looked at one another.

"The same story," said Brother Marshall. The others nodded.

"We're convinced this man is your brother, Ketty," said Brother Marshall. "So we're going to leave you now and let him talk to you. And, seeing as he is your blood brother, we'll agree to his plans."

chapter 2

WITH a tightness in her throat, Ketty watched the broad backs of the three Elders file out of the room. As the sound of heavy footsteps died away in the hall, she felt like a woods varmint trapped in a pitfall. Her heart pounded. Time passed.

At the scuffling sound of feet, she looked toward the door. In the doorway, his coonskin cap on his head, stood the tall backwoodsman out of the West who claimed he was Anson Petrie.

He strode lightly across the room. "Ketty—" He paused. "You are Ketty, ain't you? I been a long time a-finding you."

As he stood in front of her, searching her face, Ketty remembered to look at his eyes. True enough, they were like her own, blue as chicory, warmly flecked with amber, set wide apart. His hair, too, was like hers—the rich, tawny color of ripened broomsedge. He looked older, though, than his years. His face was tanned and leathered, and there was a squint around his eyes as if all the long years he'd been away he'd been staring into the sunset in the hope of finding a pass through the high mountains.

"How did you know to look for me here," Ketty asked him, aloof, "after all this time?"

He dropped into one of the chairs facing Ketty and drew a deep breath. He took his cap from his head and hung it on his knee. "Fourteen years it's been, Ketty," he said. "Fourteen long years. I was a-building me a flatboat to go down the rivers, and one day a stranger come into the fort—that's Fort Patrick Henry on the Holston. He was looking for passage."

Anson's back-country speech fell awkwardly on Ketty's ears, marking him for a stranger even though a brother.

"We fell to talking 'bout Caroliny," continued Anson. "Just the name made me sudden homesick, Ketty, homesicker than I'd ever been the whole enduring time since I'd left. It set me craving for something a body couldn't name. Something I couldn't explain to nobody and nothing at hand would cure. All at once I was the prodigal son in the Good Book, and I says to myself, I says, 'Before the West claims me body and soul, I've got to go back to my father's house.'"

He paused and sighed.

"But when I finally found the house," he continued, "no father come a-running out to welcome me. Strangers live in the house now—strangers who hadn't any notion of what had happened to the Petries. So I set out inquiring of the neighbors. But most of the neighbors have moved away, this here war being so hard and scattering on 'em, and folks being restless and all. All I could learn was hearsay—that Mother and Father are both dead, that something or other happened to all our brothers and sisters, and that somebody had taken you away to live in this place. Can

23

that be the gospel, Ketty—they're all gone but you?"

"It's the truth," said Ketty.

Anson turned his coonskin cap in his fingers and bit his lip. "What happened?" he asked when he could trust his voice.

"Haven't you heard anything, Anson?" asked Ketty, leaning forward, wondering what distance could have put him beyond the reach of so much that concerned him.

"Nary a word," he said. "Tell me about Mother."

Ketty sifted the happenings since Anson had slipped out on the night fourteen years before and had followed the fair-talking strangers into the West. Slowly a shadowy name and a shadowy brother took on flesh and blood and became a fair firstborn son, beloved by his mother beyond all understanding.

"It all comes to me as clear as dew now, Anson," she said, her standoffishness gone. "Everything falls into place, the comings and the goings and the long watches. From the night you ran away to the end of her days, Mother never knew what it was to rest and be still, like it says in Holy Writ. Day in and day out, she tried to find you or to get some word of you. Every traveler she saw on the road coming out of the West, she hurried out to ask him had he seen her firstborn, or did he know your whereabouts. If she chanced to hear of a traveler stopping for the night at somebody else's house, she saddled a horse and rode to see if she could hear any word of you. But nobody had word."

"I always meant to come back," said Anson, shaking his head regretfully. "But the West—it's a wraithy thing, Ketty, part rich level land and part notion, always a-motioning to a body to climb the steep mountains that wall it off and

24

come closer." He paused. "You haven't said what happened to Mother. And Father—what happened to Father?"

"Father went first," Ketty told him. "It fair knocked the breath out of a body, Anson, to see him well and strong one minute and the next minute crushed to death by a tree he was chopping down."

"Father? And him the best axman in Caroliny?"

"He didn't make the proper allowance, Mother said, because his mind was someplace else. He didn't work at finding you the way Mother did. He brooded instead. Maybe Mother's way was better. Remember how Mother used to sing to us, Anson? All those songs she'd sung in Scotland? She never stopped singing, though maybe she sang to bolster up her sagging hopes."

Again Anson shook his head. "I wish I'd 'a' knowed," he said.

"Mother had hardly got Father buried," Ketty said, taking up her story again, "when she had to send for the neighbors to dig graves, one at a time, for all five of the children between you and me. First Andrew, and then Calmes and Rhea and Letitia and Campbell."

"All of 'em, Ketty?" Anson covered his eyes with his hand.

"They got sick with the throat distemper and died close together," Ketty explained. "All in one December. With you gone nobody knew where, Mother had only me left. The neighbors tried to persuade her to live with one of them. It wasn't safe for a woman to live by her lonesome, they said. But Mother wouldn't leave the home place. You'd come back someday, she said, and you'd be disappointed not to find her home. Nights after I'd gone to bed, I'd hear her quoting verses out of the Psalms. 'Be still and know that I am God.' 'My help cometh from the Lord, who made heaven and earth.' 'He that keepeth thee will not slumber.' And ever so many others. And I'd lie still in the dark beside her and whisper them after her till I'd learned them by heart."

She paused a minute. "Do you remember, when you were a boy at home, Anson," she asked, "how cool and fresh the little pine-scented winds felt when they blew over your body on hot summer nights? Saying the verses after Mother felt like that."

"Go on," said Anson. "Tell me ever'thing."

"You'd think, Anson, that when Mother had parted with six of her children, five deep in their bury holes and one gone off into silence, she'd have parted with her senses too. But it seems like sorrow only tendered her heart till she looked on all people as her children. She never turned anybody away from our door hungry—Tories nor ragged militia nor Indians. Whoever tramped by asking for a bite of hoecake, Mother invited him to come in and sit at the table proper and eat. And she served every man of them just as if he had been you come home at last."

"Not red men, Ketty! Not skulking, thieving red men!"

Ketty nodded her head. "At one time lots of red men were roaming through, mostly at night, and folks were afraid and barred their doors and slept with rifles handy. But Mother had no rifle. You had taken it away. More than that, she left her latchstring out. And every evening at owl light she'd fix up a basket of victuals and send me to hang it on the stable door within easy reach of anybody passing by."

"Whatever did Mother do that for?"

"Because, no matter what business they were bent on, they were hungry, Mother said. And every morning I'd find the basket empty."

"And the red men—they never harmed you?"

"They did mischief some places. They stole horses and killed cattle and robbed corn patches of roasting ears. But they never harmed us. And then," Ketty continued, "one fall, eight years ago it was, Mother sickened and died. A neighbor took me in, but she had eight children already, and I was one too many. One day Brother Bagge drove by in his wagon on his way from Cross Creek and stopped for a drink of water. When he heard my story, he said if I'd come along with him to Salem the Moravians would raise me. So I came. I was eight years old then."

"These Moravians have been good to you, I can see," said Anson. "Seems like I never feasted my eyes on a comelier lass. You're like Mother, Ketty. And you're different from the back country."

Anson looked affectionately at his sister. Ribbons the bright red color of cherries laced the front of her gray linen peplumed garment. Long sleeves, gray linen to her elbows, white linen, fully gathered, below, reached to her hands, and a tight-fitting waist revealed a slim, supple figure. A long white apron covered her full skirt, and a white crocheted reticule hung from her apron band. Her small snowy-white *Haube* tied under her chin with ribbons to match those in her waist sat far enough back on her head to show off her tawny hair that hung in two thick braids down her back.

"The Moravians are good to everybody," Ketty told him,

dismissing his praise lightly. "But—it was hard at first, Anson. Listening to their German all day long was like being locked outside a house when you're desperate to get in. Sister Oesterlein—she was my teacher—she seemed to know I was homesick. She always spoke English to me. Of course I learned German too, but I never quite got over the feeling that I was a Scotch Petrie among German Meyers and Voglers and Bagges and Schmidts and Hackewälders and Bibighauses and Kuhnasts."

"This teacher of yours—have you been to school?" asked Anson, his eyes bright with admiration.

"All Moravian children go to school," said Ketty.

"And can you read and write? And cipher?"

Ketty nodded.

"I think it's the Lord's doings that that feller from Caroliny come along," Anson declared. "Like I said, that fit of homesickness hit me like forked lightning, and I says to Tish, I says, 'I've got to go.' And now, finding you so comely, and being able to read and all—"

Ketty's eyes narrowed. "Who's Tish?" she asked.

"My wife," said Anson. "Three young uns we got, two lassies and a fine lad."

This knowledge brought Ketty's mind sharply to the present.

"What is your plan for me the Elders have agreed to?" she asked.

Anson beamed at her. "You're going to leave Salem," he announced.

"Leave Salem? Where am I going?"

Anson laughed lightly. "Here I been so busy listening to

you I plumb forgot my real business," he declared. "You recollect I told you I was a-building me a boat. Me and my family, we're about to set out along with upwards of three hundred others to take up land in a far-off place way to the west of the mountains. The French Lick, it's called. We're going down the rivers in flatboats. You're going with us. And we'll have to make haste, seeing as how I've lost so much time. Left Fort Patrick Henry early in December and figured I'd be a week at most a-coming and another week a-going. That way I'd 'a' been back by the time the party set out. But it stands to reason this here plague-take-it winter took a hand in their schemes too and froze 'em in solid. I figure we can get there before they leave the fort, but we'll have to hurry. How soon can you be ready?"

Ketty swallowed hard.

"What else—did the Elders say anything else?" she asked.

"Nary a thing. They said, seeing as I was your blood brother, I had a right to claim you."

Ketty tapped nervously on her chair. "Tell me about Tish," she said.

"Tish—well, you see," said Anson, picking his words carefully, "it's thisaway in Wataugy where I been living, Ketty. It ain't like your Salem. It's a wild wilderness land. Oh, don't get me wrong," he cautioned. "We ain't backwoodsy nor nothing like that. We got a government. And we have all-day preaching when a preacher feller happens along. At the mouth of Reedy—that's just below Fort Patrick Henry —we got a fine mill, and as fine ironworks as you'll see anywhere, and a nail factory. At the fort, so many boats being built there now, it's as busy as Fort Pitt, folks say, or some boatbuilding town on the seaboard. But schools now—we don't have schools like your Salem school. Tish, she's never had much chance. She can't read nor write."

"Why haven't you taught her?" Ketty asked.

"I been a-meaning to, ever since we was married," said Anson, "but with the young uns coming and all—"

"Can your children read?" asked Ketty.

"Young uns can't read neither," said Anson. "I'm afraid you don't understand quite how it is in the wilderness, Sister. No schools. No books like at Salem. Hardly ever a spelling book even. No newspapers, less'n some traveler passes that way with one in his saddlebags. The preacher, when he comes, of course he brings a Bible. But he don't leave it behind. What learning a young un gets he gets at his mother's knee. But when there ain't any books, and when his ma don't know book-learning the way you've been taught—"

"You could have taught your children to read, Anson," Ketty told him accusingly.

"Now when we get to the French Lick," said Anson, paying her no mind, "things'll be different. They'll be a sight better. That's why we're going. Once we get settled in, we'll build us fine houses, and a Presbyterian meeting house to go to meeting in ever' Sunday, and a school for our young uns. And I'm a-thinking, who's there better to teach the school than you? But here we sit, our tongues wagging like clatterbones, when we ought to be stirring our stumps." He got quickly to his feet. "We got no time to waste. Besides, I borrowed my horse from a Holston farmer. He'll be needing him to do the spring plowing. You save the rest of your questions till we start out."

30

Ketty, too, got to her feet, her mind filled with questions to ask the Elders, questions to ask Brother and Sister Meyer —Sister Meyer wouldn't take kindly to her leaving, she sensed—questions to ask of anybody who had the answers. But questioning, she remembered, was not a Moravian custom. Among the Moravians what could not be settled by the Elders was settled once and for all by the drawing of the lot. In either case one obeyed and held one's peace forever after.

"Get your things together right away," Anson directed as he followed her out of the door of the *Gemeinhaus.* "We mought be able to set out as soon as we eat."

"Sister Meyer will likely say when I'm to leave," Ketty told him. "I'll go to the Tavern now and tell her."

Sister Meyer, Ketty learned, had already been told by the Elders. And, as Ketty had suspected, she didn't take kindly to the telling. Here a body had spent eight years bringing up a girl, only to have her up and leave, Sister Meyer complained, when the Tavern was overrun with guests day in, day out. Who was this brother turning up from the backwoods, and what were the Elders thinking about? Ketty could leave at sunup the next day, and not before.

As Sister Meyer complained, she found endless jobs for Ketty to do, and Ketty, obediently if not willingly, did them, her mind all the while divided between the life she knew and the unknown life that lay ahead of her. It was only in the middle of the afternoon that Sister Meyer allowed her time to leave the kitchen and get together the few belongings she was taking with her. After that there was water to be brought from the cistern in the Square, cups to be fetched from Brother Aust's kiln to replace those the militia had broken the night before—"Tell Bruder Aust he needn't bodder to send dem cups decorated mit dem fancy flowers"—the tables to set, and supper to cook.

When finally the supper dishes were washed and light still lingered in the sky, Ketty grew bold and asked Sister Meyer if she might go across the Square to say good-by to Sister Oesterlein.

Were the buckets full of water? Were the dishes stacked neatly on the shelves? The kettles and the skillets—were they all in place? A body never knew nowadays who was apt to come riding up to the Tavern, wanting hot victuals in a hurry. Were the covers on all the beds turned back? Were no militia quartered in the Square? None at all? And no officers hanging about? Very well, then. But be back before dark caught her. The Elders, Sister Meyer said, would be thumbing off the rules to her if Ketty was out of the Tavern alone, in the dark, even though she was leaving Salem the next morning forever.

Staying to hear no more, Ketty walked rapidly across the Square, since running would have been improper, hurried up the stone steps of the *Gemeinhaus*, and down the hall to the schoolroom where a candle glowed.

"Ketty!" exclaimed Sister Oesterlein at sight of her. "Did Sister Meyer say you might come? This late?"

Ketty nodded her head. "Have you—heard?" she asked, breathing hard.

"Yes, Ketty. Brother Bagge told me. I was coming over to say good-by when I thought you'd finished your work in the Tavern."

Ketty slumped on a bench in front of Sister Oesterlein.

32

"I can't stay—long," she said. "Sister Meyer is timing me against the dark."

"When are you leaving?"

"At sunup. My brother's in a swivet to be off."

"I'll walk back across the Square with you," said Sister Oesterlein, "and explain to Sister Meyer. Don't be anxious."

That was it, thought Ketty. In that room she had not only learned to read and write. In that room too, under the sound of Sister Oesterlein's voice, often with Sister Oesterlein's arm protectingly about her shoulders, she had outgrown the loneliness that had engulfed her in the beginning, and had learned not to be anxious about the happenings of today or tomorrow. Now she had come a last time, not only to say good-by, she realized, but in the hope that Sister Oesterlein would help her blaze a trail through the wonderings and questionings and stirrings, through the fears and the fancies that had gathered and mounted during the day.

"It's like everything was turned inside out," she confided to Sister Oesterlein. "Here I was, with all my life spread out before me, marked as plain as the streets in Salem. I'd live forever in Salem. I'd be baptized by Brother Marshall, and soon I'd leave the Tavern and come to live with the Single Sisters and pin up my hair, and wear pink ribbons instead of red. Then one day the Elders would draw the lot and pick a husband for me—I've always hoped, Sister Oesterlein, they'd pick one I wanted—and I'd be married and wear blue ribbons instead of pink. And I'd have my own little house, and—" She spread her hands in a gesture of helplessness. "And now," she continued, "my brother comes riding up to the Tavern and says I should go with

33

him to the far-off land in the West. And, just because he's my brother, Brother Bagge and Brother Marshall and Brother Graff, and even Brother Meyer—they all say I must go with him."

"We Moravians are obedient to those in authority over us," Sister Oesterlein reminded her quietly.

"But my brother is like any other stranger that comes asking lodging at the Tavern," complained Ketty. "He hasn't seen me since I was two. Now the Elders say I must go with him. They don't ask me if I'd like to go. They don't even draw the lot. They just say, 'Go,' and I have to go."

"They draw the lot, Ketty, only when the direction isn't clear," explained Sister Oesterlein. "But in your case the direction is clear. God has set man in families to be protected and cared for. And now, when your brother comes wanting to protect and care for you, what could the Elders decide but that you should go with him?"

Ketty nervously fingered the ribbons in her waist.

"I hardly know my brother," she said. "From now on is he going to decide everything for me? The way Brother Meyer and the Elders have decided everything up to now?"

Sister Oesterlein studied her anxious face. "I imagine your brother, being older than you and now your guardian, will expect you to do as he says," she told Ketty.

"But suppose a time comes when I don't want to do as he says?"

For a moment Sister Oesterlein looked out the window at the dusky square. "In that case, Ketty," she said as she turned back with a knowing smile on her face, "you can do as you please."

"How will I know if I'm doing right?" asked Ketty.

34

"I'll give you two rules to follow," Sister Oesterlein told her. "They're the rules you followed every day in school. First, be present."

"Be present, Sister Oesterlein?" Ketty's eyelids narrowed.

"Every morning when I called the roll, you answered, 'Present.' Remember? As you go into the far-off land, Ketty, every person crossing your path will call to you. He may not call so you can hear. But he will call just the same because he needs somebody to listen to him—to understand him, to speak to him in a friendly voice, to care about him, maybe to laugh with him. So, when people cross your path, and when voices speak, whether or not you hear the voices, be present."

"How can I be present if I don't know what a body needs?" asked Ketty.

"By loving people, Ketty, you will come to understand their needs. By loving and caring about people—all people. See people as we Moravians see them—not as friends or enemies, but as people, red people and black people as well as white, Tories as well as patriots, the gentleman's slave as well as the gentleman. If love goes with you through the wilderness, Ketty, you needn't be afraid. There isn't any evil in the world that won't give ground before a loving woman."

"Be present," murmured Ketty, trying to plumb the depths of the words.

"And do you remember how we began every day with reverence?" asked Sister Oesterlein. "The second rule is, be reverent. Reverence God and all that He has created. Especially reverence life, Ketty—all life. Reverence and enjoy the lovely things of earth—wind in wheat fields, cu-

35

cumber vines in bloom, the smell of scythed hay in wind-rows, the noise of thunder, and the stillness of the snow. Whatever falls to your lot, lean times or times of plenty, if you care about people and walk reverently, Ketty, you will be doing right. And you can make any far-off land a good land."

"You mean—from now on it's my life?"

Sister Oesterlein smiled. "You can make it so," she said. She studied Ketty's face closely.

"If you were staying in Salem, Ketty," she said, "you'd wait a bit longer to announce that you have become a woman. But where you're going you'll need to be a woman from the first day. Wait a minute."

Sister Oesterlein hurried from the room. Soon she returned, carrying a long length of pink ribbon and six tortoise-shell hairpins.

"Unlace the ribbons in your bodice and untie your *Haube*," she ordered. Then she chuckled. "Won't Sister Meyer be surprised to see you come back to the Tavern a woman?"

Quickly Sister Oesterlein exchanged the red ribbons of the girl for the pink ribbons of a woman. Then she caught up Ketty's long braids, wound them about Ketty's head, and pinned them in place.

"How does that feel?" she asked.

Ketty felt the circle of braids with her fingers.

"Like a crown," she said.

"And you wear it as a sign that you're ruling yourself," said Sister Oesterlein, tying the ribbons of Ketty's *Haube* under her chin. "Come, now. Sister Meyer will be wondering. I'll cross the Square with you."

36

On the steps of the *Gemeinhaus* they paused. Darkness hovered in the Square. The wind had died. Early stars glittered above the black-twigged crowns of the trees.

"There'll probably be a lot of darkness where you're going, Ketty," said Sister Oesterlein.

"I know," said Ketty. "There'll be darkness. And there'll be no Brother Nissen blowing on his conch shell to tell us all is well."

"Don't be afraid, Ketty. Keep the stubborn counsel of your heart, and don't be afraid," Sister Oesterlein said to her. And then, as if to exact a promise, she asked, "You won't be afraid?"

Ketty turned the question about in her mind thoughtfully.

"What you've taught me will be like an 'all's well'," she said. "Maybe," she added, "I'd better get used to the dark. I'll go across the Square alone. Sister Meyer can only scold."

Sister Oesterlein lifted Ketty's face between her palms and kissed her on the forehead. "Go quickly, then," she said, "and love go with you."

chapter 3

ONE week later, in the middle of the morning, Ketty, mounted behind Anson, sensed new life in the tired, plodding horse as he suddenly raised his head and broke into a brief trot.

"You can't fool a horse, Ketty. We're on the home stretch," said Anson. "This here"—he indicated with a sidewise nod of his head the stream flowing beside the rutted wagon road—"is the Middle Fork of the Holston."

"How much farther?" asked Ketty, weary with seven long days on the horse.

"In 'bout an hour now . . ."

Anson studied the river thoughtfully as it brawled noisily down its rocky bed. "Surely the ice can't have been melted long," he said, talking to himself.

Mist-laden clouds hung low over the wide valley and the encompassing ring of hills—clouds that in no way lifted as the riders neared their destination.

Where the Middle Fork flowed into the Holston, Anson switched the horse and dug his heels into the beast's ribs.

"Looky!" he said, suddenly stiffening in the saddle. "There 'tis. There's Fort Patrick Henry."

Peering around Anson's right shoulder, Ketty saw a graying fort beside a gray river bulking against a gray sky.

"Stockade gate's open," Anson observed. "That's a good sign. No red men about." A few paces farther on he added, "Looks like nobody's about."

As the horse stumbled wearily through the stockade gate, a blockhouse door swung open and half a dozen curious backwoods farmers turned militiamen hurried out.

"Well, 'pon my word and honor!" declared one.

"Ye be n't hants, be ye?" asked another, blinking his eyes.

"We done give you up for scalped, Anse," another told him.

"And who's this you fotched, Anse?" still another asked, gazing approvingly at Ketty as he elbowed his way to the front.

To their remarks Anson had one brisk reply. "Donelson —he still here?"

The men scoffed. "That man? And him a-rarin' like a filly when you left here?"

The door of the blockhouse in the southwest corner of the fort opened, and the doorway framed the gaunt figure of a woman Anson's age. Fair-haired children crowded around her, staring with wide blue eyes. Two women peered over their heads.

To this doorway Anson guided the horse. Not until he had climbed out of the saddle did anyone speak. Then the woman in the forefront said in a voice icy with censure, "So you brung one of 'em back with you!"

"This here's my sister Ketty," Anson announced to the staring group. "She's all of my folks that's left. The rest are dead."

He started into the blockhouse, but the figure in the doorway obstructed his entrance. "Whar all in this world have you been?" the woman asked both in anger and anxiety. "Might' nigh three months. Rest of them boats left long ago."

"Left 'long 'bout Christmas time," another of the women told Anson.

Ketty sat behind the saddle, waiting for what she did not know, while curious eyes continued to stare.

"Donelson, he said he'd done give you fair warnin' not to leave here," the first woman told Anson. "Said he couldn't hold up thirty boatloads a-waitin' for you."

"But they didn't go a fur piece, Pappy," spoke up one of the boys in the doorway. "River froze over, so they was camped at the mouth of Reedy more'n two months."

"Shubeal says they've gone now," reported the second woman. "Left 'bout two weeks ago when the hard water melted and the river riz."

"Just two weeks ago? Then we can overtake 'em," said Anson. "Traveling so many together, they'll be bound to get held up for one reason or another. Where are Shubeal and Baptist? Cal, you run find 'em. Everybody begin loading things on the boat. Nothing to keep us from leaving soon's we get loaded."

"Pappy and Baptist went a-huntin'," the tallest boy in the doorway told Anson. "Meat's plumb out."

"That ain't all that's out," said the first woman. "Hit's foolish to talk about settin' out, Anse, when we got so little to eat. A few dried apples and a half a bushel of parched corn and some walnuts and hickory nuts. That's all we got left. All. D'ye understand?"

40

Anson stared at her. "What in tarnation did you do with all them vittles you had when I left?" he asked.

"We had vittles to last two months. Did you think we was a-fastin' all the time you was a-traipsin' over them mountains?"

"We can start on the meat Shubeal and Baptist'll bring in," Anson decided. "After that we can live off the land. Spring's here, ain't it?" He moved briskly toward the door. "Ever'body come along. Let's get to loading. Be ready to shove off soon as Shubeal and Baptist get back."

The boy who had spoken first pointed a finger at Ketty. "Mammy," he asked, "is she a-goin' with us?"

The woman did not answer. Instead she looked accusingly at Ketty. "Vittles plumb give out, and another mouth to feed. A grown mouth to feed," she muttered. "You needn't set there on that horse," she said to Ketty. "I reckon hit ain't your fault."

Under the gaze of eyes intently staring, Ketty grasped the saddle and slid down from the horse's back. Sick at heart, she watched Anson crowd past the women and the children into the blockhouse, leaving her to face her accusers alone.

"Cal, you and Squire," Anson called from inside the blockhouse, "don't stand there gaping. Let's get to loading. No time to waste. Come on, ever'body. Tish, you and Rachel and Lettice—you womenfolks pack things up. The rest of us'll fetch and carry."

And what did Anson want her to do, Ketty wondered. Help the womenfolks?

At the thought she rebelled. Two of the women had not been unkind to her, to be sure. But before the sharp tongue and the cold, accusing stare of the woman who was evidently Tish she smarted like a slapped child.

"I—I'll help the children fetch and carry, Anson," she said.

Their arms filled with household goods, Ketty and the children walked in single file along the muddy path to the river bank, where Anson's flatboat was tied up.

The girl directly in front of Ketty looked back. "What's your name?" she asked shyly.

Tish's spite toward her hadn't worn off on the child, Ketty thought gratefully. The question had been friendly.

"Are you a Petrie?" asked Ketty.

"Um-hum," said the child. "I'm Lennie Petrie."

"Then I'm your Aunt Ketty. You can call me Ketty."

"I'm eight a-goin' on nine," Lennie informed her.

"What's the name of the girl in front of you?" asked Ketty.

"Betsy Petrie. She's five. And the girl in front of her, she's Pegg. She's seven. She's Rachel's girl."

"What's the rest of Pegg's name?"

"Given," said Lennie. "And the two boys in front, they're Squire Given—he's eight, same as me, 'cept I was birthed three days before he was, so I'm the oldest, goody—and t'other un is Calmes Petrie, 'cept we call him Cal. He's seven. He was named for Uncle Calmes."

"Let me see if I can name all of you now," Ketty said. "Cal Petrie. Squire Given. Pegg Given. Betsy Petrie. Lennie Petrie."

"You can name us all good," declared Lennie warmly. "That's all of us 'cept Farrer. You didn't see him."

"Who's Farrer?" asked Ketty. "Is he out hunting with the menfolks?"

42

"Farrer out a-huntin' with Baptist and Shubeal!" Squire Given said with scoffing laughter in his voice.

All the children were listening, open-eared. They had now reached the gangboard, slippery with mist, laid between the river bank and the deck of the boat. At Squire's remark they fell into such a fit of laughing that they all but lost their footing.

"Farrer ain't a-huntin' nothin'," Lennie told Ketty. "He's a-hidin'."

"Hiding? From what?"

"Hidin' from ever'thing," called Cal from the head of the line. "That thar young un hides if you jist whisper his name. Don't he, Squire?"

"That's why you didn't see him," spoke up Pegg Given. "He was scart of you. He was a-hidin' behind Mammy."

They laid their plunder on the deck of the boat and started toward the fort for another load.

"Whose boy is Farrer?" asked Ketty.

"Why, don't you know that?" asked Lennie. "He's Patsy and Rob's boy. But they're scalped and he's Rachel's boy now. He was named after that thar king that the Good Book tells about."

Ketty puckered her brow. King David? King Solomon? King Uzziah? "King Pharaoh?" she asked.

"That's hit. King Farrer," said Lennie.

Well into the afternoon, back and forth from the blockhouse down to the flatboat, the children and Ketty trudged, loaded with rakes, hoes, saws, feather beds, bolsters, blankets and quilts, wooden stools, wooden trenchers, iron pots, steel knives and forks, baskets and bowls and piggins, gourds full of seed corn, gourds full of garden seeds, and

43

one gourd in which were a few spoonfuls of salt. Anson, with the help of the militiamen, carried down the heavy plows, the log chains, the ox yokes, the barrels and kegs, and Tish's big loom.

"Hey, looky!" called Cal as the children and Ketty left the blockhouse for the last time. "Here come Baptist and Shubeal! And they've killed 'em a deer!"

At sight of the two men, followed by a droop-tailed dog, the children broke into awkward trots, leaving Ketty behind. Across the gangboard they teetered, dumped their loads on the deck, and hurried to join Anson and the womenfolk gathered about the hunters.

"So, Anse, you're back!" boomed the younger of the two as the men dropped to the ground the deer they carried slung from a pole on their shoulders. "Just two months later than you said you'd be. You ought 'a' sent me."

"That so?" said Anson dryly. He stooped and poked a finger into the deer's ribs. "Lean as a fence rail," he said.

"What d'ye expect?" asked the young man. "This hard winter, woods critters had no more to eat than us humans. Take a look at us, man. We're all skinny."

Ketty stood lonely on the edge of the little group gathered about the deer. No one noticed her or paid her mind. If Baptist and Shubeal saw her, they weren't curious enough to ask questions, and no one bothered to explain who she was.

"Mammy," asked Cal, "can we eat now? I'm as holler as one of them empty gourds we've been a-loadin' on the boat."

"I'm so holler I don't even rattle," said Squire.

"No time to eat now," decided Anson. "We'll just skin this critter and load it on the boat and shove off. Dark's soon enough to eat."

"Pappy," complained Squire, "you said this mornin' when you started a-huntin' you was a-comin' home with a deer *and* a bear. Whar at's the bear?"

Lennie, catching sight of Ketty, left the others and came to stand beside her.

"Which one is Squire's pappy?" Ketty asked.

"That there un," said Lennie, pointing to the older of the two men. "His name's Shubeal. Shubeal Given. And t'other un's Baptist Ramsay. He's Lettice's man."

"Are we all here now?" asked Ketty. "All who are going on the boat?"

"Um-hum," said Lennie. "Do you know the boat's name? The *Dragonfly.* I named her."

Ketty turned and studied the boat. Built with thick gunwales of heavy oak, she sat like a hulking tub in the water. Her forward deck was squared at the corners, and a square cabin, built of pine, covered her afterdeck. Three oars were pivoted in forked sticks fastened to the cabin roof— a steering oar at the back to serve as a rudder, and a long sweep on either side, forward.

"You're a poet, Lennie," said Ketty, smiling.

"What's a poet?"

"A poet is somebody who can see things ordinary mortals can't see," Ketty told her. "A poet can look at this big, lumbering boat and see gauzy wings shimmering in the sun and skimming fast over the water."

45

Shyly Lennie took Ketty's hand. "I'm glad you're a-goin' on this trip," she confided.

"Since I am going," Ketty said, holding Lennie's hand tight, "I'm mighty glad you're going too."

"We can eat right hearty while this meat lasts," said Anson as he helped Shubeal and Baptist skin and gut the deer. "If we just had enough salt to salt it down, it'd last quite a spell."

"You'll be a-wantin' salt many a time before you get hit," Tish told him.

When the chunks of deer meat were stored aboard the *Dragonfly*, Anson examined once more the household goods piled on deck and in the cabin. Tish checked to see that the loopholes along the gunwales and in the cabin walls were clear, that oakum, mallet, and calking iron were handy in case the boat sprang a leak, and that the great ball of pawpaw rope she had busied herself braiding while Anson was away was on board.

"Well," said Anson, "nothing more to hold us here. Ever'body aboard? Untie us, Baptist. Let's shove off."

Baptist, on the river bank, loosened the chains that secured the flatboat to trees, threw them over the gunwale, and ran up the gangboard, followed by his dog.

When the gangboard was pulled on deck, severing all ties with the land, Anson, Baptist, and Shubeal climbed the crude ladder to the top of the cabin. Anson picked up a cow's horn that he had laid beside the steering oar and blew a blast that went ringing across the flat bottomlands and came echoing and echoing back from the low-lying hills.

Lennie caught Ketty's hand. "We're a-goin'!" she said breathlessly, her eyes dancing in her lean face.

chapter 4

D RAWING Ketty after her, Lennie joined the other children crowded against the gunwale. Tish, Rachel, and Lettice, left standing in the middle of the deck among barrels and kegs, plowshares and log chains, wrapped their linsey shawls tightly about their shoulders against the chilling, mist-laden wind.

Baptist and Shubeal on the land side of the cabin set their iron-shod poles against the river bank. With the other ends of the poles embedded in their shoulders, they shoved. The *Dragonfly* trembled, and inched into the river.

"Send us word, Anse, if we ought to come," called a militiaman from the river bank.

Baptist and Shubeal reset their poles and shoved again. The distance between boat and river bank widened. Once more they shoved. Then they laid their poles on the cabin roof and swung their broadhorn oars into the water. Over the voyagers a silence fell.

It was proper, thought Ketty, watching beside Lennie, that, as the *Dragonfly* was loosed from her safe moorings

48

and entrusted to the mercies of the rivers, men should hold their peace. The earth, too, was silent, as if paying respect to this puny handful of voyagers pitting themselves against the unknown rivers and the far-off unknown land. Not a blackbird whistled. Not a crow cawed.

Tish moved to the bow of the boat and stood noting every riffle that bespoke what lay hidden beneath the water's surface, as Anson, with the long steering oar, guided the flat toward the swift current.

Caught up by the current, the boat shivered from bow to stern. One final lurch she gave as she squared herself in the deep, rolling water. Then she began slipping smoothly and easily downriver.

At once voices shattered the peace.

"I never believed hit'd come to pass."

"I allus was afraid of deep water."

> "I am bound for the Pro-om-ised La-a-and,
> I am bound for the Pro-om-ised Land.
> O, who will come and go with me?
> I am bound for the Prom-ised Land."

And, like a verse from the pages of the Good Book, "They's a man's wilderness, and they's a woman's wilderness, and they be different wildernesses."

"You never spoke a truer word, Tish Petrie," declared Rachel Given. "I'm a-goin' inside that thar cabin, dark as hit is, where I can't see this here water." She began herding the children like sheep. "You can't stand here till you get to that thar promised land Baptist's a-singin' so loud about," she told them.

Tish followed her toward the cabin door. "Though what

49

on earth we're a-goin' to do with 'em underfoot till we get to the promised land, I don't know," she said. She stood holding the door open for the children to file inside. "I've said a hundred times, and I say again, I don't favor goin' down these here rivers by our lonesome. And I'm a-knowin' we'll never overtake them others, spite of Anse's big talk."

Lennie was the last in line. Pushed unwillingly inside by her mother, she looked back.

"You come too, Ketty," she begged.

"I'll come after a while," Ketty promised.

When the cabin door was shut behind the children, Ketty turned to find Lettice Ramsay still on deck. With the cold mist blowing on them, the two looked shyly at each other.

Lettice was sixteen, Lennie had said, Ketty's own age. Besides being young, Ketty noted, she was soft and wondrous pretty. And she was heavy with child.

"Hit's a-goin' to be a long spell to set in that thar dark cabin," Lettice said, her voice so gentle it was like to be carried off unnoticed by the wind.

"Have you ever made a journey through the wilderness before?" Ketty asked.

"Oncet," said Lettice. "When I was a young un, I rode a horse from the Tidewater all the way to Wataugy. Tied in a creel." She laughed softly, remembering.

It was the first time that day that Ketty had heard a grown-up woman laugh. The sound was soothing, like a poultice on a mashed finger.

"I ain't never been on a river trip before," said Lettice.

"Do you think you're going to like this?" Ketty asked.

"A woman likes what her man likes," said Lettice. "She goes where he goes."

Her voice, her words, and her winsome face put Ketty in mind of a patch of blue-eyed grass she had come upon one March day in the Salem meadow where Brother Herbst pastured the Brethren's cows. The next day when she went to see the blossoms again, she found them crushed by a man's foot as he mended fence, without a thought to their winsomeness, and they prettifying the pasture so trustingly and meaning no harm.

"The others—Tish and Rachel—are going where their men go," said Ketty, "but they don't seem to like it."

"Tish is mad. And Rachel's scart," Lettice told her.

"Of what?"

"The river. Red men. A spell of sickness. Travelin' by our lonesome through the wilderness like this, all manner of things can happen."

"Are you afraid?" asked Ketty.

"I don't think about hit," said Lettice. "I go where Baptist goes."

She glanced with proud, trusting eyes at Baptist manning his broadhorn on top of the cabin. At that moment his head was thrown back, and he was singing,

> "Swing your ladies to the right,
> Then to left around we go,
> And we'll rally in the canebrake,
> And shoot the buffalo,"

as if he were saying to the wily wilderness, "Here comes your match!"

"What time his mouth ain't full of singin', hit's full of braggin'," said Lettice, giggling.

"At least he doesn't seem to be afraid," said Ketty.

"Baptist? He don't know there's such a word as 'fraid," said Lettice. "Why ain't you married?" she asked bluntly.

"Girls in Salem where I lived aren't married at sixteen," Ketty explained.

"You'll find hit uncommon hard in the wilderness 'thout a man to fend for you," Lettice told her. "Anse—" She hesitated. "Anse, he says you've got no folks."

"Nobody but Anson," said Ketty.

"And Tish," Lettice reminded her. "But Tish, she don't take to you like a body'd think a sister would."

"I've noticed," said Ketty.

"Don't mind her," advised Lettice. "Hit's her way, and she can't help hit any more'n a body can help havin' a wart on his nose. She ain't mad at you."

"Then what's the matter?" asked Ketty. "I can't help it that Anson brought me."

"She's mad at Anse," explained Lettice. "From the start she was agin his goin' back to the home place. She knowed them other boats wouldn't wait for him to come back. But Anse is like that. He takes keer of today and he's satisfied. But Tish, she keeps a-tellin' him somebody has to take keer of tomorrer too."

"How many boats were there?" asked Ketty.

"Must 'a' been thirty, all told," Lettice said. "Course, like Anse says, so many a-travelin' together, they're bound to get held up sometimes. But with thirty boats, folks can look out for one another when they's trouble. Tish ain't lived in the wilderness all her life for nothin'. You ever made a wilderness journey before?"

"Once," Ketty told her. "When I was two. On Anson's back."

"Anse," said Lettice, "seems like he dotes mightily on you."

Ketty was silent.

"Anse told you about this far-off land we're a-goin' to?" Lettice asked.

"A little."

"Hit's a mighty fine place, folks say," said Lettice. "Wide river bottoms. Thick canebrakes for the cattle. Salt for the bilin'. We been a-hearin' 'bout it two-three year. Any time hit was norated around that somebody was back from the French Lick, nothin'd do Baptist but we must strike out and stay all night and hear the talk 'bout hit."

"Come to think of it," Ketty said, musing, "people are always trying to find some far-off land—leaving behind the fields they've tended and the friends they love and crossing ocean seas and climbing high mountains to get to it. How are we to know when we get to the French Lick if it's the far-off land we're looking for?"

Lettice looked startled. "I ain't never had such wonderments," she said. She wrapped her arms in her shawl and turned toward the cabin door. "I declare, I'm a-gettin' chilled to the marrer in this here mist," she said. "I guess I'll go indoors for a spell."

When Lettice had closed the cabin door behind her, Ketty continued to stand on deck alone, gazing at the brown hills lying in wait for spring on either side of the river. On top of the cabin the menfolk were calling out landmarks and saying, thanks be, the river was high. Now and then Baptist spoke to his dog, which lay beside him, his voice big and bold in the March wind. "I'd sooner go to the far-off land 'thout my wife than 'thout my dog," he confided to Anson and Shubeal.

"Ain't you cold down there?" Anson called to Ketty. "Why don't you go inside out of the wind?"

"I—I'm not ready to go in," Ketty told him. She wished she could tell him more—that her safe moorings, like those of the *Dragonfly*, had been cast off; that, unlike the *Dragonfly*, which could be guided into safe channels with steering oar and setting poles, she was adrift on the broad current of life, no longer a child, but not yet a woman; and that she was afraid. But Anson, she sensed, had little understanding of, and less patience with, such notions.

"I think I'll come on top of the cabin awhile," she called up to Anson. She picked up a gum bucket by the stave serving as a handle, and climbed the ladder, thinking how scornfully Tish would stare at her. For that matter, all Salem, including Sister Oesterlein, she knew, would lift its eyebrows to see her sitting among the menfolk.

"How long will it take to get to the French Lick, Anson?" she asked when she had seated herself on the upturned bucket beside her brother.

"Depends on who's going there," Anson told her. "The Indians, they say it takes two paddles, two warriors, three moons. Me, I say three weeks. With the river high like this, three weeks."

Ketty looked down on the river, which was swollen with the waters of spring-fed creeks flowing into it. It was roll-

54

ing along, as peaceful as Salem on a Sunday, and the *Dragonfly* was riding easily on its current.

"Better throw in some luck, Anse," Shubeal warned.

"What's a puny thing called luck?" scoffed Baptist. "Me, I make my own luck."

"Ain't no boat built that can't use some good luck," said Shubeal.

"You take this here Holston now," continued Anson, paying no mind to the argument between Baptist and Shubeal. "Once a feller knows the river, he only needs to keep his wits about him."

"Yeah?" Shubeal said. "This here river's like a pet bear. You think you got him tamed, and all of a sudden, when you ain't a-lookin', he turns and claws you. You float along trustin' like, and 'thout no warnin' this here river runs out a shoal and grounds you. Or snags you on one of them drownded logs they call a sawyer and busts a hole as big as a bucket in the bottom of your boat." He spat far into the river. "And what about the Tennessee?" he asked. "Folks say the current in the Tennessee behaves like the devil when somebody's a-pinchin' his tail."

"It mought be a little rough when we hit them places called the Suck and the Boiling Pot," said Anson, belittling Shubeal's fears.

"And what about that stretch called the Muscle Shoals?" asked Shubeal.

"What's a-eatin' you, Shubeal?" asked Baptist. "I say again, a feller makes his own luck. Give him a good boat, and the rest is up to him."

Ketty wondered about the *Dragonfly*. Her bottom, built of thick planks, was well calked with tow. Her stout gunwales gave off a pleasant oaken odor, and the walls of the cabin above the gunwales were pungent with the smell of pine. But the Moravians, Ketty knew, would shake their heads solemnly at her unseasoned planks fastened together with tree nails of white oak.

"I ain't against luck," announced Anson. "Fact is, I'm counting mightily on one piece of luck—overtaking them other boats."

"That ain't luck," Baptist said. "That's a matter of pushin' down this river 'thout a let-up till we catch Donelson."

"And I'm counting on finding a message from James Robertson at Muscle Shoals," said Anson. "Remember he said, soon as he got settled at the Lick, he and couple of others'd go overland to the Shoals—way he figured it, the Shoals is just a short stretch by land south of the Lick— and leave a message telling us folks making the river trip if we could abandon our boats there and finish the rest of the journey by land. You'd call that luck, wouldn't you, if we could skip the Shoals and the rest of the river?"

James Robertson and most of the other menfolk planning to settle at the French Lick had left Fort Patrick Henry in November and had gone overland, Anson had told Ketty on their journey from Salem, taking with them cattle and horses, sheep and dogs, and leaving their womenfolk and children and household goods to follow by boat.

"I reckon, Baptist, you'd call hit luck if we was left in peace by the red men when we get to them Chickamaugy towns on the Tennessee," said Shubeal.

"I hain't changed my mind one whit," said Baptist. "I keep my rifle clean, my powder dry, and my wits sharp as a locust thorn. In Indian country, my rifle's my mainstay, not luck."

Ketty glanced about her. Anson, Shubeal, and Baptist each had his rifle within easy reach. The rifles set her to questioning.

"Are you—counting on killing Indians?" she asked.

"What do you think rifles are for?" asked Baptist.

"In Salem rifles were only for hunting," Ketty told him. "And for hunting only when meat was needed."

"Then I'd say you and the folks you've been with hain't never met up with red men," said Baptist. "The crack of a rifle's the onliest talk a red man understands."

"All of Salem met up with Indians many times," Ketty said. "Whenever Indians came to Salem they were treated like human beings. If they were hungry, as they usually were, they were fed. If night overtook them, they were given a warm place to sleep in the hayloft, since that was more to their liking than a proper bed. And the next day they went on their way."

"Yea, and I'll bet Salem was minus a horse or two. Or smokehouse provender. Or somethin'. Ain't a red man a-livin' that won't steal whatever he can lay hands on."

"Once," said Ketty, "after Brother and Sister Meyer had fed some Indians, two of them showed up at the back door of the Tavern with a deer they'd killed."

Baptist laughed uproariously. "You know any more fairy tales?" he asked.

"I know some more true tales," said Ketty. "I know one about Little Carpenter."

"The Cherokee chief? He's the biggest rapscallion of 'em all," declared Baptist.

"One day Little Carpenter came to Bethabara," said Ketty. "That's a Moravian town close to Salem. In the *Gemeinhaus* there they have an organ that Brother Bulitschek built. So the brethren took Little Carpenter to the *Gemeinhaus*, and Brother Stauber played the organ for him."

Baptist roared with laughter. "And I reckon Little Carpenter was plumb charmed with that," he said. "Did he take the organ with him when he went?"

"He did want to take something," Ketty said. "He wanted to take one of the Brethren home with him to teach the Indian children."

"Teach an Indian young un!" Baptist laughed scornfully. "I hain't never seen the redskin that could learn anything but devilment. Man, jist you wait! You're a-goin' to see a sight of things on this here journey the like of which you hain't never seen before," he prophesied.

"You've left Salem behind, Ketty," Anson told her. "Out here in the wilderness folks live by a different law. It's a fight to the finish 'twixt the red men and the white, and nobody's a-thinking he can make Indians over by teaching little red rapscallions their ABCs."

"But wouldn't it be better if we lived in peace with the Indians?" Ketty asked.

"Sure," said Anson. "Ever'body wants to live in peace. But out here in the wilderness, ain't but one way to live in peace."

Ketty fell silent. Questions raced through her mind, but she didn't ask them. No one, she sensed, had the answer. Nor was there any place on the boat where she belonged, neither inside the cabin with the women nor on top of it with the men.

And what would the Moravians think of her, she wondered, sitting with empty, idle hands? Moravian hands were never idle.

She got up from the bucket and stood beside Anson.

"Teach me to steer the boat, Anson," she said.

"You?" Anson laughed. "Steering a flat ain't exactly a woman's calling. Why ain't you inside with the rest of the womenfolks?"

"Because," answered Ketty.

Anson turned and looked at her, puzzled. "All right," he agreed. "Main thing to bear in mind is, keep her in the current."

Ketty took the handle of the steering oar in her hands.

"Swing it a bit to get the feel of it," advised Anson.

Ketty swung the oar, and, as if in answer, the big flat changed its course ever so little.

"Will you let me steer, Anson, till we tie up for the night?" she asked.

"Let her learn, Anse," said Baptist, "so she can take over when we start runnin' the gantlet of them Chickamaugy towns on the Tennessee—them friendly Indians with Tory rifles in their hands and murder in their kind hearts. She can steer while we take care of our friends."

"You can steer," Anson told Ketty, "till something shows up ahead—a rock, or an island of driftwood. They're dangerous as rattlesnakes. Right now I see a riffle ahead, and I don't aim to court bad luck just for the fun of it, so I'd better take over now."

Ketty handed the oar back to Anson. Her work on the journey was not the steering of the boat, she told herself. She had asked to steer only because she wanted to put off something unpleasant as long as she could.

With a sigh she started toward the ladder. "I guess I'll go inside," she announced.

She picked her way among rifles, stepped over Baptist's sleeping dog, climbed down the ladder backward, and opened the cabin door.

A child's screaming greeted her.

"Here comes Ketty!" shouted Lennie above the screaming.

"Goody! Here comes Ketty!" shouted Pegg.

The three Petrie children and the two Given children crowded around her in the dimly lit cabin while the wailing continued.

"Is that Farrer crying?" asked Ketty, looking in the direction of Rachel Given, from behind whose skirts the screams were coming. "What's the matter with him?"

"Aw, he's scart!" scoffed Cal.

"What's he scared of now?" asked Ketty.

"Indians," the children told her.

"Why is he scared of Indians?"

"We done told you," said Squire. "'Cause they scalped his mammy and pappy. We was a-talkin' 'bout hit, and Farrer, he started a-bawlin'."

"Hit was my sister Patsy that was scalped," explained Rachel. "She was Farrer's mammy. Her and Rob Lilburn —that was the young un's pappy. Happened two moons ago, and Farrer, he seen hit all with his own eyes."

"Please!" begged Ketty, remembering how the Moravians shielded their children from fear. "Let's not talk about it now, not where Farrer can hear."

"But hit's the truth," declared Squire. "Red men scalped his pappy and mammy. Only reason they didn't scalp Farrer was 'cause they figured worse than a scalpin'd be to leave him there by his lonesome a-cryin' in the wilderness and let the wolves eat him up."

"But the wolves didn't eat him"—Cal took up the story breathlessly—"'cause his Aunt Rachel and his Uncle Shubeal went to borry some cornmeal two days after that in the mornin'. And that's what they found—Patsy and Rob scalped, and their cabin burned to a crisp, and Farrer a-settin' by the ashes, half starved to death and a-cryin' like a lost lamb."

"And scart!" broke in Squire. "Sakes alive, he's scart of the littlest noise a body can make. Farrer's scart of a little-bitty old noise like this. Ain't you, Farrer?" Squire reached out his left hand, placed the nail of his thumb underneath the nail of his middle finger, and forced it up with a sharp click.

Suddenly the cabin seemed like to fly apart with Farrer's terrified screaming as he climbed wildly on Rachel and hid his face against her neck.

"Tish," asked Ketty above the noise, "do you care—you and Rachel—may all the children come on deck with me?"

"Take 'em and welcome," said Tish.

chapter 5

"WHAT are we aimin' to do out here?" asked Lennie as soon as the last child had crowded through the cabin doorway.

Ketty studied the ring of children around her, their faces turned expectantly up to hers. If they were in Salem, she reflected, they would all be in school—Lennie and Pegg and Betsy in Sister Oesterlein's school, Cal and Squire in Brother Fritz's school. When lessons were over for the day, the girls would be put to learning from their mothers, or from the Single Sisters, cooking and house-keeping and sewing, spinning and lace-making, embroidering and weaving, nursing and planting gardens and making hay. The boys would be apprenticed to such master workmen as the Elders should decide, from whom they would learn the skill of masons or carpenters, sawyers or cabinet-makers or wagon-makers, weavers or dyers or tailors, blacksmiths or gunsmiths, locksmiths or silver-smiths or nailsmiths, saddlers or dressers of deerskins, makers of fine Queensware, bookkeepers or tobacco manu-facturers, basket-makers or shoemakers or makers of leath-ern breeches.

So much to learn in Salem! So much to do! So much to do it with! Ketty sighed. And here, on board the *Dragon-fly*, were five children with empty hands and upturned faces, wondering what she aimed for them to do. How did a body encircled by wilderness start doing, she wondered.

Salem, she reflected, not so long ago had been a wilderness. Starting with stout hearts and a few tools they had carried on their backs from Pennsylvania, men had cleared land, raised cabins, and sent for their womenfolk. They had built workshop and carpenter shop and kiln, church and schoolroom and council hall, and all these they tended and fostered with loving care. No one in Salem, man, woman, or child, ever stood around idly wondering what to do.

Around Ketty the children waited, putting her in mind of the multitudes that followed Jesus, waiting to see some miracle done.

"Want me to teach you a song to sing?" she asked.

Hurriedly she searched through the songs stored in her memory—German songs sung by the Moravians in Salem. Life in Salem had been set to music: the ringing of the big bell that had been cast in the Moravian town of Bethlehem in Pennsylvania and hung with pomp and ceremony, and struck solemnly three times a day so that folks, if they had got somewhat awry, could reset their lives to sweet-toned music and march on again; the silvery, clarion singing of the trombones that announced with festive tunes the arrival of personages such as Bishop Spangenberg from faraway Herrnhut in Germany, coming to bring loving greetings and strict instructions to the Moravian offspring in Salem, or with radiant tunes the passing of a little child

63

through the golden gates of Heaven; the full-throated singing of the hymns on Sundays, on feast days, and at evening *Singstunde,* when choir and congregation were caught up in an ecstasy of joyous harmony.

"*Holdselig Kindlein in Kripp und Windlein,*" Ketty sang.

The children stared at her.

"That's not singin'," said Squire.

"Well, let's see," said Ketty. She began again:

"*O Haupt, voll Blut und Wunden.*"

"I don't like that kind of singin'," announced Cal. "Let's play somethin'."

"You be the Indians, we'll be the white men," shouted Squire. And before Ketty's astonished eyes the five children scurried to cover behind barrels and piles of plunder, the three girls on one side of the deck, the two boys on the other.

Cal, stretched flat behind an ox yoke, raised his head. "What do you aim to be, Ketty?" he asked.

"What are you playing?" asked Ketty.

"Scalpin'," Cal told her.

"How do you play it?"

"You watch this time," suggested Lennie. "Then you can play next time."

Ketty made her way to the bow of the boat and leaned against the gunwale to watch. At once there began a battle of wits between boys and girls as they peered over piles of plunder in search of one another, brandished imaginary knives and tomahawks, shot imaginary rifles, and made stealthy advances toward the others' hideouts. At last Betsy ventured too far into the open. Quick as a wild varmint, Cal lunged at her from behind a salt kettle and

64

caught her by the skirt. Squire leaped over a piggin, gathered up Betsy's hair in his hands, and pretended to scalp her, while Betsy screamed and Lennie and Pegg took cover behind Tish's loom. Finally Betsy, stretched limp on her back, stopped her screaming. Cal and Squire retreated to their side of the deck, whooping their joy over the pretended scalp they carried.

When the hubbub had died down, the children clustered around Ketty, each one begging, "You be on our side, Ketty."

Ketty studied them through narrowed eyelids.

"Do you play this game where Farrer can see you?" she asked.

"Of course," said Squire.

"Doesn't it scare him?"

"That young un's scart to death anyway, so a body can't scare him any worse than he is already," said Squire.

With a sense of their need, and of hers, Ketty groped for ways to stretch herself out of girlhood into womanhood.

"Would you like to learn a new game?" she asked.

"Oh, yes," agreed the children. "What's hit like?"

Ketty set to thinking. The Moravian children had not played many games, she realized. The girls had had their dolls, the boys their balls. But dolls and balls seemed much too tame for these wilderness children.

Farther back, among the games her mother had played with the Petrie children, Ketty searched. Peesie Weet? Green Gravel? Jack, Jack, the Bread's a-Burning? They all seemed dull beside the fierce game of scalping.

"Let's play The Old Woman from the Wood," she suggested.

65

"How d'you play that?" the children asked.

Ketty explained the game to them.

"The girls will be on one side, the boys on the other," she decided. "Remember, each side plays like it's doing something, and the other must guess what it is. We girls will go first. When you boys guess what we're doing, we have to run back to base before you catch us. Whoever gets caught must change sides."

She took the girls to one side of the deck and whispered to them. Then, holding hands, they started to the middle of the deck to face the boys, calling, "Here comes an old woman from the wood."

"What canst thee do?" asked Cal and Squire.

"Do anything," answered the girls.

"Work away," ordered the boys.

At once Ketty squatted on the deck and pretended to heap some things together. The three girls went a short distance away, pretended to fill their arms, returned to Ketty, and pretended to drop something beside her.

"Pickin' beans," guessed Cal.

"Skinnin' a varmint," guessed Squire.

The girls kept on working away.

"Pickin' berries," guessed Cal.

Lennie stooped beside Ketty and blew hard on the deck.

"Kindlin' a fire!" shouted Squire, and at once the girls scurried to base before the boys could catch them.

"I like this game," declared Lennie.

"I do too," chorused the others.

"Now, it's your turn," said Ketty to Cal and Squire.

The two boys retired to their side of the deck, whispered and started toward the girls, calling, "Here comes an old woman from the wood."

At that moment Rachel Given came on deck from the cabin, with Farrer clinging to her skirts. They stood watching as the two groups met in the middle of the deck.

"What canst thee do?" called the girls.

Hardly was the dialogue finished when Squire grabbed Cal about the waist, tripped him, threw him to the deck, and with weird shrieks made hacking motions at his head.

"Scalpin'!" shouted the three girls.

At the word Farrer clutched at Rachel, wrapped himself about her legs, and screamed.

"Listen, Farrer," Lennie tried to console him. "Hit's not a real scalpin', honey, hit's jist a game we're a-playin'."

"You see," Cal said to Ketty. "We can't do nothin' that he don't begin to bawl."

"Looks like you young uns jist try your dead level best to torment him," complained Rachel.

Ketty stooped beside the child and put an arm about him. But he pulled away from her and screamed even louder.

She got to her feet and faced the other children. "Come with me," she said. "I want to tell you something."

She led the way to the bow of the boat. The children clustered around her. "Do you like to play The Old Woman?" she asked.

"Um-*hum*," they said. "Let's play again."

"I'll play with you again," said Ketty, "if you'll promise you won't choose scalping again."

"Aw, shucks!" complained Squire.

"Why?" asked Cal.

"Because you scare Farrer."

"He'd be scart anyway," said Squire.

"What's the matter with playin' scalpin'?" asked Cal. "Folks get scalped all the time. Rob and Patsy got scalped."

"Pappy says we'll be lucky if we get to the French Lick 'thout some of us gettin' scalped," put in Pegg. "He says, when we get to them Chickamaugy towns—"

"Don't you think there'll be time enough for scalping when it really happens," asked Ketty, "without playing at it too?"

"Then what are we aimin' to do?" asked Lennie.

Like the ringing of a clear-toned bell from some far steeple, Ketty heard Sister Oesterlein's words: *All people are in need, Ketty. Be present.*

"Let's—let's—why don't we have school? On the *Dragonfly*, every day till we get to the French Lick—would you like that?"

"School?" echoed the children.

"What's school like?" asked Squire.

"Do you know readin'?" asked Lennie, awed and proud. "And writin'?"

"And cipherin'?" asked Pegg.

"All of them," said Ketty.

"How are you aimin' to teach us 'thout books?" asked Squire. " 'Thout a spellin' book?"

"Um-m-m," said Ketty, "well, when you haven't a spelling book and you want to learn, you make a spelling book, don't you?"

"Let's see you make one," said Cal.

68

"You'll have to let me think," she told the children. "There's surely some way to teach you to read if all we need is a book."

"See there, Ketty?" called Anson from the stern of the cabin roof. He pointed to a mill built of logs on the right bank of the river. "That's Colonel King's mill I told you about. Further on you'll see his iron works. And look! Looky there, ever'body!" The pitch of Anson's voice rose as he pointed to the mouth of a creek emptying its swollen, fast-flowing waters into the Holston. "That must be where Donelson laid by for two months."

Ketty made her way to the gunwale where Rachel and Farrer stood. The children followed her. The cabin door opened, and Tish and Lettice came on deck. Together they stared at the creek bank that had the appearance of a campsite only lately abandoned. The underbrush of rhododendron had been cut away from the bank. A path was worn from the edge of the river among the sycamores to abandoned shelters of logs and cedar branches. Beside the path was a pit for broiling meat, and from the river could be seen the sodden blackened remnants of many fires doused for the last time as the voyagers broke camp.

As the boat rode the current past the scene, Shubeal said, "I'm shore proud we're past Reedy!"

"Afraid if we tied up thar for the night we might get hexed and have to stay a couple of months? Like Donelson?" asked Baptist. "If Donelson had a used his head, that wouldn't 'a' happened. He knowed the water was low when he started. I told him so."

"But hit stood to reason the water'd rise with the meltin'

69

snows and the freshets," Shubeal said. "Couldn't nobody, Donelson or nobody else, 'a' said beforehand how long this ice'd last and how pestiferous this winter'd be."

"He could 'a' beat the ice if he'd a started the first of December like James Robertson warned him to do," said Baptist. "In this business a feller's got to depend less on luck and more on his head. And my head tells me," he added, "we'd better tie up soon."

"Keep floating awhile longer," ordered Anson. "Take up all the slack we can 'twixt us and Donelson. If the ice hadn't a caught him at the mouth of Reedy," he added, "it stands to reason it'd 'a' caught him further down. Maybe on the Tennessee."

"And that," declared Shubeal, "with them red men a-hangin' 'round, could 'a' been as downright onhealthy as a plague of smallpox."

Lennie plucked at Ketty's sleeve. "Can we start school now?" she asked.

"How about tomorrow?" asked Ketty. "I haven't figured out yet how to teach you to read without a book."

chapter 6

"In Scarlet Town where I was born,
They was a fair maid dwellin',
Made ev'ry lad cry well-a-day,
And her name was Barb'ry Ellen."

BAPTIST sang to pass the time as he wielded his broad-horn. Anson and Shubeal took up the song while Lettice, on deck, tapped her small foot in time with the music.

"I like to hear singin' like that," she confided to Ketty.

"Seems like hit helps a mite to keep a body's mind off this here everlastin' river," said Rachel.

For a half-hour beyond the mouth of Reedy the *Dragon-fly* floated smoothly on the current, rocking gently as a baby's cradle to the sound of Baptist's singing. The pattern of the river bank slowly changed. Cane patches and quiet coves where otters played came and went.

"See that there?" Anson called to Shubeal and Baptist, pointing ahead to a bank of land that jutted into the river on the right. "Let's run her in just below there."

Baptist's song trailed away. He and Shubeal waited.

The boat floated past the point of land.

"Pull her in!" shouted Anson.

Straining their muscles against their broadhorns, Baptist and Shubeal swung the boat into the quiet eddy and eased her to the bank.

"Haw!" shouted Baptist. He swung his broadhorn from the water, laid it on top of the cabin, hurried down the ladder to the deck, and jumped to the bank. Shubeal tossed out the chains, and Baptist made the boat fast to sycamore trees. Shubeal slid the gangboard over the gunwale. Baptist planted the far end on the bank and tried his weight on it.

"Stiddy as the North Star," he pronounced.

"Young uns," said Tish, like a militia captain giving orders, "line up. Help carry things off before dark catches us."

Into each outstretched hand she placed a cooking utensil, an elk hide, a quilt, or a piece of the deer meat. In single file the children trooped across the gangboard.

"Fine place to land," said Anson, studying the quiet cove. "Water deep enough so's we don't run no danger of grounding."

"And now for some vittles," said Baptist. "I'm as hungry as a bear a-comin' out of a holler tree at the shank end of winter. Young uns, get to gatherin' up firewood."

"Any Indians around here, Pappy?" asked Cal.

"Naw, naw." Anson quieted his fears. "Militia at the fort ain't allowing red men in these parts. Bring the wood a-running."

The children scurried along the river bank in search of driftwood. Shubeal brought two big stones and set them up opposite each other near the river bank. A short distance from the campsite Anson nicked from a dead tulip poplar a handful of dry punk and laid it between the stones. He

72

picked up twigs from the ground and laced them across the punk. Over the twigs he sprinkled powder from his powder horn.

"Better be careful of that powder, Anse," Tish warned, watching him. "We're a long ways from that thar French Lick."

Paying her no mind, Anson took the deerhide lock cover off his rifle, held the flintlock close to the punk, and pulled the trigger. The spark from the flint flew into the punk, and a bright blaze shot up.

Baptist, armed with an ax and with his dog at his heels, disappeared into the woods and came back carrying three stout crotched limbs. One end of each he pinned to the ground with rocks and rested the limbs on the stones Shubeal had brought so that their crotched ends were tilted over the fire.

With practiced hands and few words Tish sliced sparse pieces from the haunch of the deer with Anson's sharp hunting knife and handed them to Rachel and Lettice, who stuck them on the crotched ends of the sticks above the fire.

"I'll help, Tish," offered Ketty, holding out her hand for the next slice of meat. Tish put it into her hand without looking at her.

Ketty stuck the meat on the prongs of a stick. Flames sputtered up with little explosions when blobs of fat dripped onto the coals. Ketty's mind, however, was not on the broiling meat. It was on Tish—on Tish and all the others who had gone their several ways without so much as saying once, "You come and help, Ketty."

"Your meat's a-scorchin', Ketty," Lettice warned her.

73

With a start, Ketty stooped and turned her stick. Better put her mind on what she was doing, she scolded herself. And better figure out how to teach children to read without a book—or what to use in place of one.

"Seems like deer meat never did taste right 'thout hoecake," complained Anson as the voyagers stood about the fire, eating their meat from their fingers, with now and then a few grains of parched corn or slices of dried apples that Tish had doled out.

"We had cornmeal last December," Tish reminded him.

"Be long 'bout October or November 'fore you have hoecake," said Shubeal. "Figurin' we get to the French Lick by corn-plantin' time. Figurin' nothin' happens to our seed corn."

"We'd best not let any chance for vittles slip by, either," spoke up Tish. "I seen a rabbit trot alongside the river when we was a-comin' up. Cal, you and Squire go and set some snares."

"Let's go, Squire," said Cal.

"Reckon hit ain't worth while to smoke this here deer meat like hit was a-goin' to last forever," Tish said to nobody in particular. "Smoke hit all night and then heat hit up for eatin' long as hit lasts. We'll need some green wood for smokin'. Shubeal, while you and Baptist chop some, Anse can cut cedar for pallets. You young uns," she added, "go with Anse and carry the cedar in."

And what did Tish want her to do? Ketty wondered.

Since she received no order, she followed Anson, Lennie, Pegg, and Betsy into the woods and filled her arms with the cedar branches Anson chopped from the tree with his tomahawk. On the way back to the campfire she stopped and stared at the cinnamon-colored bark peeling off a river birch in curly papery patches.

"Know what I call that tree?" asked Lennie, who had stopped when Ketty stopped. "A raggedy old woman."

Ketty laughed. "She is wearing rags and tatters, isn't she?" she agreed. "I think, though, she may be what I need." For a minute longer she studied the tree. "Yes," she added, "I think this old woman may be just the person I'm looking for."

When they had heaped their cedar boughs beside the campfire, Ketty borrowed Anson's tomahawk and started back along the way they had come.

"Want to come, Lennie?" she asked. "You and Pegg? And Betsy?"

"Where are we a-goin'?" asked Lennie as the three girls started after Ketty.

"We're going back to find that raggedy old woman," Ketty said. "We're going to get ready for school tomorrow."

With the sharp blade of the tomahawk Ketty hacked out on the bark of the birch tree a rectangle the size of a page from a small book.

"What are you a-doin' that for?" asked Lennie.

Ketty pried up the edges and stripped the thin rectangle of bark from the tree.

"See? she said, peeling off the outer ragged patches. "This is going to be a book."

"Aw, I seen a book oncet," said Pegg. "Hit didn't look like a piece of old bark."

"Hit don't have readin', Ketty," Lennie told her.

"It's going to have reading," declared Ketty, running her fingers over the smooth surface of the bark. "You'll see."

She laid the piece of bark on the ground. "This will be your book, Lennie. We'll need one for Pegg, one for Betsy, one for Cal, and one for Squire."

The girls watched as Ketty pried four more pieces of bark from the trunk and laid them in a row on the ground.

"We need one more," said Ketty.

"Who for?" asked Pegg.

"Farrer," said Ketty.

"Farrer! That young un's too scart to learn readin'," declared Pegg.

"Farrer's going to learn to read just like the rest of you," said Ketty.

When they had carried their pieces of bark to the campsite, Ketty found straight, slender sticks among the driftwood and set the children to charring the ends in the fire.

"What're we a-doin' now?" asked Betsy.

"Making pencils," said Ketty.

"Um-m-m!" declared Lennie. "I like school."

As darkness settled down on their quiet river cove, the campers stretched on their pallets of cedar boughs and elk hides with their feet to the smoking fire Anson had kindled under the scaffold of deer meat, and covered themselves with quilts and blankets. They lay in a circle with their clothes on, children croodled close between father and mother for warmth against the raw night air and the cold ground beneath. The menfolk lay with their long rifles beside them. Tish, Ketty noticed, lay with Anson's tomahawk close at hand.

Ketty lay in the circle near Tish, but alone, her mind astir with plans for the school she would begin the next day. The voyagers began one by one to breathe with even rhythm. As the night blackened, the plans for teaching emptied from Ketty's mind and a feeling of loneliness filled it—loneliness and uncertainty and, as she remembered the readiness of rifles and tomahawks, foreboding.

Occasionally grease dripped from the scaffold where the deer meat hung smoking, exploded into flame, and blazed briefly. For an instant the flame lighted up the voyagers, outlined the black tree trunks, dimly glowed on the cabin of the *Dragonfly*, played shadowlike on the ghostly white bark of the sycamores, and then went out.

Off in the darkness something stirred. Quick as a wild varmint, Ketty sat upright. For a long time she listened. Against her face she felt the dampness of a fog that rolled in from the river and misted the voyagers over.

Still she listened, for a while propped on her elbow, finally with her head laid lightly on her pallet. The sleepers breathed heavily. Somebody—Shubeal? or maybe Baptist, since it was so loud and cocksure?—snored deeply. Now and then one of the children tossed in sleep.

How good, how very good and quieting it would be, thought Ketty, to hear Brother Nissen at that moment blowing on his conch shell and calling out in his deep German tones that all was well! Well, she told herself, she had a voice, and she knew Brother Nissen's nightwatch song. Why not sing it? It must be eight o'clock, and a proper hour for singing.

At that instant, like a hand lightly placed there, something quietly settled on her blanket.

Stifling a scream, Ketty sat upright. Baptist's dog on the other side of the circle growled low and cautious-like.

"You hain't slept yet," said someone—Tish—low and quiet.

77

"I—somebody—something touched my blanket," Ketty stammered, close to tears.

"Jist a piece of sycamore bark," Tish told her. "Hit's always a-scalin' off thataway."

With her heart pounding, Ketty cautiously ran her fingers down her blanket, found the piece of bark, and tossed it away. Then she lay down again, pulled the bedclothes about her, and tried to sleep.

But her mind was a ferment of questions. Why should she be afraid of red men in the wilderness when she had not been afraid of them in Salem? How did anybody, gripped in the ice of fear, break out of it? Where was this strange voyage among strange people taking her? Who was Tish? And what were she and Tish to each other?

"A body needs her night rest." Tish's voice broke across her torment, a tired voice—tired but kind. "Fog's better than a sentry"—a wilderness-wise voice, Ketty realized.

When voices speak, Ketty, be present. By loving, you will come to know what a body needs. By loving and caring.

The voice of a mother, tired at day's end. The voice of a tired wife—tired of bickering and complaining, seeking a cove made safe with love where she might anchor and rest a spell before going on.

"Can you go to sleep now too, Tish?" Ketty whispered across the space between them.

The peace of the dark wilderness settled on them, and they slept.

It was Tish's voice Ketty heard first in the morning.

"Cal! Wake up! You and Squire run see about your snares."

Ketty got up quickly from her pallet. As she folded her

78

bedclothes, damp with the fog that still hovered over their camping place, she looked hopefully at Tish, thinking maybe Tish would speak kindly to her as she had in the night. But Tish went her way, paying Ketty no mind.

"While the fire's being kindled I might as well go with you, Cal," Ketty said, wondering how in Tish's eyes she could be useful.

Along the fog-enveloped river bank they hurried, on a narrow path pressed and padded by small rabbit feet. Around the cove they came upon the snares—the whips of little bushes to whose tips had been attached slip-noosed loops of the inner bark of a cedar tree. Dangling from the loops bent over the trail were four rabbits, damp and cold.

"They're mighty skinny," said Cal, slipping the noose from the neck of one of the rabbits.

Squire loosed another rabbit and turned its stiffening body in his hands. "Hit's the hard winter," he said.

Back at the campfire Tish, having stacked the smoked deer meat to be carried onto the boat, took the rabbits and, one at a time, with Anson's skinning knife, nicked the pelt at the breastbone and slit it down to the crotch. Ketty, watching her, knew that not even Brother Meyer himself could skin a rabbit so deftly. Next Tish cut off the rabbit's pads, made slits in the skin on the legs, slid the skin over the rabbit's head, and cut the head off. Then she gutted the rabbit, threw the entrails into the fire, and sliced the meat into chunks. These she placed on a stone close to the fire and tilted it up with a small stone at the back edge.

As the fire browned and roasted the meat, Anson, anxious to be off, sent the children to carry the bedding on

79

board. Hardly had the voyagers eaten the last of the rabbit and tossed into the dying embers the little bones picked clean of meat when Anson ordered, "Let's get moving, ever'body. We've wasted too much time already."

"Seems to me we'd better wait till this fog lifts a mite," Tish advised him.

"If you was the captain, Tish," said Anson, "we'd sure catch Donelson in a hurry."

chapter 7

THE fog—and Tish—had the last word. An hour passed before the voyagers could set out in safety—an hour during which Anson fumed and fretted and paced the river bank and declared he'd never have left Fort Patrick Henry if he'd a knowed fog was going to yap at his heels at every turn and twist in the river. Sawyers and rocks and shoals and such like he'd counted on, he said. Even red men he'd counted on. But not fog.

At last, however, the fog lifted as willfully as it had settled the night before, and Anson gave orders to board the flat. To allow no dawdling on anybody's part, he stood last in the line and pulled in the gangboard after him.

"When do we begin school, Ketty?" asked Lennie when the *Dragonfly* was under way.

"Right now," said Ketty. "As soon as all of you find places to sit."

The children crowded into the small space around Ketty's feet. Tish, Lettice, and Rachel stood watching. Farrer clung like a brier to Rachel's skirt.

"Farrer," said Ketty, "do you want to learn too?" From

the top of the barrel where she had laid the birch bark, she took a piece and knelt beside the child. "See," she said, "this can be your book. You can learn your ABCs. And you can learn to write words and read them, like Cal and Squire."

"Like us too," Lennie corrected her, pointing to the girls.

"Like all the children," said Ketty.

Farrer wrapped himself more closely in Rachel's skirt.

Ketty turned back to the other children, picked up one of the charred sticks, and wrote on the piece of bark.

"See?" She held up the bark before the children. "Here are four letters, and they make a word that says *boat*." She showed them how she made each letter, with straight lines and rings and curlicues.

Tish watched a minute. Then she walked stiffly to the cabin, opened the door, and disappeared inside. Rachel followed her, complaining that she couldn't take a step without tromping on Farrer, and whatever was she going to do? Lettice drew her shawl about her, sat down on an upturned gum bucket, and continued to watch.

"Now, children, you may write *boat*," Ketty said.

The children laid their pieces of bark on the deck and, on their knees, bent over them. Ketty walked about the circle, helping the children form their letters.

"I know a word to learn, Ketty," said Cal. "Indian."

"Not today," said Ketty.

"I like school!" declared Lennie warmly.

"I do, sorta," said Squire. "What do we aim to do next?"

"Let's play a game," said Pegg.

"Old Woman from the Wood," said Cal.

"Do you remember"—Ketty looked into their faces—"one

thing you're not to do when you're playing Old Woman?"

"I remember," said Lennie. "We won't do hit."

"Why can't we do hit?" Squire wanted to know. "Farrer ain't here."

"You promised, children," Ketty reminded them. "And I want you to promise me something else. Promise you won't jump at Farrer, nor boo at him, nor click your fingernails at him, nor whisper his name. Don't do anything to scare him."

"Aw, shucks!" complained Cal.

While the children played, Ketty leaned on the gunwale and watched. A bird, its back as blue as the sky above it, flitted across the river.

Reverence God and all things He has created, Ketty.

The bird settled on the limb of a sycamore and sent its clear, rich warble curling through the softening March air. Ketty noticed then how the sun with its warm, life-giving rays was wooing the winterbound earth, and how the earth was stirring shyly to the wooing. Fat catkins dangled from hazel bushes bending low over the river's edge. On the steep hillside, among the bare trees, spring beauties spread their narrow, pale green leaves above the brown leaf carpet. On a solitary beech tree near the water's edge, tightly rolled buds were swelling, looking like fairy flutes for piping ethereal music.

"Seems like that'd be a mighty fine place to go a-huntin'," Shubeal called to Anson. "Lay us in a good supply 'fore we hit them Chickamaugy towns."

As long as the *Dragonfly* was moving easily downriver, Anson turned a deaf ear to any suggestion of hunting. Alert and tense, he steered the boat past the mouth of Big Creek.

A few miles farther, as the flat neared the mouth of Cloud Creek, Baptist whistled long and low. "From the looks of things," he said, "I'd say Donelson was held up here for a spell too."

His words brought Tish and Rachel out of the cabin to see the telltale signs that a multitude had indeed camped at the mouth of Cloud for a spell. Tish knitted as she gazed. The children quit their game and hung over the gunwale.

On they floated, slow minute after slow minute. The children busied themselves calling out to one another that yonder in an oak tree was a squirrel's nest, or up on the mountainside was a bare patch where they were sure strawberries grew.

"Betsy," said Ketty, "if you move over a little, Farrer can stand beside you and see the sights too."

Betsy moved to one side. "Come on, Farrer," she invited.

Farrer looked at the place opened for him. Ketty waited.

"I see a turtle, Farrer," she said, "sunning himself on a log."

Farrer looked at Ketty.

"If you stand beside Betsy you can see the turtle too." Ketty coaxed him. "I think he's asleep."

Farrer did not move, either toward Ketty or toward Rachel. But the ghost of curiosity lighted his dark eyes where the awful fear had lurked.

"No, Farrer, he isn't asleep!" exclaimed Ketty. "He's crawling!" Without waiting longer for the child, she picked him up and stood him at the gunwale beside Betsy. "There!" She pointed. "See?"

Farrer grasped the gunwale and leaned over to watch the turtle.

"Look at the young un!" hollered Cal. "He's done broke loose from Rachel!"

"Reckon we ought to blow Anse's horn to norate the news around?" asked Squire.

Ketty hurried to the boys. "I reckon you'd better do nothing at all," she warned. "Play like you don't even see Farrer. And don't you scare him!"

In the middle of the afternoon, when Cal and Squire complained of empty craws, Tish brought from the cabin a handful of hickory nuts and doled them out among the children.

"Can Ketty have some too?" Lennie asked Tish.

"Oh, no!" said Ketty, hastening to head off Tish's answer. "Snacks are for children."

But a body couldn't fend off hunger with words, she realized. For a minute she felt dizzy with an almost uncontrollable craving as she remembered the tables at Salem set with plenty—bread and meat, cabbages and turnips, potatoes and peas and beans, apples and peaches, plums and grapes, kraut and pickles and cheese, puddings and stews and rich, fat gingerbreads.

It wasn't wise, she reminded herself, to think about tasty victuals that weren't to be had at any cost. It was best to keep busy. Maybe, she decided, that was why Tish had taken to knitting.

"As soon as you finish your hickory nuts, children," she said, "we'll learn another word."

Picking the meat from the last of her nuts, Lennie crossed the deck to Ketty. "Why do you lace up your dress with them ribbons?" she asked.

"All womenfolks in Salem lace up their dresses with ribbons," Ketty told her.

"They're mighty pretty," said Lennie.

"When I marry," Ketty said, "I'll change these pink ribbons for blue ones. Girls your age in Salem wear red ribbons."

"I wisht I had some to wear," said Lennie.

"I wish I had brought some to give you," said Ketty.

The children gathered around Ketty with their pieces of bark. They learned *river* and *fire*.

"Can we play Old Woman now?" Pegg asked as they put away their pieces of bark.

"I've thought of a new game," Ketty said quickly, always fearful of scalping. "Hopscotch. I'll show you how to play it."

Taking one of the charred sticks, she sketched on the deck a rectangular scotch and divided it into five equal spaces. She looked about the deck until she found a pebble. While all aboard watched, she dropped the pebble into the first space, hopped from the first to the fifth space and back, picked up the pebble, threw it into the second space, again hopped from the first to the fifth space and back, picked up the pebble, threw it into the third space, and so on. After throwing the pebble into the fifth space and picking it up, she turned about in the space, threw the pebble into the first space, hopped for it, hopped back with the pebble on her palm, threw it in the air and caught it as it fell. She threw it into the second space, returned with it on her thumb, and again threw it in the air and caught it; into the third space, returned with it on one eye, threw it, and caught it; into the fourth space, returned with it on her

86

head, threw it, and caught it. Then she dropped it into the fifth space at her feet, stooped for it, placed it on her back, hopped once, caught the pebble, threw it high in the air, caught it as it fell, and slumped on the deck, laughing.

"Whoop!" shouted Squire.

"Ket-tee!" praised Lennie. "How could you do that?"

"Hit's my turn now," said Cal, shoving his way to the front of the scotch.

The children crowded about Ketty, all begging for turns.

"In hopscotch," Ketty explained, "if you drop the pebble, or fail to catch it, or throw it in the wrong space, you have to quit and let the next one try. Cal, you go first. The rest of you get in line."

Above the noise of the children Ketty heard Baptist's booming voice. "You got to treat this here spot mighty nice. That's Poor Valley Creek a-comin' in up ahead, and hit's planted as many shoals in this here river as they's teeth in a crocodile's mouth."

"I know what we can do," said Lennie. "We'll all learn hopscotch and see who can go the furthest 'thout a mistake. Us girls'll whup Cal and Squire, I bet."

Ketty smiled. It was good, she thought, to have hit upon something over which they could have a contest without claiming scalps.

"You hop oncet more, Ketty, to show us how hit's done," begged Lennie.

Ketty began hopping forward and back, tossing the pebble and catching it. A harsh, scraping noise along the bottom of the boat stopped her short. The boat jerked to a standstill, throwing her against Cal.

"Con-*sarn* it!" Anson growled.

The womenfolk and the children crowded to the bow of the boat.

"Back!" Anson shouted at them. "Get back from there!"

Baptist and Shubeal grabbed their setting poles, planted them on the gravelly bar on which the *Dragonfly* rested, braced their shoulders against them, and pushed with all their might. But the *Dragonfly* only settled more snugly into the gravel.

"Get into the cabin, all of you down there!" Anson ordered. His voice was raucous. "Get as far aft as you can."

Tish led the way into the cabin. The others crowded after her.

"Why did we come in here?" Lennie asked.

"Hush!" commanded Rachel.

"To lighten the load on the forward deck," whispered Ketty. "Be quiet," she urged the children. "Then we can hear when they get the boat free."

Overhead the three men poled and pushed and persuaded. But the *Dragonfly* made no move.

"Now we're in a mighty fix!" they heard Shubeal say.

"One thing, sure and certain," Anson answered. "We got to get her off before dark."

"You tell me how and I'll go do hit," Baptist said.

More pushing and grunting followed. Then those in the cabin heard Baptist's low whistle and his voice full of wonderment. "Thar's one of Donelson's pirogues or I'll eat my leggins."

"What's he a-talkin' 'bout?" Rachel asked, panting, close to tears.

"We've overtook Donelson!" shouted Cal.

"Praise the Lord!" cried Rachel, clasping her hands.

88

Cal pushed the others aside. "Let me out of here," he said. "I'm a-goin' to see."

Once the cabin door was opened, they all went crowding after Cal. Ketty picked up Farrer in her arms and carried him on deck. She felt as if she had caught a wild bird-thing that any second might go flying away.

"Whar's Donelson's pirogue?" asked Rachel, her eyes searching the river.

"Right thar," Baptist told her, pointing downriver, close to shore.

Eager eyes followed his direction. There, with its prow standing out of the water, was indeed a pirogue, half sunk in the sand.

"Lord a-mercy!" Rachel's voice quavered.

Anson, his face full of worry, studied the water around them.

"We'll have to lighten the boat," he said. "You women-folks and young uns down there, you'll all have to get off."

"In the water?" asked Rachel, her voice breaking.

"In the water," ordered Anson with barbs in his voice. "If it was deep enough to drown you, Rachel, we wouldn't 'a' grounded."

From the moment the boat had stuck on the shoals, Tish had said nary a word. Now she spoke quietly as she took command. "Young uns, line up. Help carry things off. We're here for the night."

"We're here till a freshet kindly decides to move us, I'm a-thinkin'," said Baptist.

Tish handed part of the deer meat to Cal, part of it to Squire. She put one blanket in Pegg's hands, another in Lennie's. She took off her shoepacks, and, tying them together, hung them about her neck. She raised the hem of her full skirt and tied it about her waist. Ketty, Lettice, and Rachel, watching her, did the same.

Anson slid the gangboard over the gunwale and rested the far end on a sand bar.

"Betsy," Tish said, studying the water between the sand bar and the river bank, "you ride on my back."

Ketty stooped before Farrer. "You get on my back, Farrer," she said. "I'll be your horse and set you across."

Farrer climbed on.

"Pegg, you ride on Rachel's back," ordered Tish. "The rest of you young uns wait your turn. You'd get wet to your middles."

Rachel hesitated as she looked at the water. "Why did we ever leave home?"

"Pegg," said Tish, "you wait for Ketty, you and Lennie. Cal, I'll come back for you and Squire. Bring your pappy's rifle, Cal. We'll need hit. Squire, you bring an ax."

Ketty, tingling with the sudden knowing that Tish had decided she was good for something, walked down the gangboard with Farrer on her back, crossed the sand bar, and waded through the cold water to the river bank.

"I declare," said Rachel when finally they were all safe on the bank, "one of them menfolks ought to come and kindle us a fire. We'll all catch our death of cold, a-bein' so wet and all."

"Menfolks got their work cut out for 'em," Tish said. "Young uns, gather me up some driftwood."

While Tish lighted a fire with Anson's rifle as expertly as Anson had lighted one the night before, and with much less powder, Ketty, Lettice, and the children brought driftwood, cut crotched sticks, and set up stones for broiling the smoked deer meat.

"Here, Rachel," said Tish, handing her the first piece of meat to broil. "Somethin' to do'll keep your mind off trouble."

On board the *Dragonfly* the menfolk pushed and strained and grunted in their effort to float the boat free of the gravelly bar. But the big flat didn't budge.

When Baptist sniffed the broiling meat, he threw down his pole. "Ain't nothin' but a freshet a-goin' to move us off this here shoal," he said, "and ain't no freshet in sight. Me, I'm a-goin' to eat my vittles and put up for the night and dream how to get this here boat a-floatin' oncet more."

"While you're a-worryin' 'bout the boat, you mought as well get your fill of worryin'," Tish said to the menfolk as they waded ashore. "We got enough deer meat left for one-two days. Oncet that's gone, we got precious little of anything else. And we hain't hardly left Fort Patrick Henry. What we got, we'd better save for desperation."

"All right," said Shubeal, drawing on his shoepacks, "I'm a-goin' huntin' tomorrer. Stuck or no stuck, a feller's got to have vittles in his craw."

"You'd better bring in more than one skinny deer, too," Tish told him. "We're stuck here nobody knows how long."

"Tish ain't got no faith in rain," commented Baptist.

"Nor in my huntin'," said Shubeal.

"I ain't a-countin' deer till they're skinned," answered Tish.

As soon as the voyagers had eaten, they settled themselves for the night. Beside her own pallet of cedar boughs Ketty laid another, smaller one and covered both with elk hides. "This, Farrer, is your bed tonight," she said to the child. "You want to lie down and let me cover you?" she invited.

Farrer stood looking at her. With a motion so slight a body might have imagined it, he leaned toward Rachel.

"Go on, Farrer," urged Rachel.

"I'll sing you a song to go to sleep by," coaxed Ketty.

Pulled in both directions, Farrer scuffed hesitantly to the pallet and lay down. Ketty covered him with blankets and lay down beside him on her own pallet. The others, too, lay down, their feet stretched to the glowing coals of the fire. To the accompaniment of the water breaking against the hapless *Dragonfly*, Ketty, with her hand over Farrer's, sang softly to him a song she had learned from her mother:

"Come o'er the stream, Charlie, dear Charlie, brave Charlie,
Come o'er the stream, Charlie, and dine with Maclean,
And though you be weary we'll make your heart cheery,
And welcome our Charlie and his loyal train.

"We'll bring down the track deer, we'll bring down the black steer,
The lamb from the bracken, and doe from the glen;
The salt sea we'll harry, and bring to our Charlie,
The cream from the bothy, and curd from the pen."

"I helped my pappy feed the lambs," came from the small pallet when the song was finished.

Ketty caught her breath. It was the first time she had heard Farrer speak.

"So you were a little shepherd!" she said.

"My lamb was black," Farrer said.

"Did it have a name?"

"Midnight," said Farrer. He turned over, nestled into his pallet, and was soon breathing deeply.

Soon, too, the others were breathing deeply as heat from the embers baked their feet and dried their shoepacks stuffed with leaves to keep them from shrinking.

But sleep did not come easily to Ketty. Long after Shubeal began snoring—or was it Baptist?—she lay awake, listening to the restless rushing of the river, the slow croaking of frogs in the mud banks, the March wind in the trees. The night, she discovered, had a music all its own, its rhythm drumming strong and clear against the darkness.

Pegg, you wait for Ketty.

Ketty pulled an arm from under her blanket and felt the braids about her head. Sister Oesterlein, by pinning up her hair, had prepared her for the solemn state of womanhood. But it was Tish who had anointed her. Contented, she snuggled under her blankets beside Farrer and slept.

chapter 8

LONG before there was a hint of day in the sky, songbirds
that outdid the Salem trombonists trumpeting glad
tidings awakened the voyagers. At once men and women
were up, stretching their arms and legs, stamping their feet,
shaking the children awake, rekindling the fire. At dawn
clouds covered the eastern sky.

"Looky thar," Baptist said to Tish. "Freshet's on the way
somewheres."

Tish, too, studied the sky. "We'll be lucky if hit's of a
size to do us any good," she said.

"Shubeal, before you light out hunting," said Anson
when they had eaten their slim portions of deer meat, "we'd
better unload a lot of that plunder so's the boat'll float
when the water rises."

Rachel groaned. "How?" she asked.

"On our backs," Anson told her. "How else?"

He slipped his shoepacks off his feet and pulled his
tight breeches high on his legs. Baptist and Shubeal, too,
made ready to wade the river to the sand bar, while Tish
raised the hem of her skirt and tied it about her waist.

"Lettice, you don't need to help," Tish said.

"Keep the fire going," Anson ordered Tish as he shouldered his rifle and waded toward the boat, "so's we can warm ourselves once in a while. You young uns," he added, looking back at the children, "you can best help by staying clean out of sight."

"Goody!" said Lennie. "We'll have school."

"You'll have to have it by your lonesome," said Tish. "They's work for grown hands on the boat."

"We can't have school 'thout a teacher," complained Lennie.

"You can write your words on your pieces of bark," said Ketty. "When we start floating again we'll learn some new ones."

"What's Farrer a-goin' to do?" asked Lennie.

Ketty looked down at Farrer holding tightly to her hand.

"Farrer's going to sit here by the fire and char some sticks. Aren't you, Farrer? Maybe Lettice'll help you."

Ketty felt Farrer's fingers tighten their grip. It was not a good omen, she thought.

"You can char sticks for everybody, Farrer," Ketty told him. "You can learn to count that way."

Ketty gathered a handful of driftwood twigs. Then, squatting beside Farrer in front of the coals, she put a twig in his hand and showed him how to burn and blacken the end of it.

"See if you can have one charred by the time I carry a load off the boat," she coaxed him.

Through the stretch of cold knee-deep water Ketty waded, and walked up the gangboard to the deck of the *Dragonfly*, where the others had gone before.

"Just the heavy things," Anson directed as he clanked toward the gangboard with an armload of log chains.

Baptist's dog, standing on deck, stiffened and growled low.

"Sh-h-h!" Baptist warned above the clank of the chains. He laid one hand on the dog's back and with the other he picked up his rifle. All on board froze and listened. In the hush they heard men's voices upriver.

Watching the river bend, Baptist dropped to one knee, primed his rifle, and rested the barrel on the gunwale. Anson laid his armload of chains on the deck, picked up his rifle, and rested it beside Baptist's. One minute, two minutes, long as eternity, flowed by.

The sound of voices grew clearer, "Hear that?" Baptist, still watching, asked in a half-whisper.

"What, Baptist?" asked Rachel.

"They're a-talkin' like us," Baptist said. "We're a purty sight, ain't we"—he laughed—"scart teetotally out of our wits at the sound of a man a-talkin', and us two days out of Fort Patrick Henry?"

Seconds later a dugout canoe with three men in it floated around the bend in the river.

"I never in my life seen a purtier sight," declared Rachel, her voice quavery.

"Howdy, strangers!" Baptist shouted, his big voice booming along the watery path to the men in the canoe.

"Howdy, folks!" one of them answered.

The canoe floated nearer. The three men, the voyagers could see, were dressed in stout hunting clothes. The two in front appeared to be Anson's age. The man in the stern was younger.

"Bad luck?" called the man in the bow.

"That's too purty a name for hit," called Baptist. "Hit's plain disaster."

The canoe floated alongside the *Dragonfly.*

"You're not the first to get stuck on these Poor Valley shoals," said the man in the stern. "This is a mean spot to navigate."

As he talked he kept a watchful eye on the main current and on the cross current set up by the inflow of the creek.

"We'll tie up and help you," he said.

The travelers aboard the *Dragonfly* watched the canoe float past. It was not like the ordinary dugout a body usually saw on the rivers, the clumsy, heavy craft gutted by adz and fire from the trunk of a sycamore tree. Instead it was fashioned of a cedar trunk, smoothly molded to glide through the water, and its appearance revealed a man's patient work and careful chipping as he stood on the log and swung his sharp ax, now on this side, now on that, hitting between his feet. Its four ribs were natural bulkheads carefully carved from the trunk. On the near side of its prow was painted in bold black letters: *Walk-on-the-Water.*

"Now that thar's my notion of travelin' down the rivers," declared Baptist as the canoe sliced the current smoothly and easily. "Hey, Lettice," he called, "see that thar thing? What say you and me borry hit and set out by our lonesome?"

Lettice, watching from the river bank, giggled.

The handful aboard the *Dragonfly* watched as the men paddled the canoe to the river's edge, stepped on land, tied up the craft to a tree, and came walking along the river bank.

"Landing your load?" asked the young man as he studied the *Dragonfly*.

"The heavy stuff," Anson told him.

"Rain fell on Reedy this morning. The river ought to rise soon now," said the man. "While you folks unload a few more things," he added, "we'll get rollers ready to put under the boat. Take advantage of the rise when it comes." He noticed Farrer charring sticks. "What are you doing here, young fellow?" he asked.

"He's a-makin' writin' sticks," Lennie explained. "For teacher."

"So you're having school on the boat!" exclaimed the man. "Who's your teacher?"

"That un," said Lennie, pointing to Ketty, who at that moment was wading toward the bank, carrying a plowshare. She blushed under the man's gaze.

He met her at the edge of the water, took the plowshare, and laid it on the ground. Ketty hastily untied her skirt from about her waist.

"Suppose I take over your share of unloading, and you get back to your books," the man said. "Or do you have books?"

"We—we didn't, at first," Ketty stammered. "We made some—out of birch bark."

"Birch bark?" The man chuckled. He turned to Anson, who by then had reached the river bank.

"You're bound for—"

"The French Lick, on the Cumberland," said Anson.

"Alone?" the man asked, raising his eyebrows.

"We was supposed to go with a big party," Anson told

him. "But we was held up and set out from Fort Patrick Henry just the day before yesterday. We're thinking maybe we'll overtake Donelson—that's the name of the man heading the party."

"Oh, Donelson," said the man. "He's not far ahead of you. Depends on the trouble he runs into whether or not you catch him." He shook his head. "But traveling alone—"

"You heading some place?" asked Anson.

"Surveying," the man told him. "My name's George Soelle. These are my deputies." He nodded toward the other two men. "We've been surveying grants through here for two weeks. On our way downriver to finish up the last plot."

"Then, praised be the Lord!" said Anson. "If we had to run on them shoals, I'm glad it was yesterday and not tomorrow."

At once the surveyors set to work. They chopped down small trees for rollers, trimmed the limbs, and dragged the trunks to the *Dragonfly.* Then began the straining and pushing, the grunting and heaving and sweating that were to go on until early afternoon, when the river rose ever so little on the gunwales, and the *Dragonfly*, with a loud shout from the menfolk, slid once more into deep water. Anson plunged through the water and clambered on board, with Shubeal and Baptist following. With directions from George Soelle they poled the flat into a safe landing place just below the canoe.

While the surveyors chained the flat to trees, Anson hurried ashore, in a swivet to be loaded and floating once more.

"You're forgettin', ain't you, Anse," Shubeal reminded

him, "this here's the place I'm a-goin' huntin'? I'll scour the woods for vittles while the rest of you load up."

"But there's still three hours of daylight in the sky," grumbled Anson. "We could float an hour, leastways. Take up some of that slack."

"Anse," announced Baptist, "I don't aim to pole that flat one little-bitty inch away from this here bank till we get vittles aboard her."

"I never before knowed a body that had to be told when he was hungry," said Shubeal.

"Hit won't hurt if ever'body dries out too," said Tish.

Anson breathed a sigh of defeat. He turned toward George Soelle and the two deputies. "You mought as well stay and snack with us," he said.

"Our last grant is down the river a ways," said George Soelle. "We ought to finish by sundown. We'll camp for the night with you and set out for New Bern in the morning."

Anson turned to Shubeal. "What you waiting for?" he asked.

Shubeal shouldered his rifle and, calling Baptist's dog to follow, set out north along the bed of Poor Valley Creek.

"Be back before dark," he called as he disappeared among the black tree trunks and underbrush. "Have a bed of live coals ready. I'll likely fetch a bear."

"Jist see that that thar bear don't turn out to be a weasel," warned Baptist as he picked up an armload of log chains and started toward the *Dragonfly*.

At owl light the three surveyors came back to camp.

"Sit by the fire and rest yourselves," Anson said. "Shubeal ought to be in any minute now."

100

"With that thar bear," added Baptist.

"I don't know," Anson said, "what's a-keeping him."

Like a tapestry woven all of dark threads, evening spread over and around the mountains, and night hemmed the voyagers in. While the womenfolk tended the last of the deer meat broiling over the fire, the menfolk sat listening to George Soelle tell tales of wild varmints and woods creatures he'd met up with while surveying in the wilderness. Ketty, watching the firelight play on his lean face and in his friendly dark eyes, thought him as much at home in the woods as any of the creatures he told about—the crow that took up with him and stole his tally pins, the chipmunk that traveled with him in his shot pouch, the barred owl that flew from tree to tree through the woods ahead of him as if to show him the way.

Was he telling his tales to keep folks' minds off Shubeal? Ketty wondered. When the deer meat was doled out, he ate his share in silence, and now and then glanced furtively in the direction Shubeal had gone, listening, like all the others, for the faint, far-off rustle of footsteps on dry leaves or the snapping of twigs under a man's foot.

But they heard nothing—nothing but the purling of the creek water across the shoals as it emptied into the river, the slow croaking of frogs along the mud banks of the creek, and the restless rushing of the river toward the sea.

"What d'ye reckon's a-keepin' him?" asked Rachel.

"Did you ever know Shubeal to come back from any place on time?" asked Tish. "I say we'd better get our pallets down. Young uns' heads a-noddin' already."

When the children had been put to bed, menfolk and

womenfolk seated themselves again by the fire. And again the listening began—the listening and the uncertain, question-filled waiting.

After a while Baptist got to his feet. "I'll fire my rifle. See if that'll bring him in," he said. "He's got my dog."

"Got powder to waste?" asked Soelle. "Shubeal'll know enough to climb a hill somewhere and look for a fire."

"Hit mought be he's in a holler somewheres and can't see the fire," said Rachel.

"Reckon it's safe to keep the fire a-going?" asked Anson.

"Here, yes," said Soelle. "Further downriver you couldn't take a chance." He watched Baptist priming his rifle. "The sound of a horn carries pretty far," he said. "Don't you have a horn?"

"You go and fire anyway," Rachel said, pleading with Baptist.

Baptist shouldered his rifle and started along the creek in the direction Shubeal had gone. Beyond the puny circle of light the eternal great darkness swallowed him quickly. Ketty, watching, knew that, for all his bragging, he was still a mortal thing.

For a few paces the listeners heard his footsteps. Then all was still save the crafty wilderness speaking in its many tongues.

Five minutes they waited. Ten. Then they heard the crack of Baptist's rifle.

"Be still now," begged Rachel, "so's we can hear."

But out of the wilderness came no answering shot from Shubeal.

Rachel could no longer hold back the tears flimsily

102

dammed inside her. "Somethin's happened to him, sure and sartain," she said between sobs.

"Aw, Rachel, nothing's happened to Shubeal. He's just got turned around in the woods and lost his way," Anson told her.

"Losing yourself in the woods is the easiest thing in the world to do, especially with night coming on," spoke up George Soelle.

"You—you didn't hear nothin'?" Rachel asked as Baptist trudged back into the circle of light.

"Nary a thing," admitted Baptist. "But that don't mean Shubeal won't be here by sunup a-wantin' his breakfast and a-wantin' hit in a hurry. And what's he a-goin' to say when he catches you a-snivelin' thataway?"

"I don't care who catches me a-snivelin'," screamed Rachel. "Shubeal's done been scalped, and you know hit."

Across her frenzy Tish's quiet voice fell as soothingly as a song a body might sing to a peevish young un. "You been so long in the wilderness, Rachel, and hain't learned that half a woman's life is waitin'?" she asked. "Hit's time we was all asleep."

"Hit wouldn't be so bad a-waitin' if a body knowed," said Rachel, still sobbing.

"What else is waitin' but not knowin'?" Tish asked.

chapter 9

"RECKON I'll try bringing Shubeal in with the horn," said Anson the next morning.

The moaning sound of the horn traveled along the creek bed and up the hollows and to the mountains that ringed the voyagers in, calling and calling to a man lost. A dozen times Anson raised the horn to his lips and blew. After each blast the voyagers listened, the moaning ringing in their ears after the sound had spent itself altogether. But Shubeal did not come.

"We'd better all set out looking," said Anson, his face glum. "Reckon you three can help us?" he asked George Soelle.

"We aimed to head for New Bern today," said George.

"We could look for Shubeal on the way a-goin' east," said one of the deputies. "Could be we'd find him in that direction. When a feller's lost he's apt to get all mixed up in his easts and wests."

"Specially when the sky's overcast like it was yesterday," said the other deputy.

"We can do that much," agreed George. "As we paddle upriver, we'll tie up every little while and scour the woods.

Anyway," he added, "we've got to do some hunting ourselves."

"Keep smoke a-rising, Tish," ordered Anson, nodding toward the fire. "Could be smoke'll lead Shubeal in. And while we're held up, it'll be a mighty good time for you womenfolks to go fishing."

"Rachel, we'll be back before suppertime with Shubeal and two bears," Baptist promised as he and Anson, glum-faced and fidgety, set out north along the creek.

A few minutes later George Soelle and the two deputies climbed into the canoe and paddled upriver, toward the east.

Ketty, watching until they disappeared around the bend, stood for a spell alone, feeling the wilderness pressing in upon her. Stirring powerfully with new life in every tree and blade and creature, the wilderness was a thing to raise a body on tiptoe singing. But it was a cruel thing too, exacting its full price for every misstep that mortals took. Its sounds—the songs of water and winds and timorous wild things—could lull a body to rest and quiet sleep, or they could drive a body outside herself with torment. They could magnify themselves and drown out all other sounds and all other thoughts and make a body sore afraid.

Quickly Ketty scotched her thoughts. A body could go clean out of her mind, she warned herself, the way Rachel seemed about to do, if she dwelt on such things. Wait a woman surely had to do in the wilderness, with all her questions echoed but never answered in the wilderness sounds. But while she waited, she must work.

"Tish," she asked, "would you like the children and me to go fishing?"

"The fishin' poles are a-standin' in a corner of the cabin," Tish told her. "The creek'll be a good place to catch crawfish for bait."

Ketty brought from the *Dragonfly* the fishing poles and a gourd to hold the crawfish. Taking Farrer by the hand and calling the other children to follow, she walked along the creek bank, looking for a shallow place where she might find crawfish under rocks. She was grateful for a chance to get Farrer away from Rachel, who had fallen into a fit of silence that was harder to endure than her crying.

"Ketty," said Squire, "do you reckon—"

"Your pappy's coming back?" Ketty finished his question, trying to head off any talk of scalping in Farrer's hearing. "Count how many men are out looking for him. I'll name them and all of you count," she said. "Anson."

"One," counted the children.

"Baptist."

"Two."

"George Soelle."

"Three."

"One deputy surveyor."

"Four."

"Another deputy surveyor."

"Five."

"Five men looking for Shubeal," Ketty said.

"Know who's a-goin' to find Shubeal?" said Cal. "Baptist. He's got eyes sharp as an old hoot owl. He can see things in the dark."

"I bet George Soelle can see things that Baptist can't see," said Lennie.

Ketty wondered. Lennie, she remembered, was blessed

106

with a poet's eyes. Baptist could see the thing before him. But as George Soelle talked, it did seem that his eyes, which sometimes seemed brown and sometimes murky blue, were looking not at but through the thing before him. It seemed that his eyes were piercing sham and shoddy pretense and looking into the deep corners and along the corridors of the heart.

"I believe he can too, Lennie," said Ketty.

Lennie, last in line, crowded past the other children, caught Ketty's hand, and walked beside her.

In the afternoon Tish and Lettice, Ketty, Cal, and Squire fished in the river. From their catch Tish selected half a dozen catfish, strung them on a crotched limb, laid the limb in the river, and fastened it to the bank with a rock.

"They'll taste good for breakfast," she said.

When she had cleaned, cut in chunks, and broiled the others, she carried a chunk to Rachel.

Rachel glanced at the offering. "You didn't salt hit, did you?" she asked.

"Savin' the salt," Tish told her.

Rachel shook her head. "I never could abide fish 'thout salt," she said.

At the shank end of the day Anson came out of the woods with a passel of squirrels tied together by their feet and dangling limply across his shoulder. After awhile Baptist stumbled in, scratched with briers. "Consarn hit!" he grumbled. "Couldn't find nothin'. Shubeal, bear, deer, coon, squirrel, possum, pigeon—nothin'."

Anson groaned as he sat down on the ground. He rested his back against a tree while Tish skinned and gutted the squirrels. His sagging shoulders, as catching as a rashy sickness, infected the others so that they all stood about glumly, saying little.

"Looky!" cried Cal suddenly, pointing upriver. "Looky yander! Ain't that—"

Tish, looking upriver, laid her skinning knife on a rock. Anson, in spite of his weariness, got to his feet and stumbled to the river's edge. The others—Baptist, the womenfolk, and the children—followed and stood full of wonderments as they watched a slim canoe float downriver toward them.

"That's his'n, ain't hit?" said Baptist.

The canoe floated closer. Only one man was in it.

"That's him, too," said Tish.

"That's him if hit ain't his hant," said Baptist.

Closer floated the canoe.

"Ain't his hant," said Lennie.

"Wonder what's happened now?" Anson said. "Reckon—"

"Maybe he's found Shubeal," said Lennie, her voice lifting.

"Hush!" commanded Tish.

They kept on staring and wondering as George Soelle, a thing of flesh and blood, guided his canoe into sheltered water and climbed out on the bank.

"I thought you was heading for New Bern," Anson said.

"The deputies have gone on," George said, "on foot. I sent my papers with them. Thought I'd wait another day. Back in the woods a piece I shot a deer. We can bring it out before dark if we hurry."

"You didn't—did you—" began Rachel.

"No, Rachel," said George kindly. "We didn't see any sign at all of Shubeal."

If it was the work of the menfolk to find Shubeal, thought Ketty; it was her work to shore up the children's minds with hope, at least until hope had to be abandoned. While Anson, Baptist, and George Soelle, back at the campfire, skinned the deer and cut up the meat for broiling, Ketty took Pegg and Squire down to the river bank away from the others.

"Even though your pappy hasn't come back, we won't quit believing he's alive," she told them. "Until we know differently, we'll believe he's only lost, and he'll find his way back. And," she added, looking steadily at them, "you won't talk about your pappy where Farrer can hear, will you?"

George Soelle came hurrying along just then.

"These Shubeal's children?" he asked, stopping.

"Yes," Ketty told him.

He stooped between Pegg and Squire and put an arm about each of them.

"It's the easiest thing in the world to get turned around in the woods and lose your direction," he told them. "Once I got lost when I was out hunting. The sky was cloudy, like today, and it took me four days to find my way in. Four whole days. Know what?" He turned to Squire. "You're going to have to be extra brave because of your mother. And you," he said, lifting Pegg's chin with his finger, "chin up!"

Squire and Pegg, awe in their eyes, stared at him.

"I'm going down to my canoe to fetch something," he told them. "Want to come? All of you?"

That night the fire was kindled higher than the night before in the hope that Shubeal might somewhere in the pitch-dark wilderness climb a hill and see its beckoning glow. But as the voyagers lay on their pallets no one said what he was thinking—that either Shubeal had been scalped by red men or else he had come to harm through some woods mischief and could make no headway in the wild underbrush of rhododendron and twisted grapevine.

The children slept. But the womenfolk turned fitfully as they listened to Rachel sobbing and moaning into her cedar pallet, while the menfolk, dozing lightly, raised on their elbows with every nearby noise of inquisitive night varmints prowling beyond the light of the campfire.

Day brought the sun to cheer the voyagers, but they could not be cheered. Rachel sat dazed, looking into the fire and refusing to eat, even though Tish had sprinkled a pinch of salt on the chunk of catfish she had broiled for her.

"We'll go out oncet more, Rachel," Baptist told her. "And before dark we'll bring Shubeal back *and* a passel of bear meat or my name ain't Baptist Ramsay."

"While we're out, you womenfolks smoke this here deer meat George brought," ordered Anson. "Don't waste a single morsel of it, Tish, and we won't get hung up thisaway again when somebody decides he has to go hunting." He picked up his rifle and counted the shot in his pouch. Then, thoughtfully, he turned to Baptist. "Maybe," he said, "one of us'd better stay around here. You and George go."

In the middle of the afternoon Anson called Ketty to walk down to the boat with him. As he shifted the load on deck he asked, "Reckon you can handle Shubeal's oar?"

Ketty startled, sensing what was in his mind.

"If they don't bring Shubeal in tonight, we'll have to go

110

on 'thout him," he explained. "We'll never catch Donelson thisaway."

"What will Rachel say?" asked Ketty.

"She'll carry on. But what's done is done. It can't be holped. And I'm a-thinking," Anson added, "it's time you learned to shoot a rifle."

"I?" Ketty stared at him. "What would I shoot?"

"All right," said Anson, his voice rising tensely, "Shubeal's done been picked off. There's a-coming a time, and it ain't far off, maybe, that we'll all be in danger."

Ketty stared at her brother. "Are you talking about shooting Indians, Anson?" she asked.

"Don't hand me none of that Salem stuff," Anson warned. *Keep the counsel of your own heart, Ketty.*

"But what I've told you is true," said Ketty. "Nobody ever shot at Indians in Salem. And Indians never shot at anybody there."

"But I'm a-telling you, this here ain't Salem," Anson answered angrily. "This here's the wilderness. And in the wilderness red men are going to kill you dead if you don't kill them first."

Ketty had seen Anson displeasured many a time since they had reached Fort Patrick Henry, but she had never before seen him fighting mad. She trembled as she tried to think of the right words to say to him. In spite of anything that had happened in Salem, she knew that what Anson said of Indians in the wilderness was true. But why should one rule hold in Salem and another in the wilderness? she wondered. A great gulf stretched between the two. And a gulf stretched between her and Anson. She stoutly dis-

111

believed what Anson believed, but could she make him understand her?

"Remember what I told you Mother used to do?" she asked. "Put the basket of food out for the Indians?"

"But that was North Caroliny and this here is the wilderness, I keep telling you." Anson's voice rose to a shout. "They're different things. Can't you understand?"

Keep the counsel of your own heart, Ketty.

"Different things? It's you who is different from Mother, Anson," said Ketty, trying to quiet the turmoil in her mind.

Anson's face turned red with rage. "I don't want to hear another word about them baskets of vittles!" he thundered.

The sound of the thunder died away, leaving Ketty shaken but standing firm. "Red men have never harmed me, Anson," she said quietly. "Why should I harm them?"

"I reckon it ain't nothing to you that they've done scalped Shubeal? And Farrer's pappy and mammy? And a whole passel of other folks?"

"And what had the other folks done to the red men?" asked Ketty.

"Nothing! Nary a single thing!" declared Anson. "And if you're a-thinking you're better than anybody else on this here boat, scrub that notion out of your head right now, with the stoutest lye soap you can lay hands on. 'Cause you're not better. You're cut out of the same cloth as the rest of us. And you make just as good a target for the red men too. You're not one whit different from the rest of us."

"You and I are different, Anson."

"We are, are we?" said Anson. "You love folks so much

112

that you hang out baskets of vittles for murderous red men and think that's going to pacify 'em so they'll leave folks in peace. Well, I know red men. And I love folks too. I love 'em so much that I don't mean to stand by and see 'em burned out by red men and scalped or driven off to Detroit. I love 'em so much that I do something about it. A year ago when nine hundred men gathered on the Holston, I was among 'em. We went down these here rivers and burned eleven filthy Chickamaugy towns and killed ever' red man we could sight. That's how much I love folks. I'm willing to lose my life to save 'em."

Ketty stared at him. "You and I are more different than I thought, Anson," she said.

Anson narrowed his eyes. Through clenched teeth he declared, "I'm going to learn you to shoot a rifle if it's the last thing I ever do."

Keep the counsel of your own heart, Ketty.

Singed in the fire of Anson's wrath, Ketty trembled like a leaf on an aspen sapling. But she heard herself saying, "I'm not learning to shoot red men, Anson."

Across the clutter of the deck they faced each other. Twice Anson started to speak, but anger dammed his words. His clenched fists shook. He swallowed once, twice —hard. Then his shoulders wilted, and he turned on his heel.

"I've been a-wondering," he muttered, "and now I mought as well wonder out loud, why I ever took the time and trouble, and risk getting left behind, to hunt you up and fetch you."

"Maybe, Anson," Ketty told him thoughtfully, "it was for some good purpose."

113

chapter 10

IN THE soft owl light, Ketty watched Anson laying driftwood on the fire. She reckoned he meant to light one last mighty beacon to show Shubeal the way back to camp, in case life was left in Shubeal. She reckoned, too, that Anson in his mind was imagining the words she would say to him, and practicing to himself the words he would say to her, should he make up his mind to tell her once more he aimed to teach her to shoot red men—hard, brawny words against puny, petticoat words.

The wood crackled and snapped in the hot blaze. Up the creek along the mudbanks frogs croaked. Off a ways from the campfire Lennie and Cal played a game of tag. Unceasingly the river roared in its bed. Not another sound could a body hear save these four voices—the fire's, the frogs', the children's, and the river's.

It was a thousand days' wonder, thought Ketty, that in so peaceful a place there should be so little peace. Anson was stewing like a kettle of squirrel meat. About the fire stood the womenfolk, waiting, saying nary a word, turning as if they were on spits to look off yonder in the woods for somebody coming along Poor Valley Creek.

And in herself there was no peace, either. What was she going to say to Anson if he told her once more he aimed to teach her to shoot red men? Was he going to lord it over her every time he got a notion she ought to do something? A body might crown her head with thick braids of gold and take a solemn vow she'd govern herself till the stars paled. But what was she actually to do when red men came skulking and scalping?

As she watched the flames from the fire leap bright against the darkling evening, she thought long and hard of her mother, and in her mind there was at last a semblance of peace. Her mother's way had been a good way. In the far-off land to which she was going, she would follow it. On the way there she'd follow it, too, let Anson rant and roar as he was bound to do, and let come what may.

A little before dark Baptist and George came out of the woods together. One of them carried two limp squirrels, the other a ringtailed coon.

"I thought you was aimin' to bring two bears, Baptist," called Cal.

"Hold your tongue, young un!" Baptist answered.

But Rachel's questioning gaze he couldn't silence so easily.

"We teetotally ransacked ever' hill and holler and creek bed, Rachel," he told her. "He ain't thar."

Rachel, numb with crying, stared vacantly at Baptist.

"Maybe—tomorrer—" she said, pleading-like.

"Rachel," Anson said, "this whole enduring day smoke signals have been going up. And now this here fire's big enough so Shubeal can see it for miles, granting he's on a high enough hill. If this here fire don't bring him in, we'll

115

blow the horn again. And if the horn don't bring him, we'll even try firing once more, though our powder supply ain't getting any bigger. But if Shubeal ain't in by sunup, we'll go on."

"And leave him?" asked Rachel piteously, her hand at her throat.

"At sunup we're setting out," announced Anson.

Rachel broke into sorrowful sobs. "Whatever will I do, me and the young uns, 'thout Shubeal to fend for us?"

George and Baptist busied themselves skinning the squirrels and the coon.

"It may be possible, Anson, to get a flat down the rivers with two oarsmen," said George quietly, "but it's taking a mighty chance."

"Looks like this whole enduring business is getting to be a chancy thing," grumbled Anson. Then he brightened. "Stands to reason, so many folks going to the Lick, we could pick up another hand at the mouth of the French Broad," he said, "or the Clinch."

"There'll be three oarsmen," Ketty said. "I'm manning one oar."

George, his knife poised for nicking the coon pelt, looked up at her. The firelight fell full on her face, in her amber-flecked eyes, and on her tawny gold braids of hair.

"You don't know how," he said. And he went back to skinning the coon.

"I've had one lesson," Ketty answered. "And I can learn —quickly."

George slit the skin along the underside of the coon's body and peeled it off the flesh before he spoke again.

116

"If you're going to pull an oar," he asked, a half-smile lighting his face, "who's going to teach school?"

"Tomorrow will decide," said Ketty.

Tish broiled the chunks of coon and squirrel and carried the tenderest piece of the squirrel meat to Rachel. But Rachel stared past the meat into the fire and refused to eat.

"A feller needs tommyhawk teeth to eat this here critter," complained Baptist as he tore the meat off a coon bone with his teeth. Couldn't they all have a helping of the deer meat Tish had smoked and stashed away on the boat? he wanted to know.

Anson, too, was full of complaints. He'd eaten tough, stringy meat, but he reckoned he'd never in all his borned days eaten any as tough as that. What's more, they'd better be saving their powder for big game. They'd better use rocks for powder if squirrels was all a hunter could find. But, no, he said, nobody was touching the deer meat now. It was being saved for what lay ahead.

"Anson," said George, "We counted four dead deer. Animals starved to death during this long freeze."

"Yea," said Baptist, "I reckon we're lucky to be eatin' stringy coon and skinny squirrels."

"We can set our fish poles," said Anson. "Catch enough fish for breakfast. You mought boil up a mess tonight, Tish," he added. "Have it ready."

After supper, while Anson heaped wood on the fire till it seemed the flames were licking the treetops, Tish, sharp-tongued with anxiety, sent the children to their pallets. A body couldn't hear herself think above the racket they made, she complained, though they were making no racket, being infected with the fear that beset their elders and, like their elders, hushed.

Ketty tucked Farrer's blanket about him on the pallet beside her own. She thought gratefully how like a cocoon he had clung to her the last few days. How much he was aware of Shubeal's fate and Rachel's fear she couldn't guess. It was enough that fear had left him somewhat in peace.

When the child was asleep, Ketty joined the womenfolk and stood off from the hot blaze of the fire, listening. But the fire did not bring Shubeal.

After a spell Anson took his horn, walked a few steps from the others, filled his lungs with air, and blew a loud blast. When half a dozen blasts of the horn did not bring an answering shout from Shubeal, Baptist slanted the barrel of his rifle toward the tree crowns and pulled the trigger. The roar of the big rifle went echoing through the dark woods. But no rifle cracked in reply. Nobody hollered faintly from some far-off place in the pitch-dark night.

"Baptist," begged Rachel, "shoot oncet more—jist oncet."

"It ain't one bit of use, Rachel," Anson told her. "And we ain't got another grain of powder to waste. What's more, if we go getting held up thisaway again, we'll never catch Donelson. Fact is," he muttered sullenly, "I'm beginning to wonder why we ever started for that French Lick at all. Ever'body get to bed now, so's we can get an early start."

chapter 11

WHEN day was only a scant promise in the morning sky, Anson called the others to get up. Quietly the womenfolk roused the children and shook them out of their groggy sleep. Quietly the voyagers ate their breakfast of cold boiled fish; quietly they got together their belongings. In all they did, stillness brooded over them as they continued to listen on the chance that, somewhere along Poor Valley Creek, a lost man might be calling.

"Ever'body quit dawdling and get on board," ordered Anson. He looked sharply at Rachel, who was making no move toward the boat.

"Anse," said Rachel, hollow-eyed, "I been a-thinkin'. Me and the young uns, we'll be a-goin' back."

Anson snorted. "Going back! You and Squire and Pegg and Farrer." He counted on the fingers of one hand. "Four good wolf snacks."

"Rachel," said Tish, her voice as soothing as bee balm on a feverish sting, "you can't go back by your lonesome. Anyway, what'd you go back to?" She started toward the boat. "You come on with us," she coaxed. "And stop snivelin'.

Nothin's ever cured by snivelin'. We'll find some way to make out."

"But I made up my mind in the dark," Rachel said stubbornly. "Me and the young uns, we'll go along with George Soelle, in the canoe."

All eyes turned to George. He started, as if Rachel's words had trapped him when he wasn't paying attention. He looked at the faces about him and then turned to Rachel. "I too made up my mind in the dark, Rachel," he said. "I'm not going back. I'm going on the *Dragonfly*."

Mouths gaped. Question-filled eyes stared.

"A bit ago I bought up a claim on Drake's Creek," George explained, "somewhere north of your French Lick. So I said to myself in the dark, if you folks'll let me go along with you, what better time to go and survey my claim than now, when I'll have company down the rivers? There's nothing keeping me any place. I can lash my canoe to the flat."

"Reckon then you can man Shubeal's oar," said Anson, uncommonly pleasured.

"Maybe thar is a thing called luck," put in Baptist. "Too bad Shubeal ain't here to say 'I done told you.'"

George turned again to Rachel. "I'm not settling with the notion that we've seen the last of Shubeal," he told her. "Not yet. He's not behind us. At least, the deputies and I found no trace that he'd been that way. And he's not anywhere along Poor Valley. Baptist and I scoured that creek bottom clean. If he's alive, he's someplace downriver, ahead of us. So it behooves us to get aboard and shove off as fast as we can."

Rachel listened to George as if he were saying Gospel

verses. Without another word she went on board the flat and took her stand beside the gunwale where she could keep a sharp eye on the cane that crowded down to the river bank.

"You'd just as soon teach school as man Shubeal's oar, hadn't you?" George said to Ketty as they went aboard.

"Didn't I tell you tomorrow would decide who would do the teaching?" Ketty reminded him.

When George's belongings had been stowed away on the *Dragonfly* and the canoe securely lashed to the side of the big flat, Anson took up his horn.

"I'll try once more before we start floating," he said.

The sound of the horn moaned upriver and downriver and off into the wooded mountains. Nothing but echoes moaned in answer. Baptist, ready to pole away from the river bank, cupped his mouth and halloed cannon-loud. Only echoing hallos answered him.

"Better get going," said Anson.

"Ketty!" Squire pulled at her sleeve as she stood watching Baptist and George pole the boat toward the current. "Do you reckon Pappy is downriver? Like George says?"

Squire's eyes pricked Ketty like thorns. What right had a stranger to kindle hope in Rachel and her children? she asked herself. She turned from Squire and glanced accusingly at George Soelle. But he didn't look to her like the sort who would willfully deceive a body. He was older than Baptist, she noted, but not by many years. And he had book learning. A surveyor, she knew, had to have a paper from a college named William and Mary, in Virginia, saying he had studied surveying, else he could get no license to survey lands. George was sun-tanned and wind-burned, like Anson. But whereas Anson wore a look as if whatever he wanted with all his soul and body was always getting away from him, George Soelle looked like a man who'd bide his time until, by and by, what he wanted would come to him.

"In Holy Writ," Ketty told Squire, "some verses begin, '*Und es begab sich*'—'And it came to pass.' Like, 'And it came to pass, as the angels were gone away,' 'And it came to pass that He went out into a mountain.' We can make up a verse of our own. 'And it came to pass, as the *Dragonfly* floated down the river, Shubeal—'"

Quick as a thunderclap she stopped herself. It wasn't fair to kindle Squire's hopes on a notion as flimsy as George's.

For a long moment she looked at George Soelle. Then, laying her arm across Squire's shoulders, she said to him, "George wouldn't have said so unless he'd had some reason to think so."

She gathered all the children about her. "We have a little room left for words on our pieces of bark," she told them. "How would you like to learn the words for the things we use to let Shubeal know where we are? *Smoke*, and *horn*, and *rifle*. When we've learned our words, we'll let Squire choose a game to play."

"Hopscotch," said Squire.

Little by little the long day wore away. As the sun slanted downward and shadows began nibbling at the daylight, Rachel still stood gripping the gunwale and watching the north bank of the river. When were the last embers of hope going to blacken in her breast, and when was she going to turn on George Soelle, Ketty won-

122

dered, for having kindled the hope? Most of the day Tish had stood near Rachel, knitting. Sometimes Lettice had stood with them, and sometimes, for spells, she had sat on an upturned gum bucket, watching the children at their lessons or their play. All day long, as the menfolk tended their oars, they had watched and listened. Every now and then Anson had blown his horn, but a body could see that he expected no answer. And there was no answer, except moaning, mocking echoes. No sign was there at all that Shubeal had been that way.

At sundown Anson spied a likely spot above the mouth of a small creek for chaining up the *Dragonfly*. "Right ahead, there," he directed the womenfolk as the voyagers went ashore. "Looks like there'd be a good place to camp."

A few paces they walked, their arms laden with blankets. Tish, in front, stopped suddenly.

"Somebody's done been here," she announced.

Hurriedly menfolk and womenfolk crowded to see. In a sheltered place among the trees stood blackened fire stones. Cedar pallets lay about in order.

"Couldn't 'a' been Donelson," said Baptist. "Not enough pallets."

"Shubeal—maybe hit's Shubeal," whimpered Rachel, the gush of tears inside her ready to overflow.

"Couldn't have been Shubeal, Rachel," Anson told her. "Count the pallets—five of 'em."

"Looks like whoever hit was left in a hurry," commented Baptist. "This far from Fort Patrick Henry you'd think a body'd cover up his tracks—throw them rocks in the river and scatter them pallets."

George studied the gray ashes between the fire stones.

"They couldn't have left more than two days ago," he said. "At least, it hasn't rained since they left."

Tish still held on to her blankets and to the portion of smoked deer meat she had brought ashore. "This ain't the only place in the whole endurin' wilderness a body can camp," she declared. "Why don't we go somewhere's else?"

"Just because somebody's been here and got things ready for you, you want to camp someplace else," Anson twitted her. "It's good we got that dear meat smoked," he added. "Reckon it's just as well to get along 'thout a fire."

"Supposin' Shubeal's near about," pleaded Rachel. "And him a-lookin' for a fire?"

"We'll listen for him," Anson promised, "Here," he ordered, "before dark overtakes us, let's separate them cedar branches into as many pallets as we need. Save us going into the woods. Tish, put down your blankets and pass around the vittles. Soon's we eat we can go to bed. Get an early start tomorrow."

The sun, gone from sight, bloodied the sky. River and forest and mountains, boat and voyagers, were bathed in a strange and awesome light.

"Look!" cried Ketty, pointing into the woods.

The others stared where she directed.

"What is it?" asked Anson.

Baptist stepped forward, trying to see. "You see Shubeal?" he asked.

"Oh, no," said Ketty. "I see a birch tree. See it there?"

At that instant the blood-rose sky lighted up the tattered bark of the birch, setting it apart from its black-trunked neighbors.

Baptist let out his disgust in a mighty sigh. "Yea," he

said, "go norate hit on all the mountains, we've found us a birch tree."

Ketty paid him no mind. "Anson," she said, "lend me your tomahawk, will you? We've used up our last bark."

"Some folks shore do occupy their time with strange and uppity notions," commented Baptist as Anson handed over his tomahawk to Ketty.

George followed Ketty into the woods. "Two can gather twice as much bark as one, Ketty," he told her. "That's what I learned in arithmetic."

"Look!" said Ketty as they neared the tree. "There are two trees. Two trees will give us twice as much bark as one. That's what I learned in arithmetic. You gather bark from one, and I'll gather it from the other."

Busily they hacked at the bark and peeled pieces of it from the trees. Ketty, working her way around the tree she had chosen, stepped back, lost her footing, and crumpled to the ground.

Instantly George was beside her. "What happened?" he asked.

"I—I don't know," said Ketty, trying to get to her feet. "I'm mired to my ankles."

George took her hand and drew her to firm earth. Together in the fading light they studied the ground about them.

"Ketty," said George, his voice low, "this is a grave." He stooped, the better to study the patch of soft earth. "A new one, made yesterday—or maybe today."

Ketty, her heart drumming in her ears, drew near him.

"Can you keep a secret?" he asked.

"Yes," she whispered.

"Let's not tell the others. Not unless we need to."

"You think it's—Shubeal?" asked Ketty as she drew away from the grave.

"Not unless he fell in with other white men who buried him. It could be Shubeal. Death stalks the wilderness in many guises," George explained "—frostbitc, gangrene, an accidental wound that festers and won't heal."

"Are—do you think red men are about?"

"This is a white man's camp."

"Are you afraid?" asked Ketty.

"Within bounds," said George, smiling at her.

"You're sure—red men haven't been here?" prodded Ketty.

"The wilderness holds its tongue, Ketty. I only know this is a white man's grave, dug by white men, for a white man. Red men don't bury their dead in lonesome places. And white men don't bother to bury red men. They leave them lying."

Quickly they gathered up their pieces of bark and returned to the camping spot. When supper was finished, Ketty tucked a blanket about Farrer and lay down beside him.

The children were soon asleep—or so they seemed. But menfolk and womenfolk alike betrayed their wakefulness by occasional clearing of throats, as if they lay listening for a sound they couldn't name.

Ketty heard someone stir on his pallet. Someone, she thought, raised on his elbow.

"That you, Baptist?" whispered Anson. "You hear something?"

"Seems like," answered Baptist.

The others froze, listened. Beyond any mistake, far off in the woods to the west of them, above the noise of the wind, the frogs, and the river, they heard what Baptist heard— a dog barking.

Farrer, nestling close to Ketty, stirred.

"Ketty," he asked, wide awake, "can we make a willer whistle tomorrer?"

"Sh-h-h!" Ketty whispered, listening above the loud beating of her heart for a sound away off yonder in the woods.

"Can we?" Farrer repeated.

"Maybe," whispered Ketty. "Go to sleep now."

Minutes passed.

"Are you a-goin' to sleep, Ketty?" Farrer asked.

"Sh-h-h! Not just yet."

"Why?"

"I'm not sleepy."

"What are you a-doin', then?"

For a time Ketty did not answer. Then, "I'm counting stars," she whispered.

Again they heard the barking of a dog.

In the breathless stillness that followed, Ketty heard muffled stirrings as first one and then another got up from his pallet. When Farrer's slow, even breathing told her that he had gone to sleep, she, too, got up. As long as eternity, it seemed, menfolk and womenfolk stood, waited, listened.

Again they heard barking, closer this time.

In the silence that followed, Baptist whistled a single note, so high and thin and piercing it might have been a passing shriek of night wind in piny woods. In reply whine after whine, ending in joyous, pleading barks, resounded from the woods.

"That's my dog!" declared Baptist, stumbling in the dark toward the barking. "D'ye hear him answer me? That's Shep!"

"Better be certain," George Soelle's voice warned him.

"Listen," said Baptist. Again he whistled, and again the dog barked and whined. The sound came closer and then retreated, as if the dog were running toward the camp and then away from it.

"Maybe it is your dog," agreed George. "Something's keeping him, though. Maybe—"

"Maybe hit's Shubeal," said Baptist.

"Then why don't you go and see?" cried Rachel. "If you ain't a-goin', I'll go myself." In the darkness she started toward the barking.

Tish caught and held her. "The menfolks'll go," she told Rachel. "Here's your rifle, Anse. You be careful now," she pleaded.

A few stealthy footsteps, and the three men were gone. Huddled together in the dark, the four women waited, scarcely breathing as they listened. The barking had stopped, but the voices of the wilderness continued on in relentless rhythm. Above the sound of the wind, the water, and the frogs, Tish's pleading with Anson to be careful rang in Ketty's ears like the chiming of a sweet-toned bell.

The dog suddenly broke into shrill, continuous, joyous barking.

"Hear that?" said Lettice, relief in her voice. "Shep's always glad thataway to see Baptist."

At last, out of the darkness, came voices—Baptist's loud,

128

George's quiet, Anson's scolding, and, once, another voice.

"Shubeal!" cried Rachel. "Hit's him!" She started in the direction of the voices.

"Wait," Tish advised, holding Rachel's arm. "They're a-comin', ain't they?"

Closer the voices came. Closer too came the noise of menfolk tearing through the undergrowth of pawpaw trees and bladdernut bushes as stealthiness was forgotten.

"Hello!" shouted Baptist.

"You got Shubeal?" called Rachel.

"Got Shubeal," answered Baptist. "And, what's more, got my pup. Can't nobody say he ain't worth his weight in wildcats."

"Reckon it's all right to kindle up a fire," said Anson as they stumbled into camp. "Shubeal says no sign of red men about. Here, Shubeal," he added, "you lay down on one of these here pallets till we get a fire going."

"Oh, my feet!" Shubeal groaned weakly as Rachel moved to his side in the dark. "My poor achin' feet! And for the love of mercy, somebody give me some vittles!" he begged.

"Here's a little deer meat," said Tish, moving about confidently in the dark.

The menfolk made short work of kindling a fire. In its light, while Baptist hovered over his dog, which lay panting at his feet, the others turned to Shubeal. Limp with weariness, Shubeal lay on the pallet, his face haggard, his clothes bedraggled and torn with briers and underbrush, his leggins in shreds, and his feet, from which his shoe-packs were gone, red and swollen.

"The Lord be praised!" chanted Rachel tearfully as she sat on the pallet beside him, her body rocking back and forth. "If I've got to go into the wilderness, I'll have a man to fend for me."

"You'd better get to rubbin' them feet, Rachel," said Tish. "Somebody bring me a piggin of water," she ordered. "Cold water'll take some of that thar swellin' out."

Ketty reached quickly for a piggin, hurried to the river, and dipped it in.

"Shubeal, you'll have to set up," Tish told him.

"Me?" asked Shubeal, unbelieving. "Woman, what are you a-askin'?"

"You menfolks prop him agin a tree so's I can get his feet in this piggin of water," Tish ordered. She turned to Anson. "He ain't got no rifle," she said.

"We already found that out," said Anson.

When Shubeal's feet were soaking in the piggin, the fire had begun to warm him, and the deer meat had put a bit of life into him, Anson said, "Now, Shubeal, tell us what happened."

Shubeal leaned his head against the tree, shut his eyes, and groaned.

"Yea, man," Baptist said, louder, "whar on earth's your rifle? What happened to hit?"

"Lost hit," Shubeal said, "in that thar blamed creek."

He opened his eyes, stared weakly at the faces about him, and shook his head. "Laced that mountain plumb up, thisaway and thataway and t'other way, a tryin' to short-cut that blamed creek."

"How in the world come you to get lost?" asked Anson. "Why didn't you follow Poor Valley Creek till you got back to camp?"

"Yea," put in Baptist, "and don't forget the rifle."

" 'Twaren't Poor Valley," Shubeal said. "Couldn't find nothin' on Poor Valley. So I went west a ways. All the game I found, hit was dead—dead deer, dead turkeys, dead coons, dead otters, dead ever' single varmint. All starved to death and froze to death in this here cold winter. Shep, Baptist, now Shep, he didn't fare so bad. Looked like he knowed how much of them carcasses he could stummick. But from the smell of things, I'd say buzzards was all dead too. When ever'thing else failed to get me down, in this here thawin' weather, stench might' nigh overpowered me."

"The bears ain't dead, Shubeal," Baptist told him. "You was talkin' mighty big 'bout bringin' home a bear, remember?"

"Where's your rifle, Shubeal?" asked Anson.

"That's jist hit," said Shubeal. "Feller can't shoot a bear 'thout a rifle, can he?"

"Let Shubeal say what he's got to say," ordered Tish.

Again Shubeal shut his eyes and, leaning his head against the tree, rested his weary body a spell before he took up his tale again.

"I kep' on a-goin' west," he said. "Reckon I crossed half a dozen headwaters before I come to this here creek we're on now. Like I done told you, I laced that mountain plumb up, like a pair of brogues, a tryin' to shortcut this here creek. Crossin' hit oncet on a tree that had blowed down, lost my balance. While I was a-grabbin' for somethin' to hold on to, that thar rifle slipped out of my hand slick as a willer whistle. Straight to the bottom of that creek hit went. Right down into a sinkhole hit went. Me, I can't swim. So what was I a-goin' to do?"

"Well," asked Anson impatiently, "what did you do?"

131

"Cut me a forked saplin' pole an' went to work, tryin' to fish that thar rifle up. Fished and fished. Fished for nigh onto two days. Best I could figure out, that rifle, hit landed in a bed of quicksand. Started sinkin' right away, I reckon. Fur's I know, may be sinkin' yet."

"What's a man worth in the wilderness 'thout a rifle?" Anson asked him.

"That's pint blank what I was askin' myself all the time I was a-tryin' to drag hit out of the water," said Shubeal. "That's why I didn't find you sooner—why I didn't come back to where you was camped. Figured you'd give me up long before this and shove on. So I follered this here creek out, hopin' I'd overtake you. If hit hadn't been for that thar pup, Baptist—he must 'a' scented you—I reckon we'd both 'a' perished teetotally, and nobody but the buzzards'd 'a' been the wiser. 'Cause I'd about took my last step."

"You're sure no red men are about?" Anson asked.

"I wouldn't 'a' been here, would I, if red men had been about?" reasoned Shubeal. "Me 'thout a rifle? I'm sorta hopin' now we will run into some red men," he added. "Mought get me a good British rifle off of one of 'em."

As they made preparations for sleeping, George announced, "I think I'll stand sentry—for a while, anyway."

Ketty's gaze wandered to the birch trees that sheltered the fresh mound of earth. The fact that a body lay freshly buried only a few yards from them had momentarily taken second place to a lost man found again.

Tish eyed George sharply. "You got reason?" she asked.

"Oh," George said, shuggin off her question, "it's just a notion. We've made a bit of clatter bringing Shubeal in. I'll wait till you're all settled before I put out the fire."

132

With the fire out, the night was as dark as piny woods pitch. Ketty listened to the sounds of breathing around her. Squire and Cal, though they had roused up and had listened big-eyed and big-eared to Shubeal, had fallen asleep as soon as they lay down again on their pallets. Lennie, Pegg, and Betsy had never waked up. Shubeal, his feet dried and wrapped in a blanket, was sleeping the deep sleep of a man plumb worn out. Rachel, exhausted by her long days and nights of wilderness waiting, slept beside him. Baptist lay with one arm around Shep. Both of them were snoring, the sounds seesawing, first loud, then low. Anson, Tish, and Lettice were breathing deeply.

Ketty lay wondering. The grave. How had death come to a body there on the river bank so lately? How did a body meet death in the wilderness with no doctor to let his blood and ease his pain, no trombonists to announce the tidings that his soul had entered heaven, nobody to stay and mark his grave and tend it lovingly with blossoms and such like?

And if Shubeal had seen no sign of red men, why was George Soelle standing sentry? George, she realized, treated the wilderness with more respect than Anson, or Shubeal, or Baptist. These three pitted themselves against it as if it were an enemy. George treated it like an equal, and a friend.

"If anybody's listening," George's quiet voice cut across her thoughts, "I'm counting stars."

chapter 12

AT SUNUP the *Dragonfly* was once more slipping down-river.

New life surged in the voyagers, now that the wilderness had given up what it had so nearly claimed and all were safe on board once more. The sunlight made the grave under the birch trees seem to Ketty a less mysterious thing. Like as not, she told herself, somebody, even though he had been bound for some far-off land, had met death as naturally as folks in Salem met death.

> Oh, sing unto the Lord a new song,
> Sing unto the Lord, all the earth!

she remembered from Moravian *Singstundes.*

Only Baptist seemed not wholly given over to enjoyment of good fortune. He crooned the praises of his dog, which lay sleeping soundly beside him on top of the cabin. But he nagged at Shubeal. A man in the wilderness without a rifle, he kept reminding Shubeal, was a sorry sight.

Tongues loosened, and talk flowed like snow water down a mountain. Above the chatter of the children at their lessons, Ketty heard the voices on top of the cabin.

"You seem to know the river," George said to Anson.

"Been here before," said Anson.

"Yeah," said Baptist, "me and Anse, we both been here before."

"Just a little less than a year ago now," said Anson.

"You were one of Colonel Evan Shelby's men, maybe?" asked George.

"Me and Baptist," said Anson proudly.

"Us folks in Wataugy," put in Baptist, "we'd had all the maraudin' and scalpin' and thievin' we aimed to take from them red scoundrels. We had treaties with 'em, didn't we? But they never paid no more mind to a treaty than a horsefly pays to a horse's tail. Switch 'em off and they come a-buzzin' right back. Only way to get rid of 'em was to kill 'em."

"Course," he added, "the red men was egged on by the British, but that didn't make us feel no kindlier toward 'em. Well, we gathered at the mouth of Big Creek, nine hundred all told, and chopped down sycamore trees and popple trees and hollered out pirogues enough for the passel of us and set out to take them Indian towns down on the Tennessee."

"Prettiest sight you ever did see, all of them pirogues riding the river," put in Anson.

"And ever' feller a-rarin' to get hisself a scalp," added Baptist. "Man," he continued, "you never seen such cowards as them red men can be when they're took by surprise. Ain't that so, Anse? Wasn't expectin' company, of course. When they seen us a-comin', they took to the timbers—flew in all directions like a flock of chickens visited unexpected—like by a fox. Didn't even fire a single one of them rifles

135

the British had been so kind and thoughtful as to put in their hands. Left ever'thing behind—ever' single thing. We landed and took out after 'em in the woods. Killed upwards of forty of 'em. Burnt down eleven of their filthy towns. Burnt all their corn. Must 'a' been twenty thousand bushel of hit. Took all their horses and drove away all their cattle. Some of the cattle scattered in the woods, and the rest we drove into the river. You ought 'a' heared them cattle a-bawlin' as they drownded!"

Ketty sickened at Baptist's words. A body by only half trying could even yet hear the helpless cattle bawling. Maybe on into eternity a body, if he listened, could hear their anguished outcry against man's cruelty. Maybe, she thought, all cruel deeds went right on echoing into eternity, and nothing could muffle their piteous sound save, maybe, an act of sheer goodness—like a woman's hanging out a basket of victuals for any hungry passer-by, be he saint or scoundrel, like a teacher's going forth into danger with books under his arm.

"I ain't counting much on running into red men this trip," she heard Anson saying.

" 'Tain't likely they'll be any hangin' around," said Baptist, "after the whuppin' we give 'em."

Ketty looked at Baptist—looked and wondered. Young and upstanding, strong as a back-country ox and sure of himself as a crowing rooster, he half persuaded her to believe against her will that his way with the red men was the right way—his way and Anson's.

"If you killed only forty red men, Baptist," said George, "you let a lot of Chickamaugas get away. And you didn't

136

get their leader, Dragging Canoe. Until Dragging Canoe is taken, I'm thinking whoever has burned a Chickamauga town had better look sharp."

Baptist spat far into the river. "Them Chickamaugy towns is miles down the river, man," he objected. "Why does a feller want to raise a cloud on a sunshiny day?"

"I'm only saying," explained George, "that we'd better tie up and go hunting—lay in whatever we can in the hope that we won't have to stop for provender again till we get to Muscle Shoals. I hear the red men aren't active in that area yet."

Below an eddy, in a quiet, sheltered place of deep, dark water, they tied up the *Dragonfly* and made camp on a ledge of rock jutting out into the river. Steep cliffs rose at their backs, and gray, spread-limbed beeches looked down upon them from high ledges.

Hardly had they landed when Baptist slung his powder horn, his pouch, and his bag across his shoulder, tested the sharp edges of his knife and his tomahawk, picked up his rifle, and called his dog. Anson, too, and George readied themselves for the hunt.

"I'm a-thinkin' one rifle had better stay here," said Tish.

"Shubeal'll be here," said Anson.

"But 'thout a rifle," Tish reminded him.

"Woman"—Anson turned on her—"there ain't a thing in this world to hurt you here."

"One of us should stay here, Anson," said George. "You or I."

"Me," Anson answered sullenly, "I'm going hunting. And I aim to bring home enough vittles to stop this everlasting

137

stalling. A body'd think all this outfit does is figure out ways to slow us down," he muttered as he shouldered his rifle and started after Baptist up the cliff.

Cal broke the stillness that followed in the wake of Anson's fit of spite. "Mammy, I'm hungry."

"Me too," said Squire. "Seems like I was borned holler."

"Boys," said George, "let's go fishing. You come too, Ketty," he added.

"Whar'bouts are we a-goin'?" asked Cal.

"Upriver a piece," George told him. "I thought I saw a spring hole a ways back. All you children come." He started along the river bank.

"Whar's your fishin' pole?" asked Cal.

"And your bait?" asked Squire.

"You come with me," said George. "This time let's go fishing without pole or bait."

Along the bank, upriver, they made their way, pushing from their faces the whips of saplings, skirting a pile of driftwood. There, as George had said, back from the river was a spring hole, its water bubbling up clear and cold and overflowing into a pebbly branch leading to the river.

George, in front, motioned the others to silence. "Come and look," he whispered.

Quietly they tiptoed to the edge of the spring hole. In the shallow water swam dozens of speckled trout.

"Sh-h-h!" whispered Ketty, drawing the children back. "Don't scare them."

George led the way along the branch toward the river.

"Off with your moccasins, boys," he said as he slipped off his shoepacks. "We'll bring rocks and build a dam here across the branch."

138

"What are we a-buildin' a dam for?" asked Cal.

"Because you're hungry," said George.

When the dam was finished, George motioned to the boys to follow him up the branch to the spring hole. Together they waded into the water. Before them, down the branch toward the dam, swam the trout, darting over the shining pebbles, their red spots gleaming. Finding their way to the river cut off by the dam, they wheeled and started up the branch.

Bending over, George scooped up a trout in his hands.

"Quick, Lennie! Hold your skirt!" he ordered.

Into Lennie's hastily gathered skirt he dropped the flopping fish.

"Here's another!" shouted Squire.

"I got me one too!" shouted Cal.

"Pegg and Betsy, bring on more skirts," ordered George. "Here's another."

Eleven trout they caught in the narrow branch.

"Skedaddle back to camp with 'em now," George said to the children. "Tell your mammies the rest of us'll be along soon."

George drew on his shoepacks and walked back to the pile of driftwood. From among the tangled crisscrossed sticks he pulled pieces of broken plank.

"Somebody's flat," he said, as he walked back to Ketty. "Well, the fellow who built that flat never suspected part of it would end up in school. Here's enough to make a paddle for each of your scholars to write his words on. Then you won't have to depend on birch bark. Just whittle the paddles off every night and start out fresh the next day."

"Why," asked Ketty, "hadn't I thought of that?"

"A body doesn't learn in a day," said George, "all the wilderness has to teach. Farrer," he said, as he began shaping one of the broken pieces with his hunting knife, "gather up the shavings. We'll use them for kindling when Anson and Baptist come back with their bear."

For a while Farrer picked up curls of shavings as they fell to the ground about George's feet. Then he wandered away along the river bank a short distance and splashed pebbles into the water.

"I heard Baptist and Anson telling you about the Indians," said Ketty, guarding her voice lest Farrer hear. "Do you—think they'll bother us? Farther along?"

"Likely," said George.

"Why can't we—isn't there some way we can make peace with them?"

"How?"

Ketty raked the toe of her shoe over the ground, puzzling. "Maybe—"

"Who wants to make peace?" asked George. "You haven't heard anybody on this boat talking about peace with the red men, have you? All they're talking about is killing red men. And you can be sure the red men are talking about killing us, too."

"But why?" prodded Ketty. "The folks in Salem lived in peace with the red men."

"Tell me about Salem," said George, "and how the folks there got along with the Indians."

Ketty told him about Little Carpenter's visit to Bethabara and his request that the Moravians send a teacher for the Chickamauga children.

"Dragging Canoe is Little Carpenter's son," she added.

"What do you think would have happened," she mused, "if Colonel Evan Shelby had taken one teacher with books down the river to the Chickamauga towns instead of nine hundred men with rifles? And why should Little Carpenter's son be so riled up against white men that he wants to kill those of us who never harmed the red men?"

George held up a paddle whittled to a satiny smoothness for the sun to shine on.

"It's a long story, Ketty," he said, "with many chapters. You've told me one chapter. But most of the chapters are different. They're filled with meanness and trickery. Once in a while you come across a Moravian, or a Quaker, or just a plain human being who is willing to share the earth with all men, even with red men. But most folks, Ketty, believe the earth belongs to the man who carries the straightest shooting rifle."

Ketty spread her hands in a gesture of despair. "Why am I threatened by the red men?" she asked. "I never wronged them. I never so much as had an evil thought toward them."

"When we're floating down the rivers, Ketty, all of us together," George said, resting the piece of wood on his knee, "how can red men tell you have Moravian thoughts in your head? All they can see from the river bank is that you are one of a crowd of people who have deceived them, cheated them, lied to them, and, through one ruse or another, taken their hunting grounds away from them. And that you're on your way to claim still more."

He began his whittling again. "You see, Ketty," he explained, "all this back country of North Carolina, and all the far-off land we're bound for, time out of mind has been the hunting ground of the red men. So long as white men killed an occasional buffalo or deer or bear or turkey, enough to feed themselves and their families, the red men didn't complain—much. But when white men began to kill animals willy-nilly for their pelts, the red men got their hackles up. Their meat supply was getting low. But that wasn't all. When the white men had destroyed the wild varmints, they claimed the land and began to raise cattle on it. And every white man's pasture pushed the red men's wild game farther away, and every deerskin and buffalo hide taken by white men made the red men's food scarcer still. The red men agree that the Great Spirit has given white men many advantages, but in their proud hearts they will never agree that white men are better than they. The Great Spirit has stocked both their pastures, they say—the white men's with cattle, theirs with buffalo; the white men's with hogs, theirs with bears; the white men's with sheep, theirs with deer. Without their pastures they'll starve."

"Why won't white men listen to reason?" asked Ketty.

"Because they're land-greedy," George told her. "They're always pushing west, and always in the same way. First one ventures out, a hunter or a trapper. Then other hunters come. They like the lay of the land, so they decide to fetch their families and settle. They cut down trees that shelter the wild game, and plant corn. Their neighbors follow and take up claims of their own. And nobody says by-your-leave to the red men. Usually by the time the red men are roused up enough to protest, the white men have moved in in sufficient numbers to raise an army and drive the red

142

men farther back. If they don't win the first round, they win the second. Then they call on their government, which they've left far behind to back them up, to make lawful what they've taken at rifle point. So the government draws up a treaty saying how much land the red men must cede and sends out a few bigwigs to parley with their chiefs. Sometimes the government goes through the motions of paying for the land, if you can call gunpowder and trinkets fair pay. In any case, the bigwigs top off the deal with whisky. And when the red men come out of their stupor, they find they've signed away their hunting grounds."

"Was Colonel Evan Shelby's army that Anson and Baptist were part of the kind of army you're talking about?" asked Ketty.

"Exactly. But Colonel Shelby and his nine hundred men didn't get Dragging Canoe. And as long as Dragging Canoe is alive, there'll be consequences, or my name isn't George Soelle. And you, being Anson's sister and one of this party, will have to face the consequences."

Ketty was silent a moment.

"What do you aim to do if we run into red men?" she asked finally.

"I'm keeping my powder dry and my rifle clean," George answered.

"Then you aim to kill red men?" Ketty asked. "Without trying to parley with them peaceably? And with no notion of being just?"

George took a turn at silence.

"You force me to think," he said, smiling at Ketty. "Not about whether I'll shoot, but why I'll shoot. When one is part of a crowd, Ketty, he is no longer wholly an individual. He thinks like the crowd. He behaves like the crowd. He no longer relies on himself, Ketty, but takes refuge in the crowd—in what the crowd is doing and thinking and saying. He makes the crowd a reason for what he does. And you and I—we're part not only of this small crowd on the *Dragonfly*. We're part of the crowd that's ahead of us on Donelson's boats. We're part of that eternal great big crowd that's floating down the Ohio from Pittsburgh by the thousands, and crawling through the passes and climbing over the mountains from the Piedmont and the Tidewater like ants, taking up the red men's land and raising cabins and planting corn on it—gentlemen and traders and speculators and scoundrels and hunters and trappers and farmers, all grabbing up the red men's hunting grounds and pushing the red men farther and farther back. And the easiest way to do it is with rifles. What," he asked suddenly, "do you aim to do if we run into red men?"

For a time Ketty did not answer.

"Anson tells me I'm to learn to shoot," she said finally.

"And what did you tell Anson?"

"That I would not shoot red men."

George looked into her troubled eyes and smiled at her.

"You can forget about Anson," he told her. "He'll buckle against straight, upstanding talk." His eyes grew tender. "Don't learn to shoot, Ketty," he begged. "For my sake, don't learn."

"It's for my sake I don't want to learn," she told him.

"But don't for my sake too," he pleaded with her. "Keep your—keep your dream, your impossible dream. Without it

144

you wouldn't be Ketty, and we'd all be the poorer. Even though we think you foolish, we'd all be the poorer."

"But you've just said I'm part of the crowd, and so I do as the crowd does," she protested.

"Unless," he said, "you can out-think the crowd." He looked downriver, his forehead wrinkled in thought. "No," he said, "it isn't enough to out-think the crowd. You have to out-do the crowd, too. And that's risky business. Folks who out-do the crowd sometimes get their comeuppance. They get thrown into jails and forgotten, or burned on a pile of faggots, or hanged. One man got hung on a cross for out-thinking and out-doing the crowd."

Ketty studied his words.

"In Salem I was part of a crowd," she told him. "But it was a different kind of crowd."

"Tell me more about Salem," he said. "What kind of crowd lived at Salem?"

Ketty searched through her memories of the Salem Moravians for the deeds that set them apart from other crowds.

"The rebels accused us of being on the side of the British, and the British accused us of being on the side of the rebels," she told George, "and both of them made it hard for us. But we refused to take sides. As the rebels grew stronger, they made things still harder for us. They levied heavy taxes on us, and fines, and they sent officers to hunt out all the young men and compel them to fight against the British. But we refused to fight. The folks in Salem have robust consciences, and they refuse to kill people. More than that, they refuse to be enemies to people, whether Tory

145

or rebel, or white or red or black. So the young men hid in the woods till the officers were gone. Sometimes they'd have to hide for days."

Ketty's face lighted with vivid memories.

"Though nothing was said about it, you'd always know who was hiding. At evening *Singstunde*, his place would be vacant, and there'd be a special fervor about the singing, and about the praying, and about the praising too, as if—as if it was a wonderful victory for a man to obey his conscience when he was being hounded and hunted."

George whittled for a moment in silence.

"Has it got the Moravians anywhere, obeying their robust consciences?" he asked.

"Yes," she answered thoughtfully. "Everybody trusts them—everybody, from Indians to Governor Caswell. And they're not afraid."

For minutes George whittled, and Farrer, a few steps away, threw pebbles into the river and watched the widening circles they made.

"I think I know what's in your mind, Ketty," said George, still whittling. "The man folks hung on a cross, He said He was the Way, remember? The Way, and the Truth, and the Life. Till people got their fill of His preaching and put an end to it. He thought a lot about how folks ought to behave toward one another. I think, maybe, He would say that truth is rooted in love—that no word is true that isn't spoken in love, and no act is just that isn't carried out in love."

"Then you think, when we get to the far-off land, we can begin a new kind of life? Live in justice with the Indians?" Ketty asked him. "Treat them like people?"

146

His hands came to rest on the paddle. "Do you know what you put me in mind of, Ketty?" he asked, watching her face. "A frail Silvery Blue butterfly—the most beautiful of all butterflies to my thinking—splitting its cocoon and flying off into a world that is going to be anything but kind to it." He raked the toe of his shoepack across the ground. "Who is man enough to follow the man on the cross?" he asked. "And do you think this crowd on the *Dragonfly* is planning to live in justice with the red men in the far-off land? You haven't even told me what you aim to do if red men set on us down the river."

"Ketty!" Farrer called. "Come see my boat."

At sunset Baptist's dog came panting out of the woods. Soon followed the sound of Anson's and Baptist's voices and the cracking of twigs and underbrush.

"Got a fire a-goin'?" called Baptist as they stumbled into sight. "We got vittles."

On a pole slung between Baptist's shoulder and Anson's was tied a black bear, secured with wild grapevines.

The womenfolk laid fresh wood on the fire. The others gathered about Anson and Baptist, watching as they lowered the pole from their shoulders.

"We saw nary a sign of red men," said Anson. "So, Tish, I want this whole critter jerked tonight. If we're saving of it, and the weather stays cool, it ought to last us till we get to the Shoals. We'll put out our fish lines tonight too. Then we're shoving off bright and early in the morning, and if I'm hung up again, I mean it to be for some reason better'n any I've heard yet."

chapter 13

"'PEARS to me like the current's swifter," said Shubeal the next morning as he sat on top of the cabin, his hands idle, while George Soelle wielded his broadhorn.

"'Tis swifter," agreed Anson. "Getting close to the mouth of the French Broad," he said, pleasured that he knew the river. "I'm counting on picking up a boat or two at the French Broad," he added. "So many folks hurrying to the Lick, and all of them wanting company."

"Could we meet up with somebody there, that'd be as good as overtaken' Donelson," said Shubeal.

"Could be," Anson agreed.

At noon the boat floated past the mouth of the French Broad, which surged with melted snows and late-winter freshets gathered high up on its brawling headwaters, and emptied mightily into the Holston. But the voyagers met up with nobody there.

The swollen river bore them onward. The tawny cane in the bottoms stirred like the ocean sea in the March wind, tempting Ketty to lean against the gunwale and watch away the hours as Lettice and Rachel were doing. But she turned her back on the pleasant scene and called the children to her.

"This morning I'll teach you to write your names," she told them. "After that, we'll play a new game called Holy Gabriel. My mother used to play it with us children when I was little." She chanted softly:

> "Holy Gabriel, holy man,
> Rantum, roarum, reeden man,
> I'll do all as ever I can
> To follow my Gabriel, holy man."

"Why can't we play now?" asked Squire. "We can write our names some other time."

"No," Ketty said firmly. "Lessons first. Besides," she added, "see what George has made for you—paddles to write your words on. We won't have to look for birch bark again." She brought the paddles and passed them out, one to each of the children.

"When I learn to write my name, I'm a-goin' to write hit big and black on my paddle," said Cal, "and that means hit's mine."

"All of you may do that," said Ketty. "I'll write your names at the top of your paddles, and you can copy them underneath."

When the children had wrestled a while with their names, Cal jumped to his feet.

"Looky, ever'body!" he showed off his paddle. "Mine's full."

"He's got such a short name," complained Lennie.

"Why don't we stop and have recess," suggested Ketty,

149

"and play Holy Gabriel? Then you can go back to your names."

At once the children joined hands and formed a ring about Ketty, as she directed.

"First," she told them, "think of something you want to play music on—bagpipes, a trombone, a harp, an organ. Anything but a fiddle. The one in the middle plays the fiddle. Ready?"

The children stared at her.

"Now," she directed, "you go round and round singing 'Holy Gabriel, holy man.' When you finish, you stand still and pretend to play music on whatever you've chosen, and I'll pretend to play the fiddle. Every once in a while I'm going to quit playing the fiddle and begin to play whatever one of you is making music on. When I do that, you must quit what you're playing on and play the fiddle, fast. If you don't change, you'll have to get in the middle. Ready, now?"

Round and round the children circled, Ketty chanting with them,

> "Holy Gabriel, holy man,
> Rantum, roarum, reeden man . . ."

At the last "holy man," Ketty, going fast through the motions of fiddling, turned in the circle to catch some child unawares at his music making. The children, however, stood dumbly watching her.

"Why don't you play?" she asked.

"We don't know what to play on," they told her.

"Didn't you have something to play music on in Watauga?" she asked.

"Nothin' but a fiddle," they told her.

"Let's play hopscotch," said Lennie.

"Play hopscotch today, Teacher," called George Soelle from the roof of the cabin. "Another day you can play Holy Gabriel."

Without waiting for Ketty's permission, the children broke out of the ring, formed a line, and at once Cal, in front, began hopping in the scotch. Ketty stood watching him. Lettice, too, watched with pleasure in her face. Rachel looked on dully, seeming not yet to have recovered from the long hours spent waiting for Shubeal. Tish, like the others, watched. But if she was pleasured, she gave no sign. Maybe, guessed Ketty, Tish was saying to herself that the young uns' hopscotching days were numbered, for as soon as they got to the far-off land there'd be work aplenty to set their hands to.

Ketty wandered to the bow of the boat and stood alone. Suddenly, in a new and revealing light, she saw Tish, Anson's wife. What was it like, she asked herself, gripping the gunwale, to be married to a man who had never loved you?

Surely, she reasoned, Anson had never loved Tish—not the way she herself wanted some day to be loved. Surely winds humming their songs in piny woods had never brought to Anson's mind the thought of Tish's head nestling on his shoulder. Creeks rushing headlong down their rocky beds to the rivers had never been his feet hurrying pell-mell home to his beloved.

Ketty's heart set against Anson. He had had no right to marry Tish without loving her. Her heart set even harder as she recollected how Anson had doomed his mother to the long heartbreaking search that had ended in her bury hole. "Anse, he takes keer of today and he's satisfied," she could hear Lettice telling her. What had been the real reason, she wondered, for Anson's decision, made in one reckless moment, to risk the rightful place of the *Dragonfly* and her passengers among Donelson's thirty boats, to cross the high mountains in search of a nameless thing for which he was homesick, and then to fetch Ketty against her will to make the voyage to the Lick?

Was she to pay for this reckless moment as her mother had paid for that reckless moment when Anson had decided to run away from home? And as Tish was paying every day of her life for that other reckless moment when Anson had decided to marry her?

You wear your crown as a sign that you're ruling yourself, Ketty.

For two days the *Dragonfly*, with *Walk-on-the-Water* lashed to her side, rode the current without trouble or mishap. The voyagers passed the mouth of Little River and the wider mouth of the Little Tennessee, but at neither place did they meet with other voyagers.

"Maybe luck'll favor us at the mouth of the Clinch," said Anson, tight-lipped.

"Ain't no river further down than the Clinch?" asked Shubeal.

"The Hiwassee, as I recollect," answered Anson. "But settlers bound for the French Lick ain't draining off that river."

On they floated, morning, noontide, evening. The river, called now the Tennessee, Anson said, rolled along swiftly through wide bottoms filled with cane still wearing its winter dullness. Beyond the bottoms patches of cedars, dark and cone-shaped among the bare maples and oaks, beeches and stately poplar trees, spattered the rising slopes. And beyond the slopes towered the hazy mountains. Ketty marveled that folks had not settled here where there was promise of green fields and golden gathering in, that they had set themselves the hard task of voyaging to the French Lick when they might have found what they wanted so much nearer their starting place.

This far-off land—why was a body tormented day and night, like Anson and Baptist, till he had got started on his journey toward it? And what was the far-off land? Ketty wondered—wide river bottoms filled with cane, salt for the boiling, wild game for the killing, sunshine to bake the cold out of a body's bones? Or was it a fancy of the mind toward which everybody was bound willy-nilly? She'd ask George Soelle, she decided. He'd likely have the answer.

George's voice broke into her thoughts.

"There they are, Anson," he said quietly, as if not to upset the boat with his tidings.

"Who?" Anson asked. "Where?"

Baptist stared ahead into the watery sunset. Shubeal squinted through half-closed eyelids. The womenfolk hurried to the gunwale.

"Look downriver as far as you can see," directed George, "to your right. That must be the mouth of the Clinch. If my eyes don't fool me, I see folks there."

Anson, with one hand on the steering oar, shaded his eyes with his free hand and stared downriver at the north bank.

"You're gulling," he said.

153

"No, I'm not," said George.

"I see!" Ketty cried excitedly. "I see a fire. And women-folks."

"Yea, I see 'em now!" Baptist slapped his thigh. "A whole passel of 'em!"

"Well, didn't I tell you?" said Anson. He squinted his eyes, the better to see. "Where are their boats?"

"Likely tied up on the Clinch," said George.

Anson, in excitement, took up his horn and blew a loud blast on it. On the river bank a man's arm raised and a white cloth waved in welcome.

"Run below 'em and tie up," ordered Anson.

As the menfolk steered the *Dragonfly* past the broad, full mouth of the Clinch, the womenfolk and the children, caught up in excitement, stared at the people watching from the river bank. Up the Clinch, as George had guessed, four boats were moored.

"I declare, seems like I never seen a purtier sight," said Rachel.

"And such a passel of 'em!" said Lettice.

"Ain't they a-cookin'?" asked Tish. "Maybe they got vittles."

"Hello, folks!" shouted Anson.

"Hello!" came back a dozen welcoming voices.

When finally Anson had found a likely place to tie up, willing hands grabbed up the chains thrown to them, eased the big flat into safe mooring, and tied it up. Other hands grasped the end of the gangboard and planted it safely on the bank.

Anson was the first down the gangboard. Hardly had he set foot on the ground when he began asking questions.

154

Where were they from? Where were they bound? Had they seen hide or hair of Donelson? The others aboard the *Dragonfly* were all ears as they filed down the gangboard, fearful lest one morsel of talk fall on the air and they not catch it up.

One man stepped forward to answer Anson's questions. McEnnis, he said his name was—Westly McEnnis, captain of the lead boat. He and his party had set out from Moore's Fort on the Clinch in time to catch Donelson, they'd thought. They had heard he'd been held up at Reedy a long spell on account of the ice. They'd been tied up at the mouth of the Clinch for three days in the hope that Donelson would pass by. They'd given him up and had decided to start again next morning.

"I thought sure and certain we'd overtake him," Anson said, "but looks like, if we ain't plagued with one sort of bad luck, the wilderness can think up another."

No, McEnnis told Anson, his party wasn't bound for the French Lick. Some were going to the Spanish settlements at New Orleans, some to the Illinois country. They'd stay together till they'd navigated the mean twists and turns in the Tennessee, where folks said red men might be hiding, and the dangerous shoals beyond. Did Anson want to join them? He could if he had a mind to. The menfolk had been out hunting all day, he said, and supper was ready that minute, piping hot. "Eat hearty as you can while hit lasts," he invited.

The prospect of hot victuals and of company down the rivers renewed the life in the *Dragonfly* voyagers. The cheery fires, the sight of people, and the sound of human voices thawed their blood and loosened their tongues. As dark came on, Anson and Baptist joined heartily in the talk about the campfires, while Shubeal told to willing listeners his tale of being lost in the woods. Even Tish looked less tight-lipped as the woman they called Allie Shanor urged her to heap her plate of bark with food. "Hit sure looks to me like hit's been many a day since you set down to a square meal," declared Allie. "You eat now, good and hearty."

Allie Shanor, decided Ketty, was good medicine for whatever ailed a body—starvation, fear, frostbite, lonesomeness. She seemed to be everywhere at once, making strangers feel welcome, making everybody comfortable, everybody eager to get floating once more down the rivers. Her voice was hearty and free of spite or fear or hatefulness. Ketty, watching and listening, found herself wishing Allie Shanor might be a passenger on board the *Dragonfly*.

A girl the age of Lennie pushed through the crowd of voyagers. "Ma," she said, pulling at Allie Shanor's skirt, "Pa, he wants you."

Quickly Allie Shanor, asking, "What is hit now, Jesse?" turned and hurried to a neighboring fire. She bent over someone covered with blankets and lying on a pallet. "Willie," she called to a young man talking to Anson, "bring me another blanket from somewheres. Jesse he's a chillin'. And Maggie, bring me some more of that hot squirrel broth."

"Jesse, he's had this fever for two days now," Willie told Anson as he came back to the fire.

"What ails him?" asked Anson.

"Jist a spell of the weather, I reckon. Fever'll likely break tonight. Betwixt the time the roosters crow for midnight

156

and day—that's the time fevers might' nigh always break."

"Hit's lucky we got plenty of hands on board to manage his boat," said another man. "Though I allus say there's nobody like Jesse Shanor to handle one of these here flats."

Morning brought no break in the fever, and when Westly McEnnis gave the order to blacken their fires, go aboard their boats, and shove off, two of the men from Shanor's boat wrapped the ailing man in the bearskin on which he lay and lifted him gently.

"Hit would be his boat's tied farthest upriver," said McEnnis as he watched the men stumble with their burden through the underbrush along the river bank. "Hit'll take them a right smart time to get under way," he said as he started for his own boat. "Petrie, why don't you fall in ahead of Shanor? Thataway we won't be held up so long."

It seemed to Ketty that everyone aboard the *Dragonfly* was giddy with pleasure to be at last part of so large a company floating down the river. Anson continually called out sights along the river. Baptist was full of singing and the old bragging, and Shubeal seemed to have recovered the life that had been in him before, though Baptist did not let him forget that he had no rifle. Even George Soelle, though he said little, seemed to be mulling over things to his liking.

"Shubeal," George said when they were under way, floating along, fourth in line, with Shanor's boat behind them, "feel like manning your oar for a spell?"

It pleasured Shubeal to take the broadhorn once more. "I may not be wuth my salt 'thout a rifle," he said to Baptist, "but as long's a feller can man his oar, he's wuth his sody saleratus, I reckon."

George swung himself down from the cabin roof, set upside down at his feet a gum bucket he carried with him, and stood near the children, watching as they laboriously wrote their names on their paddles.

"Isn't it time for recess?" he asked Ketty.

"Not yet," said Ketty. "I've told them I'll teach them a new word when they've written their names."

"Couldn't you do things differently this morning, Teacher?" he asked teasingly. "It's a special morning, you see, now that we've got company."

Ketty hesitated.

"Just this morning?"

"There won't be many more mornings for learning," she reminded him solemnly. Then she smiled. "What do you want us to do?" she asked.

"Play Holy Gabriel," said George.

Hardly had he spoken when the children deserted their paddles and got to their feet.

"But we don't know what to play on," said Lennie, remembering.

"Never mind," George told them. "Get in a ring. You, Teacher, stand in the middle to play your fiddle."

When they had done as he directed, he reached into the bosom of his hunting shirt, pulled from it several lengths of cane, each about six inches long, and laid them on the upturned bucket.

"Here are your music-makers," he said.

The children broke their circle and, with Ketty, crowded around, the better to see.

"Let's start with this one," said George, taking up a joint of cane. "Listen." He hit the cane against the cushion of his thumb and then shook it lightly three times, to beat out the rhythm of the song he sang:

> "Where be ye goin', sweet little maiden,
>   Where be ye goin' in the mornin'?
>   Where be ye goin', cheeks so rosy reddin',
>   Early, so early in the mornin'?"

The cane rattled harmoniously.

"Where, George, did you get that?" asked Ketty, amused.

"The wilderness taught me to make it." He looked straight at Ketty. "The dark, wily wilderness, Teacher, is father to all kinds of inventions. Last night I whittled this out while everybody else was gossiping. See?" He pulled a plug out of one end of the cane and poured into his hand three small pebbles. "That's what makes such sweet music. Here, Lennie," he said, "this will be yours. It's a Spanish castanet."

"Can I learn to write that word, Ketty?" asked Lennie.

"Next lesson," promised Ketty. "Let's see now what else George has made." She leaned over the children, the better to see what more lay on the bucket.

"Whar's mine at?" chorused the children, hovering close. Squire and Cal crowded against George, their hands outstretched.

"Ladies first," George reminded them. "What's good for the Tidewater is good for the French Lick. Here, Betsy."

George took up two joints of cane, each of them cracked in several places. Taking the end of one joint between the thumb and forefinger of his left hand, he held it lightly suspended while he struck it with the other joint, held in his right hand. A rattling, jarring sound came forth.

159

"A French tambourine," said George, putting the pieces of cane into Betsy's outstretched hands. "And here, Pegg, here's something for you to play."

He took up a piece of cane open at both ends and put one end of it to his mouth. In a voice to which the cane lent resonance, he hummed,

"Where be ye goin', sweet little maiden?"

"An English horn, Pegg," he said. "And you, Farrer." He picked up a joint of cane that bore four small notches in a row near one end. Putting the other end of the cane to his mouth and fingering the notches, George piped a tune.

Farrer reached for the cane.

"A shepherd's whistle, boy," George told him, tousling his tow hair. "You pipe music on it while you tend your sheep. And, Squire, let's see." He studied the pieces of cane still lying on the gum bucket. "Here's one for you."

The joint of cane he handed Squire was open at one end, and across the opening a small slip of cane was inserted. When George held the edge of the cane to his lips in a perpendicular fashion and blew into it, a hollow hissing sound came forth.

"Scottish bagpipes," he said, handing the cane to Squire.

He took up a joint of cane closed at both ends, with a narrow strip cut from end to end, over which was stretched a thin deer sinew. Plucking the sinew with his thumb, George produced a dull, monotonous sound. "This, Cal," he said, "is for you. An African jumbo."

"Come on!" called Lennie as she danced around and around on deck. "Let's play Holy Gabriel now."

"May I play with you?" asked George. He stooped,

picked up the bucket, and put it under his left arm. No one had noticed until then that a piece of buckskin was stretched across its mouth and tied with a thong. George picked up one of the charred sticks and beat on the taut buckskin. "A German drum," he said. "When we get to the French Lick and I can find some tin, I'll make you a real drum. But this one will do for now. Ready to play Holy Gabriel, Teacher?"

"The French Lick?" Ketty asked, studying his face through narrowed eyelids. "I thought your claim lay on some other river."

"So it does, so it does." George laughed, beating nervously on the drum. In courtly manner he bowed to Ketty. "My fancy, Teacher, got away from me for the moment. Now, shall we play?"

A scuffle followed as each of the children claimed the place in the ring next to George.

"You know about taking turns?" George asked them. "Squire and Cal waited till the last for their instruments. Suppose first go-around I stand between them. Next go-around, I'll stand between Farrer and Pegg. In the middle, Teacher," he ordered. "Here we go!"

Around and around they circled, chanting,

> "Holy Gabriel, holy man,
> Rantum, roarum, reeden man . . ."

For half an hour while the others aboard the *Dragonfly* pleasured themselves with watching, George, Ketty, and the children played—noisy, laughing, shouting, carefree, the thought of wilderness dangers shoved into the far corners of their minds.

Suddenly Cal, his attention caught upriver, left off plucking the sinew of his African jumbo. "Looky thar!" he cried,
pointing behind them.

The others quit their game and looked. The menfolk
on top of the cabin and the womenfolk at the gunwales
stared, questions in their eyes, as a canoe carrying two men
glided downriver to the rhythm of strong, hurried strokes.

"Shanor's boat had a canoe," said George as he and
Ketty, along with the children, crowded to the gunwale to
watch. "Likely somebody taking a message to McEnnis."

Looking neither to the right nor to the left, the men sent
the canoe cutting through the swift water, past the *Dragonfly*, past the two boats directly ahead, until it came alongside McEnnis's boat.

"Come on, Ketty. Come on, George," urged the children.
"Let's play Holy Gabriel."

Impatiently they shook, plucked and whistled through
their instruments, making a weird, unearthly noise.

"I want to find out what the men in the canoe are telling
McEnnis," Ketty told them.

"You play with us, George," the children begged.

"Another time," said George. "You can play by yourselves."

"I'm a-goin' to be Holy Gabriel," shouted Squire. At once
the children raced from the gunwale to the center of the
deck and formed themselves in a circle about Squire.

> "Holy Gabriel, holy man,
> Rantum, roarum, reeden man . . ."

they chanted. To the watchers at the gunwale their voices
sounded far, far away.

For an eternity, it seemed, the men in the canoe parleyed with McEnnis. At last they turned the canoe about and paddled upriver.

"What on earth's the matter now?" complained Rachel.

"We'll know soon," said George, "if it's any of our business."

"Travelin' together thisaway," Tish told him, "what's the business of one's likely to be the business of all."

As the men paddled against the swift current, voices from the flats ahead called to them, and the men answered, but those aboard the *Dragonfly* could not make out the words.

Anson stared with foreboding at the men. "I'll be willing to bet my rifle," he said, "some trouble's a-brewing—some great big mess of trouble."

The men paddled past the *Dragonfly*. "Anything the matter?" shouted Anson.

"Plenty!" called one of the men.

"What's it now?" called Anson.

No answer was called from the canoe. Instead, the men paddled alongside Shanor's boat.

"George, you and Ketty come now and play with us," begged the children.

"Not just yet," George told them.

"What are you a-doin'?"

"Waiting."

They did not have to wait long. Soon they saw the man at the steering oar of Shanor's boat and the two men wielding the broadhorns steering the boat out of the current and toward the north bank of the river.

"Are we a-stoppin' too? Again?" asked Rachel.

At that minute a canoe set out upriver from McEnnis's boat, with two men paddling and with McEnnis himself in it. Anxiously menfolk and womenfolk aboard the *Dragonfly* watched as McEnnis stopped to parley first with the folk on the boat following his, then with the folk on the boat directly ahead of the *Dragonfly*.

Minutes passed. Curious, suspicious menfolk let their oars drift idly. The children left their play and came to ply their mothers with questions nobody could answer.

At last McEnnis paddled alongside the *Dragonfly*.

Every ear was cocked to hear what he had to call up to Anson.

"Shanor's done broke out with smallpox."

chapter 14

"**S**MALLPOX!" Baptist took the dread word out of McEnnis's mouth and roared it over the water.

"Smallpox!" echoed Tish firmly. "Young uns, get away from the gunwale!"

"Smallpox!" Anson echoed weakly. "If this ain't the crowning glory of this here voyage!"

"Oh, why couldn't a body die in his own bed at home?" wailed Rachel.

"I've told Shanor's men to hold up his boat till us four boats get well ahead," McEnnis called to Anson. "We'll stay in the order we're a-floatin' now—you next to Shanor. Better keep a right smart distance between your boat and his'n, Petrie."

"Hit's likely ever'body down to the last young un on that boat'll die of smallpox," prophesied Shubeal.

"And what do we aim to do at night?" Anson asked McEnnis.

"When we're about to stop floatin', I'll blow oncet on my horn to signal Shanor's boat to tie up," explained McEnnis. "The rest of us'll keep a-floatin' till we've put a safe distance between him and us. In the mornin's when we're ready to set out, I'll blow twicet to tell Shanor's folks we're a-leavin'. You folks," he asked, "wasn't any of you close to Shanor last night, was you?"

"Anywheres on the same river's too close," Anson told him.

"Well," called McEnnis dourly as the men headed his canoe downriver, "what's done can't be holped. Keep your distance now."

"What confounded luck caused us to meet up with these folks?" muttered Anson as he studied Shanor's stricken boat, still waiting at the river bank. "Know what I'm a-thinking?" he said to the other men on top of the cabin. "Ain't no law that says just because we run into this here outfit we're married to it, for better or for worse."

"Ain't but one current in the river," Shubeal reminded him, "if you're a-thinkin' 'bout passin' 'em up."

"But McEnnis's horn, when he blows it for tying up, don't necessarily say nothing to us," said Anson.

"You're mighty right, hit don't," agreed Baptist.

"When the others pull out of the current," said Anson, "we can keep floating—get clean away from this pestilence."

"Wouldn't it be better," suggested George, "as long as Shanor's boat is keeping well behind, if we stayed with McEnnis till we get past the Chickamauga towns?"

Baptist spat into the river. "I thought George was a-settin' right here a-listenin'," he said, "when we told 'bout burnin' them Chickamaugy towns."

Anson, studying the boats ahead, weighed the arguments.

"Like I said," he reminded the others, "I ain't counting heavy on running into red men. Still and all . . ." His face

166

betrayed his nagging suspicion that smallpox was the fore-runner of worse trouble yet to come. "George, he's got a point," he admitted grudgingly. "We mought stay with 'em through the Suck. They'd come in mighty handy there if a body needed 'em. On the other hand . . ."

As the *Dragonfly* floated along in line, the menfolk bandied the argument back and forth, some saying go ahead, some saying stay in line.

Meanwhile, the sky that had been middling fair in the very early morning began to cloud over. A chilling rain-laden wind rose and blew upriver. Soon, over the face of the river, fog began drifting in wispy waves that hid from the voyagers the boats ahead and the hapless boat behind. Tight-lipped, Anson steered the boat. Within a half-hour a drizzle started.

At the first drops Tish herded the children into the shelter of the cabin. The womenfolk followed them.

Inside the cabin the children crowded about Ketty.

"Let's play Holy Gabriel," begged Pegg.

"We haven't enough light in here," said Ketty. "You can't see what Holy Gabriel's doing."

"I know," said Cal. "Why don't we play—"

A loud scraping noise along the bottom of the boat was followed by a thud against the hull.

"We're a-sinkin'!" screamed Rachel. "Let me out of here!"

Madly she fought her way to the door. The others followed.

"We're all right," George called to them as they swarmed on deck. "Grazed a sawyer."

"Get back inside there, you womenfolks," ordered Anson, "so's we can put our minds to the steering."

167

Back they went as they were ordered.

"Whar's Ketty?" piped up Farrer.

"Dry up, young un!" Rachel ordered.

"Here I am, Farrer," answered Ketty. "Come stand here by me and—"

Suddenly a mighty jolt knocked the womenfolk off balance and sent the children sprawling. The cabin door flew open.

"Watch out!" they heard George shout from the bow. "We're caught!"

"Lord 'a' mercy! Can't you have mercy, Lord?" Rachel begged tearfully.

Pegg and Betsy screamed. Lennie muffled her crying in the folds of Tish's skirt. Lettice, her hand at her throat, choked back frightened sobs.

Ketty felt the floor of the cabin tilting crazily. Through the open door she saw the bow of the boat rising as the floor beneath her sank lower.

"Stiddy, young uns!" cautioned Tish, gathering to her the children who were close.

"What's Aunt Rachel a-cryin' for?" asked Farrer.

For half a minute the *Dragonfly* hesitated. Then, as George in the bow pushed with the gouger, the stern started swinging in a wide arc to the right, slowly at first, faster as the current caught it broadside. With a scraping sound, the bow twisted clear of the sawyer and splashed into the water. For a few minutes the current carried the boat along, stern foremost.

Above the noises in the cabin, Ketty heard the menfolk shouting orders to one another as they struggled with their oars to head the flat downriver.

168

"What's Aunt Rachel a-cryin' for, Ketty?" asked Farrer again.

"Didn't tear a hole in the bottom, did it?" Ketty heard Anson asking.

"Not this time," George answered.

"Rachel's afraid," Ketty whispered to Farrer, her voice scarcely louder in her ears than the pounding of her heart.

"What's she afraid of?"

How many things there were, thought Ketty, to scare the living daylights out of womenfolk traipsing after their menfolk!

"Is Lennie afraid too?" asked Farrer.

"Yes."

"What's Lennie afraid of?"

Through the nightmare of her own fear, Ketty discovered Farrer's small hand resting in confidence in the palm of her hand. To her, suddenly, it seemed the hand of all men, time out of mind, who, forever lured toward some far-off land, had hungered and thirsted and been afraid, had asked questions and got only stillness for answers, had loved and waited and died in lonesome places, clutching in the fog and the willful wind and the rain for a hand to steady them.

Ketty drew a deep breath. Clasping Farrer's hand tightly, she called Pegg and Betsy and Lennie to her.

"Would you like to play Holy Gabriel now?" she asked. "The door's open and we can see."

Nobody answered right away. They were listening for another thud, Ketty sensed, as she was listening.

"Let's not play a game," Lennie said between sniffles. "You sing to us, Ketty."

As if through a door ajar on long nights of lonely waiting, Ketty heard her mother's voice: *What time I am afraid, I will trust in Thee . . . . When thou passest through the waters, I will be with thee.* Lennie, she realized, was not looking for a gewgaw to distract her from fear. She was reaching for a hand to steady her in the face of fear.

"I'll sing you a song we used to sing in Salem," said Ketty.

It took all the courage she could muster from the warmth of the hand in hers and from Lennie's searching face turned up to her in the half-light to sing as the boat made its uncertain way through the fog:

> "As little birds all safe and snug,
> In hollow trees will hide them . . ."

How was it on that other boat, she wondered—that boat banished to its fate, with a man aboard broken out with the scourge, and all with him likely to die? Allie Shanor, she with the life-giving words and ways—there was a hand to steady a body in time of trouble!

> "When dangers show, and storm-winds blow,
> And men and cattle frighten,
> So the Lord Christ my Refuge is."

Ketty glanced at Tish. One of Tish's arms rested on Cal's shoulders, the other on Squire's. There too, realized Ketty, was a steadying hand—different from Allie Shanor's, but steadying.

The sound of a horn downriver, muffled by rain and fog, threw a spell of stillness over the cabin.

"Sounds like McEnnis a-tellin' Shanor's boat to tie up," said Tish. "That means we'll be a-quittin' too."

"And nary a minute too soon." Rachel whimpered. "I

won't breathe an easy breath till my feet are on dry ground."

"Hit won't be dry, Mammy," Squire reminded her. "Hit's a-rainin'."

"I'm going on deck," said Ketty, "to see if we may come out now."

As she slipped through the low doorway she heard Anson's angry voice. "Because it's against my judgment, that's why."

"Fernenst or no," shouted Shubeal.

The menfolk, Ketty realized, were still bandying their argument back and forth.

Baptist outshouted Shubeal. "I'm with Anse. I say, let's keep a-floatin'. We've come this far by our lonesome. What's to keep us from goin' the rest of the way?"

"If you keep floating in this fog, you're likely to hit something worse than a sleeping sawyer," said George. "I still say we'll be better off sticking with McEnnis till we get past those Chickamauga towns."

Tish, who had followed Ketty out of the cabin, stood listening.

"I'm not going to have mutiny on this here boat," announced Anson. "Specially when it's led by folks that joined up 'thout being asked."

"Anse," said Tish, "if hit's mutiny George is a-leadin' by wantin' us to stay together till we get past them towns, why all of us womenfolks is a-mutinyin' with him."

"Lord 'a' mercy!" Anson groaned. He turned and looked at Tish long and hard. He spat into the river. Glum-faced and silent, he tended the steering oar.

A half-hour longer the boats floated. Then, one at a time,

the three boats ahead of the *Dragonfly*, like wraiths in the fog, pulled toward the river bank.

Anson watched, crafty-eyed, and held the *Dragonfly* steady in the current. Past the nearest boat they floated, past the next. As the big boat floated past McEnnis's boat, the hull bumped against another sawyer.

"Sawyers," George warned, "have been known to rip straight through the hull of a boat. We were mighty lucky to get off that last one."

"Must 'a' been a hurricane through here some time or other," Shubeal said, "to plant all them sawyers."

For a long silent spell Anson studied the fog that shrouded river and earth and sky like a gauzy curtain. "Pull in," he ordered bluntly. "It ain't even the middle of the morning yet."

When they reached the bank, Anson gave further orders. "Stay on board, ever'body. Don't set a foot on the river bank. Be all geared to start floating as soon as the fog lifts."

The rest of the morning Anson complained and hoped by turns. A body would think they were all bat blind. Fact was, he'd been on rivers in fogs a lot worse. Give any fog an hour or two and it would either lift or shift. If, by the middle of the day, it was still too thick for McEnnis, the *Dragonfly* could leave his pock-ridden bunch behind. Any day now corn-planting weather would be on them, and they were still a long, watery way from their cornfields.

The day wore on, dour and drippy.

" 'Twouldn't be such a teetotal loss," said Baptist, "if a feller could go a-huntin'."

"Wonder why it was," grumbled Anson, "that nobody

172

singing the praises of the French Lick, not a single solitary soul, remembered to mention we'd run into fog."

As the long day drew to an end and the fog still hovered around them, Anson directed that they should sleep on the boat.

"You aim to shove off ahead of McEnnis?" asked Shubeal.

"I ain't a-saying," said Anson.

At the faintest hint of day, two blasts on a horn roused the sleeping voyagers aboard the *Dragonfly*. The menfolk, staggering to their feet, saw the black hulking shape of a flatboat floating down the dark river.

Anson gaped.

"McEnnis, he's done beat you to hit, Anse," said Shubeal.

"Consarn it!" muttered Anson. "*Consarn* it!"

From the deck of his flat as it floated past, McEnnis called, "Goin' to be a fair day!"

chapter 15

THE day, as McEnnis had prophesied, was fair. The sun broke out of a bank of clouds, and the wind dropped. The five boats floated along in order, Shanor's boat, a ghostly, silent, pestilence-filled thing, far behind the *Dragonfly*.

The sun in good time bleached out Anson's glumness. The ease with which the *Dragonfly* floated on the current, with no further hindrance from sawyers, was as herbs and bitters that purged him of the mullygrubs.

"It's a good thing we was on that Chickamaugy hunt, Baptist," he said. "Seems like I recollect ever' turn and twist in the river along here."

"Must 'a' been scart," said Shubeal. "When you're scart thataway, things burn theirselves into your brain."

The day passed—a day during which nothing in particular happened, nothing good and nothing bad. The children learned their lessons and played their games. Tish sat on an upturned gum bucket in the sun and knitted. Rachel and Lettice sat and waited.

Late in the day Baptist, wielding his broadhorn, pointed

toward the south bank of the river. "See that little-bitty island?" he called. "I recollect that. That means we're a gettin' close to the mouth of Chickamaugy Creek." He studied the island as the boat floated past. "That's whar we caught that poor devil of a redskin a-settin' his fish traps, recollect, Anse? Made him guide us to them Indian towns. And that," he added, "means we're not far from Chickamaugy Town. That's the first un we burned."

See people not as enemies, but as people, Ketty—red people and black people and white.

As the *Dragonfly* drifted past the mouth of Chickamauga Creek, the menfolk on top of the cabin and the womenfolk leaning against the gunwale watched furtively as if some other hapless redskin might be out setting his fish traps. Willow whips growing beside the river were golden with the surge of spring, and a pair of wood ducks in search of a hollow tree where they might build a nest and brood their young winged above them and disappeared among the trees on the north bank of the river. But the voyagers paid little notice to such things, seeing only the ghosts of red men staring from behind every rock and tree.

At sunset the boats floated in sight of the place where the old Chickamauga Town had stood, its charred tree trunks now a witness to the stories of Anson and Baptist. And at that moment McEnnis blew his horn once.

"Lord 'a' mercy, we ain't a-stoppin' here!" protested Rachel.

"What's wrong with stopping here?" Anson asked. "Not a soul been here, I'd say, since we burned the red men out. You're as safe here tonight, Rachel, as you'd be sitting in front of your own fireplace in Wataugy."

"There'll be sentries tonight, Rachel," George told her.

As Ketty lay with Farrer close beside her in the dark, the campfire having been doused with water, she felt uncommonly strange to be alive in this ghostly place from which life had so lately fled. She wondered where the red men had gone when they were driven away by Colonel Shelby and his nine hundred men—nine hundred men setting fires to cabins and shooting running red men in the back and bashing children's heads against stout oak trees and driving milling, frightened cattle into the river to drown. She wondered if Anson had taken the life of an Indian child. And had he set fire to the scattered huts and burned the corn the red men had stored up to stave off starvation until another autumn of gathering in? Not content with burning the corn, Anson had said, the men had gone into the gardens and pulled up by the roots the young peas just putting out their tendrils for climbing. And Baptist? Had Baptist bashed in the heads of any children—Baptist, who soon would have a child of his own?

The Indian children, playing in the gentle shade of the trees—did any of them get away from the murderers? Ketty wondered. Had any Indian man-child been made to feel terror as Farrer had because some one of Evan Shelby's men—Anson? or Baptist?—laughing at the flames curling up from the Indians' miserable huts as they burned—had scalped his mammy and pappy before his eyes? She listened for a moment to hear if such a child, left to the wolves, might be crying in the night. But all she could hear was the March wind whistling among the blackened ruins, the water breaking quietly against the hull of the *Dragonfly* tied up at the river bank, and George Soelle, doing sentry duty the early part of the night, now and then walking slowly up and down at the edge of the circle of sleeping voyagers. Was he walking to keep himself awake? Or was he counting stars?

"Anson," said George as the voyagers ate their breakfast the next morning, "we'll be getting into the rough places pretty soon now. Suppose we ought to haul my canoe on the deck?"

"From the tales I been a-hearin'," said Shubeal, "if you don't want to shake a farewell hand with hit, you'd better haul hit in."

"'Twon't hurt," agreed Anson.

In half an hour McEnnis blew on his horn twice. With *Walk-on-the-Water* resting on the deck of the *Dragonfly*, the voyagers set out again.

"We'll be passing another Indian town soon," announced Anson as they got under way. "On the south bank. Settico, it's name was."

As they floated along, minute by minute closer to Settico, Anson, Ketty noticed, stopped his norating and Baptist his bragging. Both of them, like all the others aboard, grew wary and kept watch. Ketty tried to teach the children their words, but her gaze seesawed back and forth from their paddles to the river bank.

"Right about thar, hit was," said Baptist, pointing downriver to the bank at that moment opposite McEnnis's boat.

Suddenly he stiffened. Leaning forward, he gazed hard in the direction he had pointed. "Them scoundrels, they're back," he muttered.

There, on the ashes of the old Settico, loomed a new town. One large building it had, oblong and covered with bark. Adjoining the west end was a small lean-to, from the roof of which, through a hole, curled the blue smoke of burning wood.

Baptist felt for his rifle. His dog, lying beside him, got to his feet and stood tense and stiff, his hair raised on his back. Anson looked to his rifle, then hastily studied the north bank of the river for a likely place to pull in.

"Womenfolks into the cabin," said George, his voice only a note louder than the sound of the water.

Tish, crowding after Rachel and Lettice, swooped Betsy into her arms and pushed Pegg and Lennie, Cal and Squire, ahead of her toward the cabin door. Ketty, her first thought of Farrer, found him making marks on his paddle, unaware of the fear sweeping across the boat like a hurricane wind. She lifted child and paddle in her arms and ran after Tish.

"Whar are we a-goin', Mammy?" whispered Betsy.

Tish laid a firm finger across the child's mouth—a sign to all the children not to let a whimper escape them. Inside the cabin, she bolted the door. Rachel stood like a stone image, her mouth wide open but her screams fixed solid within her.

"What did we come in here for, Ketty?" asked Farrer, his voice high-pitched and clear.

"Sh-h-h!" Ketty laid a finger on his lips. "George told us to come," she whispered.

"Why did George tell us to come?"

Why did they go into the cabin? Ketty repeated Farrer's question to herself. Why did she, Ketturn Petrie, go hiding in the cabin—she who had never harmed a red man? She who had never nursed hate-filled thoughts toward red men? She felt stifled and strangled in the fear-tainted air of the cabin.

Suddenly, before anybody could ask what on earth she was doing, or say to her that she'd gone plumb out of her mind, she set Farrer on his feet, unbolted the cabin door, opened it, and slipped out on deck.

"Ketty!" Anson's raspy voice greeted her. "Get back in that cabin!"

Ketty shut the cabin door behind her.

"Get back in thar, Ketty!" commanded Baptist. "What fool notion—"

Ketty, standing tall and straight beside the closed door, glanced at George. He pointed to the red men's house, now directly opposite the *Dragonfly,* and with his head he motioned toward the cabin door. Seeing Ketty hesitate, he motioned again, jerking his head in a way to brook no talking back to him.

With feelings of defeat and guilt gnawing at her, Ketty opened the cabin door and slipped inside again. In torment she waited with the others while the current bore the *Dragonfly* downstream with no more sound in the cabin or on top of it than if ghosts were voyaging down the river in a ghostly ship, manned by a ghostly crew, past the new Settico, past the wooded river banks where it was possible red men might be hiding, past bends in the river that finally hid the town from view.

Then, outside, she heard McEnnis's voice calling up to Anson. "You folks see that thar Indian place back thar?"

"Settico," Anson told him.

"Hit's too quiet to suit me," said McEnnis. "Somethin'

mean's a-brewin' somewheres. They's a preacher feller on the boat jist ahead of you, says he's been here before, and says in an hour or so we'll be a-hittin' them mean places in the river. I figure, ruther than hit 'em in the pitch dark, we'd better get a good night's sleep and tackle 'em when we're fresh."

"You mean you're quitting? Now?" asked Anson.

"Figure we'd better," said McEnnis. "Don't 'pear to be any red men on the north bank. I'm paddlin' back a ways further to signal Shanor we're tyin' up. A horn hereabouts'd just be invitin' red men. We're sleepin' on board tonight," he added, "ready to shove off, jist in case. Better post a sentry."

Words were few and hushed as the voyagers aboard the *Dragonfly* waited in the waning daylight for the dreaded darkness. Quietly the menfolk speculated on the whereabouts of the Settico Indians. Maybe the men were out hunting and the squaws were home tending the fires. Maybe the men were off some place powwowing, talking up mischief for which they'd surely get their hides full of lead. Or maybe—it could be, in fact, it just might be—they were farther downriver, lying in wait where the boats would be at the mercy of rocks and rough water. Well, said Baptist, if that's where they wanted to learn their lesson, that's where they'd learn it.

The sinking sun sent its rays in a direct line across the water to the boats, lighting them up as targets. Uneasily the voyagers watched and listened and waited. When finally the sun sank behind the mountains, it left the western sky a sea of boiling red clouds.

180

"Look at that thar sky!" Rachel called attention to it as if a body could see anything else. "Hit means trouble, that sky does."

No one answered her.

"Well, why don't you say somethin'?" she demanded, holding back her tears only a little better than she did her fears.

"Rachel," said Tish, "snivelin' won't change that sky one little bit."

At dark the womenfolk crowded into the cabin with the children and lay down, croodled together on the floor. Ketty lay beside Farrer, her hand enfolding his. When the child was breathing evenly, Ketty listened for sounds on the roof of the cabin, but she heard only Baptist's snoring. Either Anson or George was standing sentry, she guessed— or both.

On a sudden impulse she got up from the floor, wrapped her shawl about her shoulders, and stole through the doorway onto the deck.

"That you, Ketty?"

Her heart leaped at the sound of the voice.

"Yes, George," she whispered.

"Come on up," said George. "You can watch with me. Here." His voice came from the top of the ladder. "Give me your hand."

"Where are the others?" whispered Ketty.

"Asleep," George answered, "behind the gunwale, where Baptist's snoring won't roll them into the river." He led Ketty across the cabin roof to the steering oar.

"It's more comfortable to dangle your feet over the

edge," he whispered. He waited until she was seated and then sat down beside her. "Now," he asked, "why aren't you sleeping?"

"Because—"

"Because you still can't bring yourself to be one of us?" he asked. "To be partner to our crime?"

She was silent a minute, sorting out her thoughts, feeling grateful for someone to talk to—feeling grateful for George to talk to.

"I don't think of you as being one of the rest of them, George," she said, "as being partner to their crimes."

"But I am," George assured her.

"But you agree with me that there's a juster way of dealing with the Indians," Ketty said.

"I know there's a juster way, Ketty," he told her. "But at this minute I've got my hand on my rifle, ready to shoot at the least suspicion."

Ketty sighed. Questions tormented her mind as a cat torments a mouse.

"The time for parleying with the red men was over before we set out, Ketty," George told her. "It's too late now. There's nothing a body can do now but watch with the eyes of a hawk and pray that his aim with his rifle is good."

"You too, George?"

They sat a long time in silence, hearing the night wind loafing among the treetops and the dark water lapping against the hull of the boat.

"You are so pure in thought, Ketty," George whispered, "so very pure in thought."

It came to Ketty, sudden-like, that George's hand lay on hers. When he had placed it there she didn't know.

182

With a feeling of guilt she started to pull her hand away. All Salem would be scandalized to know that a girl, even though she might be betrothed to a man chosen by the Elders to be her husband, was sitting beside him in the dark, her hand in his.

The warmth of their hands, touching closely, banished from Ketty's mind all fear of red men and tuned her ears to the haunting rhythm of the night as the softening wind idled among the trees and the dark river flowed unceasingly on its long journey. If a man loved a woman, sang the aching sweet night, with all his mind and heart and quiet strength, even should he die, his love would no more end than the river ends, but through all time would go flowing mightily into the glorious sea of life.

"But thoughts are not enough," said George.

Ketty strove to guard the fragile moment against assaulting words, but in vain. Words put an end to it. But the hands remained clasped—the warm, strong hands.

"Not even pure thoughts."

"What is enough?" asked Ketty.

"Deeds. Deeds born of loving thought and acted out in love, like those we talked about when I made the paddles. This bloody river of hate that has its headwaters in both red men and white men—even one loving deed might change the direction of its channel a little. But who is strong enough and good enough to do the deed?"

How far away was Salem! thought Ketty, filled with the wonder of the warmth of George's hand on hers. The wilderness, terrible in its strength, terrible in its loneliness, its cruelty, and its craftiness, was no match for strong hands warmly clasped. Like some patriarch in Holy Writ giving his blessing to the wandering Israelites, the wilderness blessed strong hands clasped in love.

"Did you ever see a map, Ketty, with rivers and mountains and cities on it?"

"Yes."

"But not roads."

"No roads."

"Let's imagine a map. And let's say a man and a woman are going on a journey from some starting place at one end of the map to some good land at the other end. They ford rivers and climb mountains and pass through territory where wicked people live. Winds howl against them, rains all but drown them, and cold stiffens their joints. But these hindrances are nothing because they're young and strong. And they're in love. And it says on the map that they arrive and that they live happily all their long lives. Because, all their long lives, they're in love."

"Any—man and woman?" asked Ketty.

George pressed her hand. "Do you know why I came on this voyage, Ketty?" he asked.

"To take up your claim."

"To take, if I can, what I can't do without," he told her. "Remember that morning back on Cloud Creek when you told me you were going to man Shubeal's oar? It was then, Ketty, that minute, that I knew why I had sent my deputies back to New Bern without me—and why I had to come on this voyage. All my life, I realized then, I've been looking for a far-off land. That morning I knew where it was."

He put his arms about her, drew her to him, and kissed her.

After a moment she freed herself. "I'll go in now," she whispered.

Tomorrow, thought Ketty—what would tomorrow bring? The Suck. The Suck with its raging, swirling waters. Dragging Canoe, proud son of Little Carpenter, gone mad with hate and bent on deadly revenge. And, within her, tenderness for the man beside her, and a sudden chilling fear for his safety.

chapter 16

HAD a body never heard tell of the Suck, decided Ketty as she stood on deck watching, he would know that somewhere downriver, not very far ahead, a mess of trouble was stewing. The mountains that for so long had kept their distance began boldly to close in on both sides of the river. As cocksure as Baptist with a long rifle in his hands, they moved in to the water's edge, crowding out the narrowing bottoms of cane altogether. High above the voyagers towered the heads of hoary rock, and the river, pinched and confined, twisted and contorted and whirlpooled around its sudden bends, roared in its narrow gorges, and splashed against the rocky walls.

The *Dragonfly* bounced and creaked in the bends, warped and wallowed in the whirlpools.

"Like riding on a chip," Anson called as he anxiously tended the steering oar in an effort to keep the flat in the twisting channel.

Shubeal and Baptist, cautious and anxious, wielded their broadhorns, while George, in the bow of the boat, shoved with the gouger against jagged rocks jutting into the river, and searched the current for treacherous swirls.

186

"When's the next town, Anson?" called George as he wiped sweat and spray from his face.

"Any time now," said Anson.

The womenfolk braced themselves, some against Tish's loom, some against the barrels on deck, not venturing to the gunwales. Tish held her knitting in her hands, but she did not knit. Lettice, her face strained as the boat lurched and warped, gazed steadily at Baptist, and now and then her lips moved in the words worn old by folks mired in trouble: "Lord 'a' mercy!" Rachel, white as a cloud, caught her breath in little gasps as if the churning water were already washing over her.

"Why don't we play hopscotch, Ketty?" asked Farrer, the only one on board who seemed to have no notion of the danger that lurked everywhere about them.

"Boy," Cal told him, "with this here boat a-switchin' hit's tail thisaway, you're apt to hop right over the gunwale into the river."

"Been a long time since we seen them three boats ahead," said Shubeal.

"We kept a-tellin' you, didn't we, we mought as well go by our lonesome?" Baptist reminded him.

"Hit sure looks like hit's ever' boat for its lonesome down this stretch," agreed Shubeal.

"So long as we don't see Shanor's boat, I'm satisfied," said Anson.

On the river bore them. Around a bend they came into a straight stretch of water, near the end of which floated the third of McEnnis's boats.

"I declare, hit does put heart in a body to see 'em," said Rachel.

187

The others on deck turned their gaze to the boat ahead and to the steep cliffs that confined the rushing water.

Anson, for the moment relaxed, searched the rocky shelf on the south side of the river. Suddenly he scowled. He rubbed the back of his hand across his eyes as if to clear his vision. "I hadn't recollected it as being right there," he said.

On a ledge above the river, where a Chickamauga town had been defiled and burned, stood a new town, risen, like the new Settico, from the cinders of the old. As the boat ahead of the *Dragonfly* floated even with it, out of a long, low building red men came pouring. Like ants they scurried about, down the ledge, and along the river bank. Then, before the horrified eyes of the voyagers, two dugout canoes carrying three men each set out from the river bank, one toward the boat ahead, the other toward the *Dragonfly*.

Shep, standing beside Baptist, growled. The hair on his back stiffened.

Rachel gasped. Tish began herding the children together. Lettice looked at Baptist with eyes gone wild.

"Inside! Get inside the cabin!" Anson ordered the women-folk.

With one hand on the steering oar, he stooped and, with the other hand, grabbed up his rifle. "Here, Shubeal!" he said, thrusting the rifle toward him.

Baptist swung his broadhorn onto the cabin roof. He dropped to his knees, spat on his hands, rubbed them together, picked up his rifle, and trained it on the red man in the bow of the canoe headed toward the *Dragonfly*.

"Don't shoot," George called from the bow. "They're not armed."

A heaviness in Ketty's chest choked her.

Be present, Ketty. See people not as friends or enemies, but as people, red people and black people as well as white.

With her hand at her throat, she watched the other womenfolk crowding through the cabin doorway, pushing the children before them.

"I'm a-goin' to stay with Ketty," Farrer said.

Lennie turned. "Ain't you a-comin', Ketty?"

"Hurry!" Ketty ordered. "Get inside and shut the door."

"Get inside yourself, Ketty!" Anson said angrily.

Ketty hesitated. The thought of the fear-tainted cabin sickened her, and in her roiled mind Sister Oesterlein's orders argued with Anson's orders.

She turned and saw the canoe plowing through the swift water toward the *Dragonfly*. Suddenly Sister Oesterlein's orders were forgotten and panic possessed her. Four quick strides she took toward the doorway of the cabin. As she reached for the door, it opened, and Tish crowded through.

"Squat behind the gunwale, Ketty, quick!" Tish called as she dashed across the deck.

Finding sudden relief in her mind, Ketty dashed after Tish.

"Menfolks mought need help," Tish whispered as Ketty squatted beside her behind the gunwale.

Ketty, her heart pounding, peeped through a loophole. She saw one of the Indians in the canoe raise an arm. She heard him call something to the men on the flat.

" 'Brothers'?" Baptist's unbelieving voice was scarcely louder than the roar of the water. He lowered his rifle. "Is he a-sayin' 'Brothers'?"

The canoe shot closer.

"Brothers!" sounded clearly across the narrowing expanse of water. "Don't go north side. North side bad for boats. This side good."

"Watch out, Anse!" Baptist warned, keeping his voice low. "This mought be a trick."

"Pull for the north bank," ordered Anson.

Baptist and Shubeal put down their rifles and took up their broadhorns. Anson steered the clumsy flat out of the current and headed it toward the wall of rock on the north side.

The boat ahead of them, trailed by the other canoe, floated around a bend and out of sight.

"Don't go that side, brothers!" the red men called again as the flat neared the north wall of the gorge. The canoe followed and drew alongside.

Baptist's dog growled.

"Easy, Shep!" Baptist laid a hand on the dog's back. "Easy!"

Coppery hands grasped the gunwale. George laid down the gouger and as the three Indians, unarmed, hoisted themselves on to the deck, he faced them. One of them held the pawpaw rope tied to the bow of the canoe.

Tish and Ketty got to their feet. The three men on top of the cabin sharply eyed the three red men.

"What do you want?" asked George.

The red men spread their empty hands. "Brothers," they repeated.

190

"Give them something down there, Tish," ordered Anson. "Anything."

Tish had not waited for orders. She was already hunting for something to put into the red men's hands.

Beside a piggin Ketty caught sight of Farrer's willow whistle, dropped when the child had been dragged into the cabin. For a second she was in the *Gemeinhaus* at Bethabara, hearing Brother Bulitschek play the organ for Little Carpenter, hearing Little Carpenter ask the Brethren to send a teacher for his proud stripling of a boy, Dragging Canoe.

She stooped and picked up the whistle. The red man nearest her snatched it from her hand. He turned it about and studied it. "Humph!" He snorted and tossed the whistle over the gunwale into the river.

Without another word or sign, the three red men climbed over the gunwale, dropped into their canoe, and paddled away toward the town on the south bank.

chapter 17

"JUMPIN' Jehoshaphat!" exclaimed Baptist, his mouth open with astonishment as he looked after the red men. "What d'ye make of that?"

George shook his head. "Something mighty tricky's going on," he said.

Ketty looked about—downriver, upriver, and up and down the steep cliffs. Suddenly her throat went dry. She grasped Tish's arm. "Look!" she whispered. "Look!" she called to the men. "On the cliff, behind you."

Turning, the voyagers saw a file of red men trotting along a rocky ledge a hundred yards upriver. As the Indians crossed an open space between clumps of trees, the voyagers could see that they carried rifles and that their faces were smeared with red and black war paint.

"Looks like their trick worked, Anse," said Shubeal.

As he spoke, from the cliff nearest the *Dragonfly* a rifle cracked. A bullet spatted the water beside the boat.

"Looky thar!" shouted Baptist. "They're above us! They're ever'wheres, the devils!"

192

A bullet from the ledge upriver splintered a corner of the cabin roof.

Baptist swung his broadhorn onto the roof, grabbed his rifle with one hand and his dog with the other, and jumped to the deck. Shubeal, with Anson's rifle in his hands, jumped close on his heels. Crouched behind the gunwale, they searched the cliffs for red men. Another rifle cracked from the cliff above, and a bullet thudded against the side of the cabin. Rifles on the deck roared in reply.

"Somebody come up here!" shouted Anson. "Quick!"

George, carrying his rifle, climbed the ladder to the cabin roof, laid down the rifle, and grabbed the handle of Shubeal's broadhorn.

"Pull in closer to the cliff, George!" Anson ordered. "That'll give us some protection."

George pulled hard on Shubeal's broadhorn. Anson left the steering oar and took over Baptist's broadhorn. Ketty, her numbed senses thawing, saw the steering oar untended in its pivot. She darted up the ladder and grabbed the handle of the big oar.

As the *Dragonfly* turned toward the cliff, all along the rim and along the ledge upriver rifles cracked. Bullets spattered on the roof, on the deck, and in the water.

On deck, Shubeal and Baptist, squatting behind the gunwale, measured charges of powder, loaded, rammed the bullets home, primed, aimed, pulled the triggers, and measured powder again. As the boat moved slowly under the protection of the cliff, the firing died down.

Baptist cautiously raised his head above the gunwale. "Whupped 'em again," he said.

"Stay close in," ordered Anson. "I'll steer, George. You

pole along fast as you can. Ketty, get down from here."

"Quick, Ketty," ordered George.

George swung his broadhorn onto the roof as Anson, again at the steering oar, studied the cliffs.

"We're just about out of range of them rascals on the ledge upriver," Anson said.

George took up a pole, and at the forward corner of the roof nearest the cliff he set one end of it against the rock and buried the other end in his left shoulder. As he walked along the edge of the roof, toward the stern, he pushed against the pole and moved the flat slowly downriver. When he reached the stern, he lifted his pole, walked back to the forward corner, set the pole again, and again walked to the stern.

"This cliff along here's so steep, if we stay close in they can't hit us from above," said Anson.

"There's no law that says they have to stay above us," George reminded him. "They likely know every toehold in this rock for miles along here."

"Well, as long as they are above us," said Anson, "we'll stay in close. It'd be plain suicide to get out in that river. If we can make it to that bend—" He studied the bend downriver and the cliff above it. "I don't believe they can get on that downriver cliff from this un," he said. "That break between 'em's too deep."

Another rifle cracked from the upriver ledge behind them, and a bullet hit the water a rifle's length from the boat. Baptist's and Shubeal's rifles answered. A bullet thudded against the side of the cabin. A shower of bullets rained in the river around the flat.

"Guess we're not out of range yet, Anson," said George.

194

"Baptist," called Anson, "you come up here and pole too—get us along faster."

"Shubeal, you go," ordered Baptist. "If they's any chance, I aim to get me another scalp."

Shubeal got to his feet.

"Give me that thar rifle, Shubeal," ordered Tish.

Shubeal thrust Anson's rifle into Tish's hands and scrambled up the ladder. As he reached the roof, a bullet from the upriver ledge shattered a board at his feet. An ugly splinter caught in his ankle. He stooped and, as he yanked the splinter out with one hand, he grabbed the pole with the other.

An arrow landed at Anson's feet.

"Where'd that come from?" asked Anson.

George glanced at the cliff above them. "From up there," he said.

Anson took a deep breath. "If they're shooting arrows from up there—" He studied the cliff. "Looks like we mought have to shove out," he said. Turning, he saw Ketty. "Ketty," he said, scowling, "you still up here? All right. You steer. Me and George'll pole and man the broadhorns. Shubeal, you jump back on deck. You can use George's rifle. You down there'll have to cover for us the best you can."

Ketty hurried to the steering oar, George at her heels.

"Ketty," he pleaded, "go down on deck. Go to the cabin. We'll get along."

"No," answered Ketty firmly, keeping her hands on the oar. "I'm all right."

A flock of arrows from the cliff above whistled through the air like a covey of quail. Some rattled against the deck, some settled in the water around the boat. One tore into the folds of Ketty's skirt. Close at hand a bullet thudded.

"They've got me!" Anson groaned. "In the leg. Somebody take this here pole! Quick!" he pleaded.

George jerked the arrow from Ketty's skirt. "Are you hit?" he asked.

Ketty shook her head. "I'm all right," she said again.

"You must get down from here, Ketty."

"I'll stay," Ketty said. "You help Anson."

For a second George hesitated. "Bless you, Ketty!" he said. Then he rushed to Anson and helped him across the roof of the cabin and down the ladder. Back on the roof again, he grabbed up his pole.

Tish propped Anson against the gunwale. "Can you stand hit till we get through this?" she asked.

Anson rolled his head in pain. "I reckon I'll have to."

Squatting behind the gunwale, Tish caught sight of a red man, rifle in hand, halfway down the cliff a short distance ahead of the boat. She snatched up Anson's rifle again, rested the long barrel on the gunwale, and took careful aim. With a steady finger she pulled the trigger.

Down the cliff the red man half rolled, half tumbled, his fall broken by stunted trees. Midway the rifle slipped from his hand and lodged against a cedar sprout. The body of the man caught against a Judas tree just beginning to turn pink along its branches. A dying twitch loosed it, and it slid into the river ahead of the boat.

"Look at that!" George gasped. "More'll be down any minute. They'll be swarming all over this boat. Shubeal!" he called. "Come up and help!"

Shubeal, with George's rifle in his hands, climbed the ladder, laid the rifle on the roof, and snatched up a pole.

George picked up his rifle. "Here, Tish!" he called, passing the rifle down from the top of the cabin. "If Anson can load, you fire both rifles."

He grabbed up his pole again. "We have to get away from here, Shubeal," he said. "Baptist," he called, "you and Tish load all three rifles and be ready. We're going to pole beside the cliff a few yards farther and then make for the current. It's a sight healthier out there than it will be here if the red men get down this cliff. Fire at every red man you see. Make 'em keep their heads down. It's our only chance. Ready, Shubeal?"

Standing on the forward corner of the cabin roof nearest the cliff, he planted one end of his pole against a protruding rock and the other against his shoulder. Shoving with all his strength and walking along the edge of the roof toward the stern, he propelled the boat forward.

Shubeal, pole in hand, took his place on the forward corner. He glanced up at the cliff. His eyes went suddenly dreamy. As the boat floated along beside the cliff, he raised the far end of his pole and prodded the cedar sprout against which the red man's rifle had lodged. The rifle slipped sidewise and rested with its butt in a shallow crevice in the rock. Shubeal, walking along the edge of the roof, prodded the stock. The rifle moved an inch. He prodded again.

"Why don't you pole, Shubeal?" shouted George as he neared the stern edge of the roof.

Shubeal prodded again. The rifle moved free of the crevice, slid down the cliff, hit a narrow ledge, and flipped over toward the boat. Shubeal, leaning crazily over the edge of the cabin roof, caught it in his outstretched hands.

"Hooray for Shubeal!" shouted Baptist.

With scarcely a glance at his prize, Shubeal passed the rifle to the deck. Baptist reached up and grabbed it.

"Hand hit to Tish," directed Shubeal. "I aim for Tish to fire the first shot with hit."

He took up his pole, set one end of it against the cliff, the other against his shoulder, and, with new life coursing through him, pushed with all his might and started walking along the edge of the roof.

"That rifle loaded, Baptist?" called George.

"Yep," answered Baptist. "All loaded and a-rarin' to go."

"See that break in the cliff?" George asked. "Soon as we get even with that, we're heading for the current."

Silent and tense, those behind the gunwale searched the cliffs for red men, while those on the roof of the cabin poled the flat slowly along.

"Ketty," said George, "when we get even with that break, hold the steering oar hard to your left. Ready down there?" he called to Baptist and Tish.

The *Dragonfly* floated even with the break.

"Shove off!" ordered George.

Setting their poles straight against the cliff, George and Shubeal pushed. Slowly the big boat labored out into the river.

"Hard to the left, Ketty!" called George as the *Dragonfly* headed toward the brawling current. "Pick up your broadhorn, Shubeal!"

George threw down his pole and swung one of the broadhorns into the water. "You're steering fine, Ketty! Keep her moving, Shubeal!" he encouraged.

Behind the gunwale, Anson, his face white and twisted with pain, wrapped bullets in greased wadding and laid them in a handy piggin. Tish and Baptist searched the cliff, their rifles ready.

A puff of smoke halfway down the cliff was followed by the report of a rifle and the thud of a bullet against the hull of the boat. Baptist fired. A red man plunged forward down the cliff, and Baptist reached for another rifle.

"I'll get the next un, Baptist," said Tish, sighting along the barrel of Shubeal's rifle. "Ain't that one behind that bush up thar?"

Before Baptist could locate the bush, smoke puffed from it and a bullet crashed into the deck close to Anson. Tish pulled the trigger of the rifle.

Suddenly, as if a hundred fires were being kindled, smoke puffed everywhere along the cliff.

"Pull, Shubeal! Pull!" urged George.

Bullets streaked toward the boat. From the boat rifles answered as fast as Anson could load. Bullets struck the cabin roof. One tore through Ketty's skirt. Another grazed the handle of George's broadhorn.

"Pull, Shubeal! Steer into the current, Ketty," directed George. "We're almost there!"

As a shower of bullets spatted the water, the current caught the flat and carried it swiftly downriver, out of range of the rifle fire.

Anxiously George scanned the cliffs along the north bank.

"You were right, Anson," he said. "I don't believe they can cross that break."

As the current carried the boat around the bend, George swung his oar on to the roof and rushed to Ketty. "I'll steer now," he said. "You get on deck."

"Your oar?" said Ketty. "Who'll man your oar?"

"We'll get along," George assured her. "It's too chancy for you to be up here. Baptist can come up now. He's a match for this stretch of river, I reckon."

Baptist, carrying his rifle and his dog, climbed the ladder and took up the broadhorn.

"If you could shoot a rifle, Ketty, like Tish," he said, "the next time we run into red men you could squat behind the gunwale with my rifle, whar hit's safe, and I could stay up here and steer."

Keep the counsel of your own heart, Ketty.

"You leave Ketty alone," said George.

On deck, Ketty looked on anxiously as Tish with a hunting knife slit a leg of Anson's breeches. As Tish folded back the bloodstained buckskin, clotting blood oozed from a hole in the side of Anson's leg, above his knee.

"That bullet went clean to the bone," Anson said, groaning.

Inside the cabin somebody—Rachel? Lettice? it didn't sound like one of the children—uttered a high, shrill moan that ended in a scream.

Tish examined Anson's leg closely.

"Hit didn't go that far, I reckon," she said. "Jist into the fleshy part. All I need do is gouge that bullet out."

She studied the hole in Anson's leg a minute longer, picked up the hunting knife, and scowled at it.

"Ketty," George called from the roof, "come get my knife. It'll do a better job."

Ketty climbed the ladder and took the knife—a small, sleek bit of cutlery with silver tracings overlaid on the pearl handle. Two sharp, narrow blades it had, of polished steel.

"Open the little un," Tish told Ketty. "You'd better hold his leg, Ketty," she added. "This here boat's a-bouncin' around so."

Sitting on the deck beside Tish, holding Anson's leg steady, Ketty looked on as Tish probed the hole in the flesh with the sharp point of the keen knife blade.

Anson gripped his leg with both hands and screwed up his face in agony. "You're a-killing me, Tish! You're a-killing me!" he cried out.

The point of the knife scraped dully against the bullet.

"Careful, now!" Tish warned. "Jist let me get this here blade behind that ball and hit'll be over quick."

Deeper she probed. Skillfully she twisted the blood-stained blade in the hole and slowly pried the bullet, a lead ball the size of a pea, out of Anson's flesh.

"Oh-h-h-h!" groaned Anson.

Inside the cabin the screams grew shriller.

Tish watched the blood oozing from the hole in Anson's leg.

"I need—" she looked around her.

"You need to bind it up, don't you?" asked Ketty.

"And they ain't one solitary thing on this boat, I reckon, that's fit to bind hit with."

"Here, Ketty!" called George. He took from his breeches pocket a little wallet of crumpled paper and lifted from it a large square silk handkerchief. Ketty climbed the ladder to take it.

"A keepsake," George explained. "Belonged to my Grandfather Soelle—a good man. I liked him."

"But, George—" Ketty hesitated to take it.

"Sooner or later," George told her lightly, "the wilderness makes good use of everything."

As Ketty climbed down the ladder she heard another scream, long and shrill, inside the cabin.

Tish doubled the handkerchief catty-cornered on her knee and folded it in two-inch widths.

"It pounds all over my body," Anson said, "right down to my fingernails."

"What hit needs," said Tish, "is a poultice. First time we tie up and somebody can find me some slippery elm bark—"

The cabin door opened a crack and Rachel's face, strained with fear, showed through. "Lord 'a mercy, Tish!" she begged. "Come quick!"

"I thought as much," said Tish, giving one glance at Anson's leg and another at the cabin door, as if she were trying to decide where her duty lay.

"I'll do for Anson, Tish," Ketty told her, taking the handkerchief.

As Tish slipped inside the cabin, Ketty knelt beside Anson, laid the folded handkerchief over the wound, and began to bind his leg.

"Lord 'a' mercy, don't draw it so tight!" said Anson, rolling his head from side to side. His face was pale and drawn. "Where did Tish go?" he asked weakly.

"Inside the cabin," Ketty told him, watching the blood seep through the handkerchief.

"What for?"

"She was needed."

"Who could need her more than I do?" Anson complained petulantly.

Ketty drew in her breath. Anson did value Tish, then. And he was willing to say so when he had need of her, and of her touch that was sure and firm and gentle.

"Does your leg feel better now, Anson?" Ketty asked, tying the ends of the handkerchief in a hard knot.

"Not one bit!" said Anson. "Go tell Tish I want her."

"Anson," asked Ketty, "what is Tish's real name?"

He opened his eyes wide and stared at her.

"First you got too high and mighty notions about yourself to learn to shoot a rifle," he said. "And now you expect a body to use his dying breath to answer fool questions."

"You're not dying," Ketty assured him. "And you can answer my question with one word. What is Tish's real name?"

Anson shut his eyes again, leaned his head against the gunwale, and muttered sullenly, "Pretitia. Pretitia Tidings —as if it mattered."

"It does matter. Why don't you call her Pretitia, instead of Tish?"

He opened his eyes. "And get my head blowed off? You forget Tish can shoot a rifle. Tish," Anson added, "is worth her salt."

"Yes," agreed Ketty, "Tish is worth her salt—a hundred times over."

Anson drew up his throbbing leg and groaned.

"Don't move your leg," cautioned Ketty, placing her hand firmly on it. "There. That's better," she said soothingly as he quieted again.

"Tish is a name for a common woman," she told her

brother. "But your wife, Anson, is no common woman. Why don't you help her to be what she is inside herself? You could begin by calling her Pretitia—once in a while, at least."

The cabin door was suddenly swung wide open on its leather hinges, and without order or ceremony Rachel pushed all the children through the doorway onto the deck. Their faces were streaked with the tears they had shed in silence as the battle with the red men had raged. Farrer rushed to Ketty, threw his arms about her waist, and began crying as if floodgates had suddenly opened.

"What's a-going on?" demanded Anson. "Keep them brats away from me," he ordered.

Before Rachel could shut the door, another scream, anguished, long, and piercing, rose from the cabin.

On the deck and on top of the cabin, where Baptist, Shubeal, and George anxiously guided the boat through the rapids, a silence settled. Baptist's face turned as white as the foam that flecked the churning water.

"That girl!" Anson said. His shoulders, which had been rigid with pain, slumped. "Picking a time like this!"

With an arm tightly about Farrer, Ketty turned back to Anson. "Keep your leg still now, Anson. The bleeding's about to stop, I think. I'll keep the children away from you."

She gathered Farrer in her arms and turned to the questioning, frightened children still huddled near the cabin door where Rachel had pushed them. "Let's sit here on the deck together and be quiet," she said to them.

Her mind was fermenting like cabbage in a briny kraut

tub as she sat among the children. She wondered about Lettice inside the cabin—Lettice with the wondrous pretty face, now in pain. She wondered about Allie Shanor. Shanor's boat they hadn't seen since morning. Nor had they seen any of the boats ahead since the red men boarded the *Dragonfly*. But that, she decided, was not to be wondered at, seeing how the river twisted and flailed like a snake whose head has been smashed with a rock, and a boat had hardly turned one bend in the river before it was in another, sharper bend.

She glanced anxiously at the cliff above them. It kept its secrets well. The cliff, Ketty realized, was on the side of the red men.

On they floated, west and south and sometimes north, the river in its narrow, twisting bed a thing of angry power threatening to crumple the *Dragonfly* like a scrap of paper. Ketty had hardly noticed the river, she realized. There'd been other things to occupy her mind.

Again the cabin door opened, and again Rachel came hurrying out.

"Lettice, she's done birthed a baby," she announced. "Hit's a boy, Baptist," she called up to him. "A big bouncin' boy. You mought come down and see hit for yourself, Baptist."

Baptist swung his oar onto the roof and started for the ladder.

"You can't go now, Baptist," George told him firmly. "We're getting close to the Boiling Pot. The boy'll keep."

They had not long to wonder what the Boiling Pot was like. The *Dragonfly*, buffeted along, suddenly, with a loud

205

noise of warping, turned half around in the willful current. At that moment a shot rang out from somewhere on a cliff above.

Ketty saw Baptist grab his rifle. She saw Tish run out of the cabin, snatch a rifle from the deck, and crouch beside Anson at the gunwale. Without thinking, Ketty pushed the children through the cabin doorway and shut the door.

"Get inside, Ketty!" George called to her.

But Ketty was powerless to move. In her ears she heard the reedy music of the organ back in Bethabara, and the voice of Little Carpenter asking the Moravian Brethren to send a teacher for his proud son, Dragging Canoe. She felt a great loneliness, and on her shoulders settled a heaviness like no burden she had ever carried before. Leaning against the cabin wall, she covered her face with her hands, and sobbed. Through her sobs she heard dimly another shot from somewhere on the cliff.

At that moment a swirl in the current twisted the *Dragonfly* crosswise. The boat careened toward the north cliff. With a harsh scraping noise and a mighty jolt it came to a standstill with the bow resting on a rock close to an overhanging ledge.

George hauled the steering oar up on the roof. With screams from the cabin ringing in their ears, he and Baptist jumped on deck.

"Consarn this good-for-nothing leg!" complained Anson as they rushed past him to the bow of the boat.

"Reckon we can pole off?" asked Baptist.

"We'll try," George said.

They heard another shot, this time from a distance.

"Don't 'pear from their shots to be so many," said Baptist.

"They may be signaling others to come," said George. "If a couple of dozen climb down this cliff before we get off this rock, we're finished."

"Shubeal," called Baptist, "you come and help George pole off. Me and Tish'd better get set for whatever's a-comin' down this here cliff."

Shubeal grabbed up the poles, climbed down the ladder, and raced to the bow. Together he and George set the poles, braced their feet, and strained. But the *Dragonfly* did not move.

George studied the rock on which they were grounded. Water swirled over its slippery surface, ankle deep. "We can do better out there," he said. He scanned the cliff above them. "Baptist," he called, "nobody's coming down the cliff yet. You come help."

Tish, watching the three men jump onto the rock, laid down her rifle, slipped off her shoepacks, lifted the hem of her skirt, and tied it about her waist. Ketty, watching Tish, wiped her eyes with the back of her hand, hastily took off her shoes, and tied up her skirt. She and Tish climbed over the gunwale onto the rock.

George set one end of a pole under the hull of the boat and the other end on his shoulder. Baptist set the other pole. Shubeal, Tish, and Ketty braced their shoulders against the gunwale.

"All together!" ordered George. "Heave!"

With the cold water washing their ankles, they pushed and pried, slipped on the rock, groaned and grunted and sweated.

"Once more! Heave!"

As Ketty strained against the gunwale, something moving at the bow of the boat caught her eyes. She looked up.

"Lettice!" she screamed.

"She gave a little!" shouted George. "Heave!"

Baptist, seeing Lettice standing at the gunwale, for a second relaxed his grip on his pole. "Lettice, what on earth? Go back in the cabin, honey!" he pleaded.

Another shot rang out in the distance.

Lettice, her hand at her throat, watched Baptist as he strained on his pole. Suddenly she turned and ran into the cabin. In seconds she was back, clasping a bundle in her arms.

"Lettice!" George called angrily. "Get back in that cabin!"

But Lettice, as if she had no hearing for voices shouting warnings to her from without but followed instead some voice calling deep within her, climbed over the gunwale onto the slippery rock, the bundle clasped tightly in her arms. Her face, always soft and pretty, was uncannily so as she waded toward Baptist through the cold, swirling water.

"I'm not a-leavin' you, Baptist!" she said, gasping. "I'm not a-leavin'—"

With a grating sound the *Dragonfly* slid on the rock. The water beneath the boat deepened.

"Get aboard!" shouted George.

Grasping the gunwale, Tish and Ketty, Shubeal and George climbed onto the deck. Baptist, holding Lettice's right arm tight, struggled over the gunwale. As he turned to pull Lettice aboard, the boat grated off the rock and lurched into deep water. Lettice, clutching her bundle in her left arm, struck the gunwale. Her body went limp, and the bundle slipped into the river.

"God A'mighty!" shouted Baptist, holding on to Lettice with one hand and with the other frantically grasping for the bundle. George reached for Lettice, lifted her aboard, and laid her on the deck.

Crying, "My boy! My boy!" Baptist straddled the gunwale. Shubeal grasped him around the waist and held him.

George ran to Shubeal's aid. "You'd drown in that water!" he shouted into Baptist's deaf ears.

Baptist fought like a crazy man. "I never even seen my boy! This here river took him 'thout so much as a little-bitty splash!" he cried madly.

Together George and Shubeal hauled him back on deck while the *Dragonfly*, steering oar and broadhorns untended, careened downriver in the turbulent current. Still Baptist struggled. Tish laid a hand on his shoulder and spoke to him gently. Freeing an arm from Shubeal's grasp, Baptist struck at her. Suddenly wrenching his body free, he struck George a blow that sent him reeling across the deck against Tish's loom. In his blind grief he barely missed Anson and was advancing on Ketty when Tish put out a foot and tripped him.

He hit the deck hard and slumped against the gunwale. When he could get his breath, he began to laugh. Clean out of his head, he laughed and laughed, his cackling bouncing back foolishly from the rocky cliffs. The longer he laughed, the louder he laughed.

Tish, watching him anxiously, dipped a piggin over the gunwale into the river and dashed the water full in his face.

chapter 18

LIKE some strange water monster dragged up from the deep river and set down dripping wet on the deck, Baptist writhed and sucked in air in labored gasps and beat the deck with his big hands.

"Tish," Anson said, holding his throbbing leg, "did you need to drown him?"

The voyagers stood watching over Baptist, powerless to help him. Tish left the circle of onlookers and, bending over Lettice, felt her pulse. Gratefully she listened to her moaning, unconscious though it was.

"George," she called, "you carry Lettice inside. She'll come around. They'll both come around. But—hit won't ever be the same again."

When George had carried Lettice inside the cabin and laid her on her pallet, he hurried up the ladder to the steering oar. Shubeal followed him to the roof of the cabin. Tending one of the broadhorns, with his newly won rifle lying beside him, he gave only half his mind to the river, the other half to Baptist.

When finally Baptist's breathing was easier, Tish bent

over him and wiped the water from his face gently with the hem of her skirt. She stood watching until, weak and spent, he covered his face with his hands and began to sob like a child.

"That's better, Baptist," she told him. "I'll go now and see 'bout Lettice."

At the door to the cabin she stopped, looked upriver, and listened. Ketty, noticing, scanned the cliffs for red men but saw none.

George, too, noticed. "You hear something, Tish?" he called.

Tish laid a finger across her lips to motion him to silence.

"Thar 'tis," she said in a minute, her voice scarce louder than the roaring river.

Somewhere upriver a rifle cracked. A man shouted. Other rifles cracked.

Suddenly the air upriver was burdened with the heavy roar of many rifles. The whooping of Indians, high-pitched and frenzied and powered with angry exultation, pierced the roar, and above the shrill whooping rose now and then the terrified scream of a woman.

George drew a long breath. "Shanor's boat," he said.

"Sounds like they're grounded too, poor devils," said Shubeal.

"And the red men are down the ledge," said George.

Suddenly the roar of the rifles stopped. The yells of the Indians and the screams of the women grew shriller.

"Fighting it out at close range now," said Anson, "with tomahawks and knives."

Ketty thought of Allie Shanor. "Can't we go back and help?" she asked, close to tears. She turned to Tish as being the one most likely to have an answer. But Tish stood tongue-tied, gripping the door to the cabin.

"Aren't we going back to help?" begged Ketty, looking up at George.

With a choking in her throat she bowed her head on the gunwale and sobbed.

"Don't take on so, Ketty," Shubeal said comfortingly. "Them red men they'll get their comeuppance. Ever' last one of 'em'll die of smallpox."

Ketty sobbed louder. Soberly Tish opened the cabin door and went in to Lettice.

"Ketty"—George's voice broke through her sobbing— "come up here."

Ketty wiped her eyes, climbed the ladder, and stood beside George at the steering oar. He took her hand and held it comfortingly.

"We can't go back, Ketty," he said. "A flat can be persuaded upriver when the current is gentle. But nobody can get a flat up this stretch of river. It's a law of the river, Ketty, and we're helpless."

Ketty listened to his reasonable words. But the loving remembrance of Allie Shanor crowded out reason. "We could—could stop, couldn't we, and wait to see if anybody escapes?" she begged.

An ominous stillness settled on the river—a stillness pierced faintly by a single scream, high and shrill like that of a little boy the size of Farrer, pricking like a thorn, and suddenly cut off.

George pressed Ketty's hand.

"There's nothing to stop for now, I'm afraid, Ketty," he said. "Even if we could have stopped earlier," he asked her, "how could we have helped? Against as many red men as there are back there we're too few, Ketty. And by corn-planting time we'd all likely be dead of smallpox."

Ketty's tears fell faster. "Everybody—sometime or other —comes to helplessness," she sobbed.

"You're right, Ketty," said George. "Baptist and Lettice, Shanor's folks, that red man Tish shot, all the red men who'll likely catch smallpox from Shanor—all men everywhere, sometime or other, come to helplessness. No man is ever so strong but at some time he stands in need of pity—love and pity."

The cabin door opened and Tish came out.

"Rachel," she asked accusingly, "why didn't you stop her?"

"Me? I could as easy 'a' stopped one of them tornadoes," said Rachel. "She'd got to see Baptist, she said. We was all like to die, she said, and she was a-goin' to die with Baptist. And then here she come a-tearin' back, a-sayin' nothin' but a-figurin', I reckon, that the young un'd want to die with Baptist too. So off she tore again, with that baby in her arms. Couldn't a yoke of oxen 'a' pulled that girl back, Tish. Didn't you see the way she looked?"

For a minute Tish stared at Rachel, her face full of censure. Turning, she called up to Ketty. "Hit's you she wants."

Ketty wiped her eyes, climbed down the ladder, and hesitated for a minute at the door of the cabin. Why had Lettice sent for her? she wondered. Was she expecting her, in the wake of death, to have some word of life to say?

At the thought Ketty knew her own helplessness. Who in the wake of death has words of life? she asked herself.

She opened the cabin door slowly.

"Shut the door, Ketty," begged Lettice weakly from the pallet where she lay.

In the dimness Ketty could see that Lettice's eyes were shut in her tortured face, as if she couldn't bear to face the light. Before the door could swing shut, Tish followed Ketty into the cabin.

"Feel her feet, Ketty," she said.

Ketty knelt beside Lettice. Gently, with her warm hands, she rubbed Lettice's feet that were clammy with cold.

"Baptist, he didn't even see his baby." Lettice broke into sobs.

"Hit's rest you need, Lettice," Tish said, smoothing back her unkempt hair from her fair forehead. "All the strength's plumb gone out of you, child. You need some good warm vittles."

Lettice shook her head. "I want to die," she sobbed. She buried her face against the pallet and cried bitterly.

"Don't talk thataway," Tish told her. "Life ain't a purty to throw away when you get tired of hit. Even when life's a burden, you don't throw hit away. You hold on to hit, hard."

Ketty's throat tightened. Tish knew what she was speaking of.

As she chafed Lettice's chilled feet, Ketty felt in memory the warmth of George Soelle's hand on hers and heard his steadying voice. "Love lightens the burden, Lettice," she said.

"Hit wouldn't be so bad," said Lettice, "if the baby had a decent bury hole—one I could tend with blossoms and

214

purties. But to be buried in that deep rilin' water, and nobody a-knowin' wharabouts—"

Ketty remembered the death of babies in Salem and the trombonists announcing the news with special gladsomeness that a little pure soul had entered Heaven before it had had time to be besmirched. She remembered the strains of singing in God's Acre in Salem in the springtime of the year that so many children had died of smallpox.

She shut her eyes and tried to find solid footing in her thoughts. Salem was far away. But Lettice, and Baptist, too, knowing nothing of trombones and their announcings, were asking, like the Moravians, for words of life, and crying piteously for some balm to soothe the jagged edges of their pain.

"Why don't you say somethin', Ketty?" begged Lettice. Ketty took Lettice's hand in hers and held it warmly.

"We can't help the bury hole, Lettice," she said. "But I can sing a song for the baby. And you and Baptist, when you get to the French Lick and clear your land—you can set aside one little corner close to your cabin and call it God's Acre. And you can maybe set out a tree in it for your baby—a tree that'll say to you that he isn't dead, but somewhere, somehow, he's alive. A tree that blooms is a good tree for remembrance—a tulip poplar tree, maybe."

Lettice, lying with her eyes closed, listened.

"Would you like me to sing a song for your baby, Lettice?" asked Ketty. "As if we were burying it proper?"

"Go bring Baptist," Lettice said, wiping her eyes.

Tish started toward the door. "I'll send Baptist," she said. As Baptist entered the cabin, Ketty started. She had not

215

seen him indoors before. She had always thought of him as belonging outdoors, stalking bear or the great-antlered elk or deer or red men, along the rivers, among the high mountains, in the canebrakes and woods. Now, inside the cabin, he looked like a captured thing, trembling, afraid, helpless—even though the cabin was much too small to hold him, much too confining for his booming voice.

Baptist, however, had no voice now. He stumbled across the dimly lit cabin toward the pallet on which Lettice lay, dropped to his knees beside her, and covered his face with his hands.

Lettice, paying no mind to Ketty or to Rachel and Tish and all the children who had crowded just inside the doorway and stood waiting, laid a hand on Baptist's bent head and stroked his thick brown hair.

"Ketty, she's a-goin' to sing for the baby, Baptist," she said soothingly, "to give him a decent burial."

"It's a song especially for a little boy, Baptist," Ketty told him. "Only I'll have to sing it in German. The English words don't fit the tune. It says that the best thing that can happen to children is to be called home to a loving Heavenly Father."

She was still afraid of Baptist—afraid that he might scorn her German song as he had scorned so many of her notions.

Was ist denn für den Kinder das Beste auf Erden?

Her voice rose clear and strong.

Peace settled on the cabin. Tish, standing tall by the doorway, looked straight ahead. Rachel and the children stood motionless, staring at Ketty. Baptist's tense shoulders relaxed as if he had glimpsed another world than the wilderness, an indescribably fair world inhabited by his first-born, on whose face he had never looked.

Ketty, when she had finished the song, walked softly across the dark cabin, opened the door, and motioned the children to come with her on deck. Tish and Rachel followed. Ketty shut the door and left Baptist and Lettice alone with their grief. Stooping, she picked up Farrer and held him close in her arms.

chapter 19

"HIT'S a toss-up," Shubeal said at the shank end of the long day. "If we land, hit's like sleepin' with rattlesnakes. If we keep a-floatin', hit's like parleyin' with copperheads."

Anson, propped against the gunwale, studied the rosy sunset. "That means fair weather," he said. "We've got a full moon. And, according to what folks say, we're past the meanest part of the river."

"Let's parley with the copperheads," said George. "We'll need one man to steer and one to watch and listen. We can take turns."

"Me and Shubeal'll take the first stretch," announced Baptist. "Then George can take your place, Shubeal. Seems like I don't care if I don't sleep tonight."

The wilderness, Ketty guessed, had matched Baptist and won—for a spell, anyway.

"I can watch with George, Baptist," she said. "You need some night rest."

At midnight George took the steering oar from Baptist.

Ketty sat beside him on an upturned gum bucket. Moonlight shimmered in long, wavering lines on the dark bosom of the water. The wind was a whisper.

"The river's gentler," Ketty said.

"We're out of the mountains," said George, studying the shape of the river banks in the moonlight. "If we can depend on what folks say, we've left the red men behind, as well as the Suck. Now we've got only the Shoals to worry about."

The stillness of the night seeped into them and gentled their voices.

"Let's not borrow trouble," said Ketty. "We've had trouble enough for one day."

"We've had trouble enough today for a lifetime," said George.

Ketty studied his face outlined in the moonlight as he watched the river ahead for signs to steer by.

"Did you hear the song I sang for Lettice's baby?" she asked.

"Yes."

"Do you think the words are true?"

"That God wanted the baby? The baby was drowned because of Lettice's foolishness—or because her love for Baptist overwhelmed her reason. We're not to judge."

Their talk was slow and set apart with silences.

"Of course," George continued after a time, "Lettice wouldn't have left the flat if the red men hadn't been threatening to come down the cliff. So you might say the red men drowned the baby. But before the red men came Colonel Evan Shelby—and Anson, and Baptist. Red men and white men together have been getting ready to drown

Lettice's baby since the day the first white man carrying a rifle trespassed on the red men's hunting grounds and a red man sent an arrow in his direction."

"And what about people who have never trespassed, even in thought?"

"Unfortunately I can count such people on my fingers," said George. "To be sure, there are plenty of indifferent ones, plenty who have never trespassed themselves but who make no outcry when others trespass. But there's nothing innocent about indifference. The indifferent ones are the allies of the trespassers. They're back of the lines, molding bullets for the trespassers to shoot."

For a long time Ketty pondered his words. "If red men and white men together drowned Lettice's baby, together they could have spared him if only enough people had cared. Is that what you're saying?" she asked.

"If even a few people, rightly placed, had cared," said George.

"George"—Ketty changed the subject abruptly—"why do you think Anson dropped everything when Donelson's boats were about to set out, and went back to Carolina? He said it was because he was homesick."

"Let's credit him with telling the truth," said George. "Anson sometime in his life lost his way. He probably went back to get his bearings."

"Why do you think he married Tish?"

"Because he loved her."

"He couldn't have loved her."

"In his floundering way," George said, "he loved her. He found in her something dependable he didn't have—some strength missing from himself that he needed."

"Then he must have got over needing it, because he doesn't love her now."

"The time may come," said George, "when he'll need Tish's strength again—when he'll know he's too weak to walk alone. Then he'll love her. But he can never love her as much as I love you, Ketty."

"Why do you think Anson brought me on this voyage?" asked Ketty.

"I imagine the closer he got to the home place, the clearer in his mind were the good things he'd turned his back on. You, being the only one left, were the symbol of all those things. Realizing how close he had come to losing his past, he wasn't going to risk losing the last symbol of that past. Anson, more than anybody else on this boat, Ketty, needs caring about."

"More than Lettice and Baptist?"

"Much more."

"I guess I haven't cared much about Anson," confessed Ketty. "From the minute I peeped at him through the kitchen keyhole back in the Salem Tavern, I guess I've looked on him as—as an intruder, not as a brother."

"Anson doesn't understand you. He's made it hard for you to care about him."

"Do you know what he's planned for me to do at the French Lick?"

"Well," said George, bristling, "whatever it is, he'll have to get used to the idea that you won't be there to do it."

"He plans for me to teach school when we settle down."

"Oh, that." George laughed. "There'll be somebody else to teach school, so many folks falling over themselves to get to the Lick."

"George," Ketty asked, "what's going to become of Farrer?"

"You'd like to take him for our boy, wouldn't you?"

"I would. I know Rachel has a claim on him. But she doesn't really want him, does she?"

"We'll sound her out."

As day broke, ragged rosy clouds went scurrying across the eastern sky, marshaling themselves into order like trombonists to announce the rising of the sun. And the sun, when it rose in fiery splendor, shone on a calm river and quietly rolling hills and bottoms filled with cane crowding to the water's edge.

"Anson," called George, "we've seen no sign of red men, no towns anywhere along. What say we tie up and stretch and go hunting?"

"Just what I was thinking about ordering," said Anson.

"We'll look first for a slippery elm tree," said George. "I imagine a poultice would feel good on that leg."

"Hit takes bilin' water to make a poultice," Tish reminded them. "Is hit safe to kindle a fire?"

George studied the river banks and the wooded hills. Silence brooded everywhere. "I believe so, Tish," he said. "One big enough to boil water, anyway."

When the others had landed, Anson hobbled down the gangboard, favoring his wounded leg and declaring that a body had no idea how good it felt to walk until he'd been denied walking for a spell.

George, his rifle in his hands, climbed the rise beside their landing place and studied the broomsedge meadow that sloped down to a cane patch in a wide bend in the

222

river. Shubeal, carrying his new rifle at the ready, scouted the woods upriver and back a ways.

"No signs?" asked Anson.

"No signs at all," they reported.

"In that case," said Anson, "we mought rest here for the night—get our second wind before we head for the Shoals, give my leg time to strengthen up a bit. I'm still counting on going overland from the Shoals."

"Hit'd be a right purty time to go a-traipsin' overland," said Shubeal, "with the sarvice berries and them thar Judas trees and the dogwood trees all a-fancyin' up the wilderness."

Anson, seated on the ground and leaning against a tree, watched Shubeal. "Looks like you're itching all over to fire that rifle," he said.

"Me? I was a-wonderin' if one of us oughtn't to stay around here," said Shubeal. "You a-bein' laid up with that thar bullet hole in your leg."

"Tish is here," said Anson.

In single file, their wary eyes watching for any motion of twig or underbrush, George, Shubeal, and Baptist set out through the woods. "Have your water boiling, Tish," called George. "I'll look for some bark first."

In half an hour he was back, bringing a ball of sweet-smelling, sticky shreds from the inner bark of a slippery elm tree. Tish dropped the shreds in the boiling water and stirred them with a stick of driftwood. "Soon's hit thickens, the poultice'll be ready, Anse," she said.

The morning passed—a quiet, peaceful morning with warmth in the air and a thawing of the numbness in the hearts of the voyagers. Ketty, reminding the children they hadn't had lessons for two days, sent them to the boat for their paddles and blackened twigs and set them to writing their words and reciting their ABCs. When lessons were finished they roamed along the edge of the woods in sight of the camping place, scuffing the fallen leaves in search of wintergreen to stay their hunger till the hunters came back with game.

"Looks like they ought to be back by now," said Cal when the sun stood overhead.

"Here, Cal," called Ketty. She heaped his hands with wintergreen leaves.

"Don't eat all them at once," Tish cautioned. "They won't stay in a craw that's been might' nigh empty so long."

Ketty picked another handful and carried them to Lettice. "I'll bring you some next, Anson," she said.

Lettice sat holding the wintergreen in her cupped hands. "Seems like I'm not hungry," she said.

As the sun moved toward the west, Ketty called the children to their lessons again.

"We've had lessons the whole endurin' day," Cal complained. "We hain't played a game for three days."

Lennie put down her paddle. "Let's play Holy Gabriel," she said.

"Where are your music-makers?" asked Ketty, remembering Farrer's whistle tossed into the river by the red man.

Cal felt in his shirt bosom, and Squire felt in his pockets, but they could find neither jumbo nor bagpipes. Lennie and Pegg walked across the gangboard and looked about the boat.

"My Spanish castanet's got to be somewheres," declared Lennie, searching in corners. They found the tambourine but nothing more.

"Never mind," said Ketty. "There's plenty of cane about. Squire and Cal can whittle out some new music-makers." Her words hurried after her thoughts. "In Salem," she told the children, "when somebody important was coming into town, the trombonists went out to meet him and trumpeted him in. Oh, it was very gay! When you hear George coming, you can go to meet him. March in before him, making music. George and Shubeal and Baptist," she remembered to say.

She climbed the wooded slope and measured with her eyes the distance to the cane patch growing beyond the sloping broomsedge meadow. Nothing stirred in the meadow and nothing in the cane patch—nothing except red-winged blackbirds swinging on the stalks of cane and fluting their springtime *konk-la-reeee, konk-la-reeee.*

"Children," called Ketty, "I'm going to get some cane for you."

"Wharabouts?" asked Squire.

"Down this hill and across a meadow. Not far."

"I'm a-goin' with you," announced Cal. "I've got a knife and I can cut the cane."

"I'm a-goin' too, Ketty," said Farrer.

All the children started up the rise.

"No," said Ketty, firmly. "I'm going by myself." A body could make no headway with a passel of children under-foot—if a body needed to make headway. "I won't be gone long. Lend me your knife, Cal."

"Where're you going?" called Anson.

"To get some cane," Ketty told him. She started down the slope.

"Some what?" shouted Anson.

Ketty did not answer. Anson, she guessed, wouldn't take kindly to her errand.

With the camping place behind her and out of sight, Ketty walked leisurely across the broomsedge meadow, through greening sprigs of grass. At the foot of the meadow, spears of blue flags thrust their sharp blades through the moist earth. It was the first time Ketty had been alone since she had left Salem. To be by her lonesome, and in love, and with spring skipping across the earth with blossoms in her hair, was a gift a body had hardly to deserve, she thought. She imagined George coming out of the woods, and the children, marching in front of him as if he were the King of Spain, tootling and rattling their pieces of cane to welcome him.

George would scold when he learned about her going into the cane by her lonesome, she realized. He'd say that a body venturing into a cane patch without a rifle was clean out of her mind.

She stopped and looked about her and listened. But all she could see was spring on the way, and all she could hear were the red-wings singing.

At the edge of the cane she stopped again and listened. She'd cut two stalks, she decided—or three. Better take plenty.

She looked back across the broomsedge toward the camping place. The sedge, bent ever so little, showed plainly the way she had come. She listened again.

She parted the cane and stepped into the thicket in

search of a large stalk. The largest ones seemed to be growing farther in. She pushed ahead, listening after each step. She cut a stalk. She listened again and cut another.

To her right she saw another large stalk. She'd cut that one, she decided. That would be enough.

As she stepped toward the stalk her foot touched something solid. She looked down. At her feet, on his face, lay a red man.

Ketty drew back. To stifle a scream, she clamped her hand over her mouth.

One leg of the man's buckskin breeches, she noticed, was torn and stiff with dried blood.

When voices speak, be present, Ketty.

No one had spoken, she told herself quickly.

She took another step backward.

Suddenly everything within her cried out to her to run to safety—everything but the memory of voices.

All people are in need, Ketty. Be present to see and to hear.

She took another step backward. She must run quickly and tell Anson. Anson would grab his rifle and hobble across the meadow—no, Tish would come with the rifle.

To change a thing, Ketty, a body has to step aside from the crowd, and from crowd thinking.

For a long time, as long as eternity, it seemed, the crowd called her toward the safety of the camp, and the quiet voices bade her stay.

With her heart pounding, Ketty stepped cautiously toward the man. One hand, she noticed, rested on his rifle on the ground beside him. She bent over his head lying limp on a limp arm. No sign of breathing could she see.

The voices of the crowd called her again toward the camp. But the memory of other voices held her. She stooped and laid her hand on the back of the red man's neck. It was warm. He was alive, then, she told herself. He was only playing dead.

What could she do for him? she wondered. Water? A man who had lost blood would surely need water. But how was she to get water to him?

Thinking she might bring a few sips in her cupped hands, she made her way through the cane to the river's edge. As she stooped to dip up the water, she caught sight of a mussel shell among the drift. She washed it, filled it with water, and hurried back to the red man still lying limp on his face.

She knelt beside him, worked one hand under his forehead, raised his head, and held the shell to his lips. He did not drink. Ketty tilted the shell and let the cool water moisten his lips. Suddenly the man sucked the water into his mouth and swallowed it. Ketty brought him another shell full, and he drank that, too, and then dropped his head limply on his arm.

Ketty laid the shell aside and bent over the man's wounded leg. A bluebottle fly was buzzing about the dried blood. A wound, Ketty knew, ought to be bandaged, as Tish had bandaged Anson's wound.

Carefully she lifted a corner of the torn buckskin pasted with dried blood to the man's leg. Had he been shot? she wondered. Had a bone been broken? And where did a body find a bandage?

For a minute she was puzzled. Then she raised her skirt, with Cal's knife slit a hole in her stout white flaxen underskirt, and tore a wide square from it. She folded the square catty-cornered, and then into two-inch widths as Tish had folded George's handkerchief. With the knife she gently pried the buckskin loose from a spot where a thick clot of blood hid the man's wound. Working carefully to avoid disturbing the clot, she wrapped the bandage around the man's leg and tied the ends tight. The red man made no sign that he knew she was present.

"Can you understand me?" Ketty asked.

No answer.

"The menfolks have gone hunting," Ketty told the man. "If they kill some game, I'll bring you something to eat."

For a few seconds longer she stood watching. Then, she turned, hurried out of the cane, picked up the stalks she had cut, and ran up the sloping broomsedge meadow to the campsite.

"What made you so long, Ketty?" asked Lennie.

Cal and Squire set at once to whittling, but Ketty's thoughts were not on music-makers, nor on the pleasure it would give George to be escorted home through the woods to the patter of feet and the piping of whistles and the rattling of pebbles in pieces of cane. How, she wondered, would she get away from the others to take food to the red man? Suppose the men found out an Indian was lying in the cane? Baptist and Shubeal would sneak through the broomsedge with their rifles and kill him. Hadn't Baptist said the only good Indian was a dead one? And would George sneak with them—George who loved her, and believed with her that an Indian was a man like other men, but couldn't bring himself to practice what he believed?

The sun had still an hour in the sky when the campers

229

heard the hunters returning. At once the children rushed into the woods and marched before the men, making music on their pieces of cane. Each hunter carried on one shoulder a kill of squirrels. George and Baptist carried between them a deer slung from a pole. Anson, hobbling about, poked up the fire, and Baptist brought spits and stones for broiling the deer meat. Tish skinned and gutted the squirrels, popped them into a kettle, and set them to boiling.

Hungry as she was, however, Ketty could not enjoy the savory smell for wondering how she was to take a morsel of the meat to the red man.

When the deer meat was finally broiled, Tish doled it out among the outstretched hands. The children, with their shares, sat down on tree roots and began munching hungrily. Menfolk and womenfolk stood about the fire, eating. Ketty, her portion in her fingers, strolled to the top of the rise. When no one was watching, she darted down the far side of the hill, sprinted across the meadow, and entered the thicket of cane. She found the red man, still lying on his face, a short distance from the place where she had bandaged his leg.

Ketty held the piece of deer meat close to his mouth. The good smell of it was more than he could resist. He snatched the meat from her outstretched hand and gnawed on it greedily.

Ketty had an impulse, now that she had done all she had promised, to run away. But had she done all she could do for a man in need?

She looked at the bandage, now lightly stained with

blood. Stooping, she untied the bandage gently from the wound and tossed it aside. She tore another square from her petticoat and placed a new bandage on the wound. Again she started to leave, but one thing more remained to be done. She found the mussel shell, took it to the river, dipped it full of water, and carried it back to the red man. He had finished the meat. While she held one hand under his forehead, he sipped the water from the shell.

"Do you feel better now?" Ketty asked.

There was no answer.

Was she free to go now? she wondered.

"I'll bring you more victuals in the morning," she heard herself saying. Then, after one more look at the man, she went back to the camp.

She slept soundly that night in spite of her hunger. The next morning, when she walked alone to the top of the rise, carrying a thigh of squirrel meat, George Soelle followed her.

"Don't the menfolks need you to help carry things back on the boat?" she asked.

"Yes," he said. "But you need me too."

She returned his steady gaze. "No, George," she said. "I don't need you." She might as well tell George. He'd ferret the truth out one way or another. "I have an errand to do," she told him. "I have to do it alone."

"Ketty, you were away from camp almost half an hour last night. Where were you?"

"Did the others miss me?"

"I don't know. But I did."

"Why?"

"You don't need to ask why. You know that what concerns you concerns me."

"If you love me, George," Ketty said firmly, "you will trust me. You will not ask me questions. You will let me do what I have to do—what I have promised someone faithfully to do."

"Ketty," he said, alarmed, "what are you talking about? And what are you doing with that squirrel meat?"

Suddenly Ketty felt weak and helpless. She was caught. Yet was she? Need she be?

"You may go with me, George," she said, "but you must leave your rifle behind."

He hesitated. "You are asking too much."

"But you must trust me. You're asking to go where I have already been twice. I had no rifle."

Reluctantly George leaned his rifle against a tree.

"Quick now," Ketty hold him, "before the others see us."

She ran down the hill and across the meadow, with George at her heels, asking what wild goose chase she was leading him on. But she paid him no mind.

Inside the cane thicket where she had left the red man, she stopped. George stood behind her, peering over her shoulder. Her hand went to her throat. "He's gone!" She gasped.

George picked up a bloodstained bandage from a clump of cane.

"Ketty," he demanded, "what is this? And who's gone?"

A light wind had risen with the morning, and, with the cane leaves rustling about them, Ketty told him everything.

232

"Don't you know the red men never leave their wounded behind?" George asked her fiercely. "This canebrake was probably filled with red men watching you."

"Then they saw that I bear red men no malice," she told him. "I saw no sign of other red men," she added.

"Well, suppose this man was by himself. He could have been out scouting. And maybe somebody on a boat ahead of us shot him. But if he was a scout, Ketty, do you realize you might have led a whole pack of red men to our camp? They could have swarmed on us in the night and killed every one of us."

"I did what I had to do, George," Ketty said. "Here was a man needing help. I helped him."

George gulped. "It isn't that simple, Ketty. You have to think of consequences."

"What are the consequences when a body helps a man in need?" she asked.

George looked at her, standing tall and straight and un-afraid, her head crowned with her braids of tawny hair, her blue eyes gentle and trusting. He reached for her hand and held it tight.

"You will marry me, won't you, Ketty?" he begged. "Soon?"

"Because I need you to protect me?"

"I'd like to protect you. You do need to be protected sometimes, Ketty. But I want you to marry me because I love you. And I love you because you are the bravest and the most beautiful woman in the world. And I need you, Ketty."

He took her in his arms. Only once a suspicion crossed

233

Ketty's mind that they would be missed from the camp-site and ought to be going back.

"Something's missing," she murmured as she turned her face up to his. "In Salem the trombonists always announced gladsome news."

"Don't you hear?" asked George. "The south wind's blowing."

chapter 20

IN THE broad light of the fresh March morning, after their night of rest and their breakfast of squirrel meat, the voyagers went aboard the *Dragonfly*. George took the steering oar, Baptist and Shubeal the broadhorns.

"I declare, hit's like bein' born again," said Shubeal, "this feelin' I got, now that I got me a rifle."

They had been floating a spell when Shubeal pointed toward the south river bank ahead of them. "Bless my soul!" he called. "Thar's somebody!"

Under a bee gum tree close to the river bank sat a man, waving his arms. "Help! Help!" the voyagers heard him calling in a weak voice as they floated closer.

"What in tarnation's a feller doing in this place by his lonesome?" Anson asked as he pried himself up from the deck and picked up his rifle. "If he is by his lonesome," he added. He searched the wooded slope gently rising behind the man for signs of Indians.

"Help! Help! I'm a-dyin'!" called the man.

"Pullin' in, George?" asked Shubeal.

"Better be careful. Could be he's a decoy," warned Baptist.

"What's the matter?" shouted George.

"Red men," answered the man weakly. "For pity's sake, help!"

"You by your lonesome?" called Anson.

"Help! Help quick, before I die!" begged the man.

The boat floated even with him.

Anson studied the river bank. "Could make a landing here," he said. "Water's deep enough. But suppose red men set him there just to trick us into landing?"

"Let's float downriver a ways," suggested George. "Pull in under that spoonwood tree, Baptist. Tie up there. I'll go back and see what's the matter."

"Me and Baptist'll cover for you," said Shubeal.

Under the spoonwood tree George chained up the *Dragonfly*.

Shubeal looked back toward the spot where the man waited. "George," he said, "we can't cover for you. Trees so thick we can't see the feller from here."

"This could be onhealthy business, George," warned Baptist.

"We've passed the feller now," said Anson. "Reckon we'd better just go on?"

George, looking up at the faces on the boat, saw Ketty. She was watching him. With her eyes she was loving him —loving him and fearing for him, and at the same time encouraging him. *A man needed help. I helped him,* he could hear her saying. Ketty, he remembered, had gone without a rifle to the red man in the cane. Suddenly his rifle felt heavy in his hands. For a second he hesitated.

236

Then, holding his rifle at the ready, he walked into the woods where a man needed help.

Anxiously the voyagers watched for his return. Minutes later he came back, carrying the man across his shoulders.

At sight of the man Ketty gasped. She turned to the children. Stooping, she whispered in Lennie's ear, "He's been scalped."

"Oh-h-h-h!" Lennie's eyes widened.

"Take Farrer away, where he won't see."

"Where'll I take him?"

"Inside the cabin. Go look for something—anything. Hurry."

With Lennie following, Ketty pushed Farrer toward the door.

"When're we a-comin' out?" asked Lennie.

"I'll come for you," Ketty whispered. "I don't want Farrer to see till I can explain." And she shut them inside the cabin.

George walked up the gangboard and set the man down on deck, his back against a barrel. Menfolk, womenfolk, and children circled him in awe.

The man leaned his bloody head against the barrel. "Water!" he said, moaning. "Somebody—fetch me water."

Ketty dipped a gourd into the river and held it to his parched lips. He sipped a few swallows, let his head drop back against the barrel again, and shut his eyes.

"You'd better be a-leavin' here," he warned. "Them red men can't be far away." His shoulders slumped. "Help me, somebody. I got to lay down."

"You mustn't lay down," Tish told him. "Hit's better

when a body's scalped thataway to set up." She picked up a piggin from the deck and handed it to Ketty. "Bring me some water," she said. "I'm a-goin' to wash this here blood off his face so's he'll look like a human bein'."

With her hands she gently washed the blood from the man's forehead, his matted eyebrows, and his cheeks, and dried his face with the hem of her skirt. George, Baptist, and Shubeal hastily poled the *Dragonfly* into the current and headed her downriver. Closely they watched the south bank for red men.

"Tell us what happened," they heard Anson say to the man.

They cocked their ears to hear the answer.

"We was a-goin' down the river in flats. Four flats they was. Started at Moore's Fort, on the Clinch."

The man kept his eyes shut as he talked. After each bit of news he parceled out, he sighed with a great heaviness as if he had spoken his last words.

"Feller named McEnnis, he was a-leadin' us."

"McEnnis!" echoed Anson. "Where's McEnnis now?"

"Feller aboard one of the flats, he broke out with small-pox. McEnnis, he ordered him to stay behind the rest of us. . . . Some other folks took up with us at the mouth of the Clinch. We aimed to stay together through the Suck and them other mean places."

The man rolled his head, opened his mouth and sucked in long drafts of air, and for a spell was silent.

"Lord . . . hit was turrible, turrible through them places. . . . At the Suck red men took out after us. We made hit through. . . . But them boats behind us, they didn't. Least-ways, from the rifle firin' and the awful screamin' we heared, we judged they didn't. We never seen 'em again. . . . Some of our folks was for layin' by. Wait to see if any-body turned up. But they wasn't no place fit to tie up. . . . So we kep' a-floatin'. All night. And all next day."

"Where's McEnnis now?" Anson repeated.

For a spell the man rested. He opened his eyes and looked weakly at the faces about him. His eyes settled on Tish. He shook his head in little jerks as if he were trying to loosen the fogginess in his brain. "Hain't I seen you before?" he asked.

"Hit was our flat joined up with you folks at the Clinch," Tish told him.

"Ah, now I recollect. But—how come you're not scalped? Nor drownded?"

"One of us drownded," Tish told him.

"I would 'a' swore you folks didn't make hit," the man said. "If I was a swearin' man," he added. "My name's Luster. Preacher Luster. . . . I'm a preacher of the Gospel. I was a-goin' to the new land to save the souls there."

"A preacher of the Gospel!" echoed Rachel. She crowded closer into the circle.

"How come you got scalped?" Anson asked.

"Oh, my head!" The man groaned as he shut his eyes and rolled his head in pain. After a spell he took up his tale again.

"We was all dog tired from wrestlin' with that thar river. And then we come out on a long peaceful stretch. Nothin' to mar hit. . . . Passin' a cane bottom, on the north bank, long 'bout the middle of the day, one young feller he thought he seen somethin' a-movin' close to the edge. . . . He'd bet another feller, this feller had, he'd get hisself ten

Indians before he turned twenty. So he pulled his trigger.
. . . All of us, we seen the cane a movin' then, so we 'lowed
he could count hisself another Indian."

He sighed again. Rachel shooed a bluebottle fly from
his head.

"Purty soon we begun to think 'bout tyin' up, we was so
dog tired. Figured if red men was about, they'd be on the
north bank, so we tied up on the south. Didn't land. Didn't
kindle no fires. Jist tied up to get some sleep soon's dark
settled. . . . Red men must 'a' been a-watchin' ever' move.
Soon's we went to sleep, they set on us. In the dark a body
couldn't tell nothin'. . . . Screamin' and tommyhawkin' and
rifle butts a crackin' agin heads all mixed up together. . . .
One of them red devils grabbed me by the hair. Sliced
my scalp clean off. Pitched me on the river bank to die. . . .
When I come to, wasn't nobody in sight."

He looked weakly at Anson. "I never seen McEnnis
again," he said.

"When did this happen, Preacher Luster?" called George
from the roof.

"Last night. Hit's God's wonder I lived till now."

"How far back was the red man the fellow shot?" asked
George.

"Oh, quite a ways. . . . I recollect hit was jist on the far
side of a wide bend in the river. Maybe ten mile. Whar
was you folks camped last night?"

"Just the other side of the bend," George told him.

"And you didn't see no red men?"

"No," said Anson.

"Not in numbers," said George. "Ketty saw one."

"Ketty—Ketty—" Anson gasped, unable to speak more.

Shubeal and Baptist forgot their oars and gaped at Ketty. The womenfolk stared at her in unbelief.

"One that had been shot," explained George. "She was gathering cane and stumbled onto him."

"Ketty saw a red man?" Anson sank his forehead into his outstretched hands and groaned. "And nary a word about it! Why, in the name of Heaven, Ketty—"

"Your man can't count that Indian, Preacher," said George. "He was still alive. Ketty bandaged his wound—your man had shot him in the leg, Preacher. Ketty carried him water to drink and took him her victuals at suppertime. This morning when she took him breakfast, he was gone."

Mouths gaped wider. Eyes bugged out. Anson tried to speak. But for the moment speech forsook him.

Preacher Luster leaned forward. His gaze settled on Ketty as the one singled out by the others. "You—you—" he began.

Anson found his tongue. "Is George telling the truth, Ketty?" he asked. "You did stumble onto that red devil? And fed him vittles? And said nary a word to me about it?"

"Yes, Anson."

"What fool notion possessed you this time?"

"You heard the story from George. There's no more to tell."

"I'd say there's plenty more to tell. George didn't say why you done such a foolish thing. I'm asking now, why?"

All eyes were on Ketty as she and Anson faced each other across the circle. Between their minds, Ketty sensed, was a space as wide as the world is wide. And Anson was asking her to bridge it.

"The man had been shot and needed help," Ketty explained. "And I was there to help him."

"So it's as simple as that!" Anson snorted. "It never once entered your head you might be leading a whole pack of the devils straight to our camping place, I reckon."

"I didn't think that by helping a man who needed help so badly I'd be putting anybody in danger."

Anson snorted again. "Well," he said, "from now till we get to the French Lick, I don't want you out of my sight. You hear me? You and your fool notions!"

Preacher Luster raised a trembling finger and pointed it at Ketty. "This girl's a Tory spy," he said, shaking his finger at her. "Them red men, they're all armed with British rifles, and egged on by the British to kill ever' last one of us. Nobody but a Tory'd be a-helpin' 'em out like she done. She's a traitor to her own folks, that's what she is."

"Baptist, take this steering oar," George said.

He swung himself from the roof to the deck and, standing beside Ketty, faced Preacher Luster.

"This girl is neither a Tory nor a traitor," he said, his eyes murky blue and flashing. "You take that back."

"I—I—said, hit looks like she's one," stammered Preacher Luster.

George bent over him. "You know what you said. Are you taking it back?"

Preacher Luster looked at George's face. His breathing was short and loud.

"Are you?" prodded George.

Preacher Luster nodded his head weakly, dropped it against the barrel, and shut his eyes. "I—I didn't mean hit, I reckon," he said.

242

George straightened his shoulders and looked at the faces in the circle, and at Baptist and Shubeal on the roof. "Did all of you hear him?"

Tish and Lettice nodded their heads. The others stared.

"Well," asked George, "did you hear him?"

All heads nodded.

"Then let this be the end of such reckless talk," George advised. "It's likely because of what Ketty did that the red men never came nigh us, for it's plain as day now that they knew where we were camped. We can't say for sure she saved us. But we can't say she didn't."

"Hit's because," Preacher Luster said haltingly, "jist because—sometimes the wilderness drives a body daft, that I thought maybe this here girl—"

"No," George assured him, "Ketty isn't daft, either. She's quite sound in mind. And, Anson—"

"Anson," Ketty interrupted, "I'm not going with you to the French Lick."

"Not—not going—" Anson choked on his words.

"Ketty is going with me to take up my claim," George explained. He turned to Preacher Luster. "Since now you understand us better," he said, "and know us both to be honorable people, we'll engage you to marry us the day we get to the mouth of the Red River. That's where we leave you."

"Now, won't that be somethin'!" exclaimed Rachel. "A weddin' shindig'd sure liven up this here voyage."

"If Preacher Luster's a-goin' to marry you," said Tish, "I'm a-thinkin' we'd better tend to that scalp of his'n. He mought not last to the Red River. Know what I'm a mind to do?" She bent over Preacher Luster and looked closely

243

at his head. "Bring me Anse's awl, Ketty. Hit's amongst a batch of tools in that thar churn a-settin' by the cabin door."

Ketty searched among the tools in the churn, and found the awl, straight and short and pointed.

"You're a-goin' to die thataway," she heard Tish saying to Preacher Luster as she hurried back, "less'n a body does somethin' for you. Can you bear a right smart pain?"

"What you aim to do?" asked Preacher Luster, eying the awl suspiciously.

"I aim to bore holes in your skull to give hit a chance to heal. Like I seen a doctor feller do this winter at Fort Patrick Henry. Man come in there with his scalp a-missin', and the doctor, he cured him. Course," Tish added, "I reckon you won't never have hair again."

The preacher shut his eyes and groaned.

"He can stay with us while he's a-healin'," Rachel spoke up. "Thataway we can hear some preachin' now and then."

"Let me think a minute," begged Preacher Luster weakly.

"Gangrene'll be a-settin' in any time now," Tish said.

Preacher Luster dropped his chin on his chest. "Let's have hit over with, then," he murmured.

Tish scowled at the awl. "Hit mought be cleaner," she said. She handed it to Ketty.

Leaning over the gunwale, Ketty dipped a piggin of water from the river, and scrubbed the awl.

"You stay handy, Ketty," said Tish, taking the awl. "I may need somethin'. I reckon you ain't as foolish as them menfolks are a-tryin' to make you out. Anse, you go steer. George, you stay right here and hold the preacher stiddy,

244

case the pain's more'n he can bear. Get ever'body else away, Ketty," she ordered.

Tish examined Preacher Luster's skull, chose a spot for operating, and with sure hand and steady nerve set to boring.

"Jist take hit easy, now," she said soothingly to the preacher as the awl probed his skull. "This here bone's awful hard. That doctor bored six-seven holes in that other feller's head. That'll be 'bout right for you too, I reckon."

When finally the last hole had been bored, and a reddish fluid filled the holes and overflowed onto his skull, Preacher Luster slumped against George and retched.

"Lean him agin the barrel gentle, now, and keep him propped there," said Tish. "He'll come around soon. But hit'll take two-three year to heal—that's what the doctor told that other scalped feller. Hit'll take two-three year to cure up teetotally. But hit'll cure."

Rachel steadied the preacher's head against the barrel.

Ketty looked anxiously at his scalp. "Oughtn't we to bandage it, Tish?" she asked.

"That doctor at the Fort, he didn't wrop up that other feller's scalp," said Tish, watching. "Jist let the air strike hit. Hit's good hit ain't warm weather yet," she added. "Not many gnats and flies a-stirrin' now to plague him. Rachel, shoo that bluebottle off him."

"Better cover him too, hadn't we?" asked George, as he chafed one of Preacher Luster's cold, clammy hands.

Ketty brought two blankets and wrapped them about the preacher. Rachel wiped cold sweat from his face and watched anxiously till the deep retching subsided. Tish, too, watched, standing tall and straight above the man and her handiwork. "Hit's good," she said simply. "In a week, maybe, his head'll be covered with proud flesh. When that begins to scab over, healin'll set in."

The cabin door opened, and Lennie stuck her head out. "Ketty," she called, "Farrer says he ain't a-stayin' in here any longer."

At that moment Farrer gave Lennie a shove that sent her flying through the doorway. Ketty went to them.

"Farrer," she said, taking him by the hand and leading him away from Preacher Luster, "the man beside the river, the one George brought on the boat, his head had been hurt."

Farrer tried to see around her. "Whar's the man at?" he asked.

"He's right over there. I think he's asleep now."

"What hurt his head?" asked Farrer.

"He was in a fight."

"Did—did—" Farrer's wide eyes looking up at Ketty, filled with terror. "Did he—get scalped?"

"Yes, Farrer. But—"

Farrer clutched Ketty's skirt. His mouth opened wide. Quickly Ketty laid her hand over it.

"Tish is doctoring the man's head," she said. "He's going to get well. And he's going to do something special for us—for George and me."

Farrer pulled Ketty's hand away and peeped from behind her. At sight of Preacher Luster, he whimpered.

"When a body's hurt, folks take good care of him," said Ketty.

Farrer listened. Ketty took his hand and drew him from

246

behind her. "See," she said, "Rachel's taking care of the man. I expect in a day or two, when he's better, he'd like you to write your name for him on your paddle. Could you do that for him?"

Farrer pulled back, continued to stare, and opened his mouth to cry. But he did not cry.

chapter 21

AS THE day wore along, the *Dragonfly* floated westerly on a peaceful river, between peaceful banks. Rachel tended Preacher Luster faithfully as he roused from the stupor that followed his ordeal. Anson, with little to say, stood in the bow of the boat, watching.

When the sun was two hours from setting, he turned to those on deck. "Seems like I hear thunder," he said.

"Now who's gone daft," Rachel wondered aloud, "a-hearin' thunder on a sunshiny day?"

"Baptist," called Anson, "you hear thunder?"

"I hear somethin'," said Baptist.

All on board grew quiet. All of them heard what Anson had heard—a rumbling noise that grew steadily louder.

"That? That thar's the Shoals," said Preacher Luster.

"George," called Anson, "get ready to tie up."

"We ain't thar yet," Preacher Luster said. "A body can hear that thar roarin' for miles."

"From the racket they make, I thought they were just around the next bend," said Anson. "When you get in sight of 'em, George," he called, "tie up."

On they floated. The rumble grew into a thundering, deafening, continuous roar. The river widened. Islands loomed ahead.

"Ain't that some feller's flat busted up thar?" asked Shubeal, pointing ahead to an island holding in check a great heap of logs, timbers, and lesser driftwood.

"These here Shoals is the graveyard of flats," said Preacher Luster.

Anson searched the north bank of the river, up and down.

"Looks like Robertson, he didn't come, Anse," called Shubeal. "Don't see Donelson's boats nowhars."

"Could be Donelson didn't find the message," said Anson. "Pull in," he directed George. "I aim to make sure."

Ashore, the menfolk walked along the margin of the river strewn with mussel shells, a mile upriver and a mile downriver, looking for a cairn of rocks in which James Robertson might have left a message. Finding no cairn, they ranged in the woods farther back from the river, looking for a message in a hollow tree, or in an out-of-the-ordinary tree crotch. But they found no message.

Returned at last to the river, they stood studying the threatening stretch of water.

"Worst is," said Anson, "a body don't know how long it is."

"One mile of this is a mile and a half too long," said Baptist.

"I've heard say it's thirty-five miles, give or take a little," said George. "Baptist," he said, starting toward the woods, "let's cut some more poles." He turned back to Anson. "Think your leg's strong enough so you can pole? You on one side and Shubeal on the other? Baptist can use the

249

gouger in the bow. I'll steer. Before we set out, we'd better trim the cargo, too."

On board, the menfolk, with Tish and Ketty helping, shifted cargo, balancing one heavy object against another, so that there might be no listing. When there seemed nothing more they could do to favor themselves, the menfolk poled away from the bank, eased the boat into the current, and headed for the Shoals.

"Believe I could set on one of them thar kegs and see better," said Preacher Luster.

Tish and Rachel got him to his feet and put a keg under him. He rested his arm on the gunwale and peered over. Ketty, looking on, expected Rachel to go rushing into the cabin where she couldn't see the menacing stretch of water. But Rachel, keeping flies off the preacher's head, stood by to tend him should he need anything. On the other side of the preacher stood Tish, tight-lipped. About her clustered the children.

"Hit's a good thing the water's high," observed Preacher Luster. "We'd never make hit through in low water."

George, at the steering oar, studied the islands ahead and looked for the deepest channel. Skillfully he steered between two islands. From that moment the *Dragonfly* was at the mercy of the Shoals. The river, suddenly unconfined by proper banks, spread out a mile or more in width over a hard, flinty bottom. Water, shallowed by the spread, cascaded downhill through a wilderness of grim rocks rearing their ugly shapes, and bucked dangerously around the islands heaped with drifting logs and brush and planks from hapless flatboats. The channel ran first here, then somewhere else. Through the thunderous din the ominous noises of the boat in trouble grated in the voyagers' ears. As the menfolk with gouger and poles guided the boat away from menacing rocks and reefs, the *Dragonfly* tossed and groaned and threatened to break to pieces.

Tish and Lettice, Ketty and the children stood at the gunwale, bracing themselves, waiting for whatever came, and looking ahead for signs of an end to their trouble. Preacher Luster clung to a gunwale and studied the careening course of the boat. Rachel, standing beside him, held her tongue and neither whined nor berated.

Unexpectedly the boat floated into placid water. The pent-up anxiety of the voyagers let itself out in great sighs of relief as Baptist laid his gouger on the deck and rubbed his hands together to get the cramps out of them.

Shubeal, on top of the cabin, stood listening. "Is that racket I hear behind us? Or ahead of us?" he asked.

George gazed downriver. "Both," he said. "I hate to tell you, Baptist, you can't lay down your gouger yet. Look what we're coming to."

In the distance spread another grim stretch of shoals.

Firmly the womenfolk and the children on deck planted their feet. Grimly the menfolk readied themselves. As best they could they eased the *Dragonfly* into a swift, shallow, uncertain channel. Until owl light, partly they guided the boat, partly they gave themselves to the mercy of the Shoals. Headlong the boat rushed, narrowly missing some jagged rocks and reefs and scraping others, until, finally, it floated once more into smooth, deep water, and the thunderous roar was unmistakably left behind.

"Steer straight for the first likely spot to tie up," Anson ordered.

When all the others had gone ashore, he limped down the gangboard and slumped against a willow tree to which Baptist was chaining the *Dragonfly*. "I'm real proud of this here flat," he said. "Time or two I thought she wasn't a-going to make it." He watched Baptist a minute. "Tie her up good and tight, Baptist," he said. "I mean to sleep tonight. If there's a spark of decency in them red devils, they surely figure that if folks can navigate that nasty stretch of river they deserve to be let alone. Poling through that brushpile of rocks has stove me plumb in."

"Now, if hit wasn't so near dark," said Shubeal, "and a body could go a huntin'—What I aim to say," he added, "is that a body'd sleep sounder if he had vittles inside him. The juicy back bone of a Wataugy hog'd taste mighty good right now."

"And broiled kidneys," put in Baptist.

"Mought as well make it the whole hog," Anson said. "Conjure up souse meat and scrappling and sausage while you're at it. And top it off with crackling bread."

As if to mock them, Tish brought the gourd in which the kernels of parched corn were kept and doled them out.

"Even if you had such things, you couldn't kindle a fire to cook 'em with," she reminded them. "We've been in Indian country too lately to take chances."

The preacher nodded. "Let my scalped head be a warnin' to you," he said, looking at Ketty.

That night, as Ketty, lying on her pallet in the cabin, devised words to persuade Rachel to let Farrer go with her and George, she heard Baptist quietly walking the length of the cabin roof, with his faithful dog at his heels. He was thinking about his boy, Ketty imagined.

No one would have believed, thought Ketty, that a little baby Baptist never saw could have wound its arms about him so tightly and humbled him. The old bragging and the big talk were gone. They'd come back, no doubt, in time. Baptist could use them when he started swinging an ax against the tough trunks of oak trees, and snaking logs into place for a cabin, and clearing new ground of stubborn stumps. He'd set out a poplar sapling for remembrance, as Ketty had suggested, and Lettice would lovingly tend it. Baptist would never mention it. But on early summer mornings on his way to plow, he'd hear the bees buzzing in and out of the cups of yellow gold and fiery flame, and he'd stop a minute to remember his first-born. In the midst of bustling life he'd remember and be humbled.

chapter 22

AT SUNUP the voyagers were on their way again. The wide river, flowing now in a northerly direction, meandered pleasantly between low willow-bordered banks.

"Looky thar!" said Shubeal, making a sweeping gesture with his arms to take in the wide stretches of gently rolling land. "If I'd 'a' knowed they was bottomland like this anywhars in creation, I'd 'a' said fare-ye-well to them steep corn patches back at Wataugy long ago."

The menfolk pleasured themselves gazing over the broad land. George Soelle stared at a distant hillside meadow set in woods east of the river.

"Anson," he said, "do you see something moving there? In that patch of broomsedge? Beyond the cane patch on the river bank?"

Anson and Baptist and Shubeal squinted into the distance.

"I see the broomsedge," said Anson.

"But look at that dark patch in the middle," George told him. "Know what I think that is? Buffalo."

"Buffalo!"

The menfolk stared harder. Cal and Squire raced up the ladder to get a better look. The womenfolk and Preacher Luster leaned against the gunwale and gazed ahead.

"For a fact, that is buffalo," said Anson. "There's our breakfast, and our dinner, and our supper—maybe enough to last us to the Lick. Get ready to tie up, ever'body. We mought rest here a day or two while the womenfolk jerk the meat."

In a flurry of hushed excitement the menfolk guided the flat to the low-lying bank and in haste chained her to cottonwood saplings.

"Looky here!" said Shubeal, peering through a thicket of smooth alders growing behind the cottonwood. "Ain't that a trace the critters 've made?"

George and Baptist turned and looked. There, packed hard and firm by buffalo hoofs, ran a trace, paralleling the river.

"The buffalo are headed this way," said George. "If we don't scare them the other direction, they'll likely make for this trace." Hastily he picked up his rifle. "Baptist," he said, "you come with me. We'll cut through the woods here south of the opening and come at the herd from the far side. Shubeal, you go downriver. Keep the cane patch between you and the buffalo till we get even with them."

"I'll go with Shubeal," said Anson.

"That's a mighty long ways, Anse, to hobble on that poorly leg," Tish told him.

Anson paid her no mind. He picked up his rifle and started after Shubeal.

"Mammy," said Cal, "I'm a-goin', too, me and Squire."

"No, you ain't," said Tish. " 'Taint no place for young

uns. And don't you talk so loud. You'll scare the buffalo."

"Pappy," called Cal, keeping his voice low, "can't me and Squire come too?"

"I told you no," said Tish.

"Ain't it about time, Tish, you cut your apron-string hold on Cal?" called Anson.

Cal ran across the gangboard, with Squire close behind him.

"You come back here, Cal!" called Tish. "Anse, send them young uns back."

"You young uns walk along quiet behind me," Ketty heard Anson tell the boys. "And mind what I say."

The three of them, heading in the direction of the canebrake, disappeared in the brushy thicket of alders that were dusting the river with their soft golden pollen.

Tish walked to the gunwale and, with worry signs marking her face, stood watching the way the three had gone.

"We can see better, Tish," said Ketty, "on top of the cabin."

She climbed the ladder to the roof. Tish followed her. Lettice and Lennie, Pegg and Betsy followed Tish. Rachel stayed on deck, watching beside Preacher Luster.

The grazing buffalo, their heads low, their shaggy humps high, looked like a choppy dark sea in the middle of the broomsedge opening.

"Looks like the Lord God A'mighty knowed we'd eat about our last vittles," said Rachel, pleasured.

"'The Lord careth for His own,'" quoted Preacher Luster.

The womenfolk, watching from the roof of the cabin, caught sight now and then of Shubeal making his way at

256

the edge of the cane along the river bank. They saw Anson, followed by Cal and Squire, disappear into the canebrake beside the trace. The trees hid George and Baptist. Stillness brooded everywhere.

"One time," mused Lettice, breaking the silence and keeping her voice low as she watched the unsuspecting herd, "I eat some buffalo meat. Hit's plumb good."

"Better'n bear meat?" asked Lennie.

"Heaps better," said Lettice. "You take the hump, now. Hit's juicy and tender."

Tish, with an effort, looked away from the canebrake to the hillside.

A buffalo raised its head.

"They've scented the men," whispered Lettice.

As she spoke, a shot rang out from the woods. The lead buffalo plunged ahead. The herd followed, galloping straight across the opening toward the trace.

Rifles cracked from the canebrake, and another from the woods. One buffalo fell. Toward the trace plunged the others. Another fell.

Tish and Ketty, suddenly cold with apprehension, watched as the panic-stricken beasts in their flight crowded the right flank off the trace into the canebrake. Past the boat the big beasts thundered, jarring the earth with their hammering hoofs. As they disappeared among the alders upriver, the thunder died to a rumble that was pierced by shrill screams from the cane.

Tish, turned white as blue john, scrambled down the ladder. Ketty ran after her, across the gangboard, and through the alders. Guided by the screams, they came on Squire standing beside a big rock inside the canebrake, his face white with fright as he poured out sharp, shrill cries of terror. At his feet lay Cal, his legs stretched wide, rolling his head and moaning.

Tish dropped to her knees beside Cal and clasped his head in her hands. At that moment Anson, forgetting the lameness in his leg, came hurrying from the other direction. "What—what's happened?" he asked. He bent over Cal. "What's the matter?"

"Them buffalo!" Squire screamed.

Tish drew a deep breath and ran her hands over Cal's legs.

Anson straightened. "I told you boys to stay behind this rock."

"Cal didn't stay." Squire was sobbing.

As Anson bent over Cal again, Tish got to her feet, turned away, walked a few steps into the cane, and stood alone, her back to the others. Ketty could see her hands clenching and unclenching, clenching and unclenching.

"Why didn't you stay where I told you, lad?" pleaded Anson.

Ketty, sickened with the agony—of Cal as he lay writhing in pain, of Tish, who, having borne so much sorrow already, must bear still more, of Anson, whose guilt, it was plain to see, was beginning to gnaw at him—turned away. She put an arm about Squire's shoulders. "Can you stop crying, Squire, and tell us what happened?" she asked.

"When we heard them buffalo a-comin' down the hill," Squire told them between sobs, "Cal, he edged out from behind the rock so's he could see. I told him to come back, but he wouldn't mind me. Before I could grab him the

258

buffalo was on us. One of 'em knocked him down and tromped on him."

"They didn't hurt you, did they?" Ketty asked.

"No." Squire sobbed. "I done like Anse told me."

"Why don't you go to the boat now?" suggested Ketty. "We'll look after Cal."

She watched as he started through the cane, still crying. Turning, she listened for a minute to Anson's helpless implorings. Then she walked past him, to Tish, put her arm about Tish's waist, and stood in silence with her.

In time, Tish, having gathered her strength, turned, knelt once more beside Cal, and once more carefully ran her hands over his legs. "They're broke," she said, without looking up. "Both of 'em."

Without a word between them, Tish and Anson carefully stripped Cal's breeches off his legs. Both legs were bruised, and, just above his knees, as Tish had said, both were plainly broken.

"Why didn't you stay behind that rock, Cal, like I told you?" Anson asked again.

He placed one arm under Cal's shoulders, the other underneath his hips. As he started to lift, Anson turned ashen white and shut his eyes.

"Leave him a-layin'," Tish ordered.

Anson slumped against the rock and covered his face with his hands. As if his heart had been made of ice now suddenly melted, tears streamed down his face.

"I'll call George," Ketty said to Tish.

She made her way through the thick cane to the edge of the opening. She could see on the hillside the craggy shapes of the two dead buffalos above the waving broom-sedge. As George and Baptist ran across the opening toward the beasts, Shubeal came up the hill from the far edge of the cane.

"How many'd we get?" he called. Seeing Ketty, he stopped. "What was all that screamin' 'bout down there?" he asked.

"Cal's been hurt," Ketty said. "George!" she called. "Tish needs you. Quick!"

"Cal's hurt?" called George. Leaving the buffaloes lying, the three men raced down the hill. "What happened?" George asked, studying Ketty's face.

"The buffalo trampled him," Ketty explained, fighting back her tears.

"What in tarnation was Cal a-doin'?" asked Baptist.

Without answering, Ketty turned and led the men to the rock where Cal lay, rolling his head and crying, "Hit hurts, Mammy! Hit hurts!"

George knelt and ran his hands over Cal's legs. For a second he rested a hand above one knee and watched Cal's face twist in agony.

"Ain't they?" Tish asked.

"Broken? Yes, Tish. Both of them," George answered. He got to his feet and stood beside her. "The skin isn't broken, Tish," he said. "That's in his favor."

"Tish," said Baptist, "what on earth was you a-thinkin' 'bout to let him leave the boat?"

"Hush, Baptist!" begged Ketty.

"Don't you blame Tish for this," said Anson. "I let him leave the boat—him and Squire. It's a thousand wonders,

260

Shubeal, Squire ain't lying here too." He covered his face again and let the tears flow. "They mought both have been tromped to death." He sobbed.

Ketty caught her breath as she realized she was listening to words she had never expected to hear—Anson confessing he'd done wrong. Suddenly she saw him as he was—trampled and bruised and broken by the heavy weight of his weakness and his willful stubbornness and folly. Pity welled up in her.

"The lad'll never walk again," Anson went on.

"Tish," said George, "we must put these legs in splints—set the bones the best we can before we move Cal."

"Hickory'd be best for splints, wouldn't hit?" asked Baptist. "Hit's light and strong. Shubeal," he said, starting toward the boat, "I'll fetch an ax. We'll have the splints in no time, George."

Tish stood watching Cal writhing in pain. "Ketty," she said, "bring me some willer twigs."

"Why did I ever let them young uns foller me?" Ketty heard Anson tormenting himself afresh as she started for the twigs. "Hit looks like the Good Book's right," she heard Tish reply. "Hit's the little children that's made to pay for the sins of their fathers." Then Tish added, in a voice heavy with weariness but bearing no bitterness, "You thought they was big enough, Anse."

A mightier miracle than that of Anson's confession had come to pass, Ketty sensed, a miracle of forgiveness, as full of wonder as any told in the pages of Holy Writ, of the deaf who heard or the blind who were made to open their eyes and see.

261

When Ketty had brought the twigs, Tish put one of them to Cal's lips. "Chew hard on this, honey," she coaxed him. "This'll ease the hurtin'."

"I can't! I can't!" Cal moaned.

Anson bent over him. "Try it, Cal. Try it, like your mammy says. Here." He cut a short length of the twig and put it in Cal's mouth. "Try it, lad," he begged.

When Baptist and Shubeal returned with a length of hickory trunk, they set to work with froe and mallet to make staves for splints.

"That about right?" Baptist asked, handing the first one to George.

George laid it against one of Cal's legs to measure the length. "That's good," he said. "We'll need enough to case both legs." He turned the stave about and looked at it. "Anson," he said, "it ought to be whittled smooth."

Anson took his hunting knife from its sheath, squatted beside Cal, and set to whittling. Between strokes his eyes strayed to Cal's legs, and sometimes to his face, still twisted with pain as Cal chewed hard on the twig. When Anson could stand the sight no longer, he got up hastily and walked away into the cane. "Tish!" he called.

Tish left Cal and went to stand beside Anson.

"He'll never walk again as long as he lives," Anson said to her, with a new onset of tears.

"That's beyond a body's knowin'," Tish told him.

"You think—he'll walk again? Sometime?"

"I aim to do all in my power," Tish said. "You must, too. Beyond that we'll have to wait and see."

"How long, you reckon?"

"George says in a matter of eight weeks or so we can maybe tell."

"Eight weeks! That's almost as long as I was gone to Caroliny!"

"For sure hit's a long time, Anse. When a body's got nothin' but spindly hope to hold him up, hit's a mighty long time."

"But—you think—he'll walk again?"

"You come now and finish smoothin' down them splints so George can tie 'em on."

"What's he aiming to tie 'em on with?"

"With some of that pawpaw rope I plaited while I was a-waitin' for you to come back from Caroliny," Tish said. "Baptist laughed at me for makin' so much."

"Tish—" Anson began. He looked at her imploringly. But he could not tell her what he had to say.

Tish led the way back to Cal. With great care George set the bones. Laying the splints, planed as smooth as a buckeye, edge to edge, he encased Cal's legs. While Baptist and Shubeal held the splints firmly in place, George wrapped them around with the pawpaw rope and tied it securely.

"Now, boy, how's that?" he asked.

"I can't walk," said Cal, whimpering.

"The rest of us'll walk for you for a while," said George.

He turned to Baptist. "Bring the gangboard. We'll carry him to the boat on that."

As the procession wound its way out of the cane, Lennie was waiting at the boat. At the sight of Cal, her hand went to her throat. "Is Cal—is he—" She began to cry.

Tish called to her. "You go fix a pallet for him, child."

263

After Cal had been settled on the deck, Baptist turned to Shubeal. "Me and you'd better look after them buffaloes," he said.

Hours later Ketty and Lettice portioned out pieces of boiled buffalo tongue, while Baptist tended ribs and chunks of hump and haunch smoking over a smoldering fire. Ketty carried a portion of the tongue to Anson. He cut it into bits and fed them to Cal. He did not join the others as they feasted quietly about the campfire. He wasn't hungry, he claimed. Even if he was, he said, he couldn't swallow a bite of that buffalo meat. "Tish," he said, "you go eat."

Tish walked down the gangboard. In a minute she returned, carrying two pieces of the tongue. One of them she held out to Anson. "Hope can't live 'thout vittles, Anse," she said. "We both got to hope, hard as we can."

Anson took a deep breath and looked at Tish with beseeching eyes. Slowly he reached for the meat.

"Tomorrow," said Tish, "before we set out again, I want Baptist to kill some squirrels for Cal." She bent over Cal. "The hurtin' better now?" she asked.

"A little," he murmured. "Can I sit up?"

"Sure you can, lad," Anson told him. Together he and Tish propped him against the gunwale. "Try not to move your legs, honey," Tish cautioned him. "Thataway they'll grow back straight, maybe. You want another twig to chew?"

"Hit don't hurt so now," said Cal.

"Tomorrow," said Tish, "I look for you to feel better."

"I'll sleep here right beside you tonight, Cal," Anson told him. "If you want anything, you just let me know. I'll be your legs till you get your own under you."

"Mammy, you sleep on t'other side of me, will you?" asked Cal.

"Sure she will, lad." Anson answered for Tish.

The next morning George and Baptist shouldered their rifles and, in search of squirrel meat for Cal, disappeared across the broomsedge meadow behind the wooded hills. On every tree and bush tender leaves were uncurling. In cane and meadow red-wings and meadowlarks trilled their songs.

"Ketty," said Tish as she picked up a piggin and started across the gangboard, "you come with me. We mought find some potherbs in the woods. They'd taste good to Cal."

Ketty walked across the gangboard after Tish. "Lennie," she heard Anson calling, "reckon you could stay with Cal a spell?" In a few minutes he followed, saying nothing. He walked better now, with scarcely a limp, Ketty noted, as he hurried ahead of her and took the piggin from Tish. It looked as if he couldn't bear to have Tish out of his sight.

At the edge of the woods Tish stooped and plucked a young green shoot with deep green leaves. "Thought we'd find hit," she said, holding it up for Ketty to see. "Merrybells. They make mighty good eatin' this time of year. And good pot likker, too. If one's a-blossomin', jist pinch the blossom out."

They ranged through the woods, picking the tender shoots pushing up through the carpet of winter-worn leaves.

"Anson," Ketty asked, "you and Tish, you think—it's all right for me to marry George? And go with him to his claim? And not with you to the Lick?"

"It's a little late to be asking them questions," said Anson. For a minute the three of them plucked merrybells in silence. "I'd had in mind that you'd teach a school at the Lick."

"There'll be schools, Anson," Ketty told him. "George says so many folks are coming to the Lick there are bound to be schoolteachers among them. Lennie—some day, Anson, Lennie will be a schoolteacher, a much better teacher than I would ever be."

Anson sighed. "Forget about the school," he said. "Seems like the real reason I brung you along was—was because you put me in mind of Mother."

Ketty laid a handful of shoots in the piggin and let her hand rest on them as she looked at Anson. "When I was most like Mother, then you were hardest on me," she said.

"I reckon folks have always been thataway," Anson told her. "Comes along somebody with a heart of goodness and we beg, 'Never leave us.' Then when he begins to behave like his heart tells him, we stone him. Like Stephen in the Good Book."

He wandered away, out of earshot.

"Ketty," said Tish, "you ain't got nothin' to housekeep with. And George—menfolks don't think 'bout skillets and stew kettles and suchlike bein' a part of gettin' married. They think a body makes out on spoonin'. I'll go through my plunder, see what I can give you to get you started."

"Tish—" It was hard for Ketty to say to Tish what she wanted to say. Tish's face seemed always to keep her kindness hidden, and her backbone made no truce with

266

tenderness. "You've been a good sister to me, Tish," she said.

"Don't let Anse nettle you 'bout marryin' George," Tish advised. "He'll come round. He needs time, that's all."

"You're glad we're marrying, aren't you, Tish?" Ketty asked.

"Time out of mind hit's been a woman's way to marry a man and go traipsin' half across the earth at his heels," Tish told her. "You're so pretty, the wonder is some man hain't persuaded you before this. Since you seem to want to hear the words said, I'm proud you're a-marryin' George. He'll be good to you."

"When you and Anson get settled at the Lick, Tish, I hope life will be much better than you've ever known it."

"Anse, he's learned his lesson," said Tish. "While we're a-waitin' to know if them legs of Cal's are ever straight enough to walk on again, he'll have time to learn hit so's he won't never forget hit. If you and George could maybe come to see us oncet in a while—"

"We will, Tish," promised Ketty. "We'll come every chance. Maybe when the corn's laid by we can come. Before snow flies, anyway, we'll come and stay a long spell, Tish. It'll be something to think about all summer long."

"I'll be a thinkin' 'bout hit too," said Tish.

Shoots of merrybells were spilling off the heaped-up piggin.

"Mought as well go," said Tish. "Leave Anse to his thinkin'."

Within an hour George and Baptist, followed by Anson,

came out of the woods, carrying a kill of squirrels and a heavy white bird.

"What's that thar critter?" asked Rachel.

"That thar," said Preacher Luster, "is a swan. Sweeter meat a body never tasted."

"And the sweetest part is for Cal," announced George. He went on deck, where Cal was sitting propped against the gunwale. "How's it going, boy?" he asked.

"I wish I could move my legs," said Cal.

"Know what I'm going to do?" said George. "Make a calendar for you on one of your splints. A calendar of fifty-six days. Every night you can mark off one day. On the fifty-sixth day—that's eight weeks—you can take those splints off."

"Are you a-goin' to do that now?" asked Cal.

"Later," said George. "Right now I'm looking for a great big gourd. Baptist and I found a bee tree back in the woods. We're going to bring the honey to you. All you can eat."

chapter 23

IN THE early afternoon the voyagers went aboard once more. For three days they floated, always in a northerly direction. On the morning of the fourth day Anson took his old place at the steering oar. But before he did so, he and George laid Cal on the gangboard, lifted him to the top of the cabin, and propped him against a keg so that he could see the sights along the river.

As Anson guided the flat downriver, he kept a sharp watch ahead. They ought, he said, to be coming to that other river John Donelson had said the Tennessee emptied into, the Ohio.

Without a sign to hearten the voyagers, the *Dragonfly* floated all day. Then, at sunset, the boat passed a low island fringed about with willow trees. Half a mile farther on, menfolk on the roof and womenfolk on deck stared in wonder at the mighty Ohio flowing down from the north.

"Hit's full of sunshine!" exclaimed Cal.

"That thar's mud," said Preacher Luster.

George whistled softly. "It looks like all the ice and snow

in Kingdom Come have melted and are running down that current!"

"Pull into the bank," ordered Anson. "We got to figure some things out. Somebody," he added, "ought to build a boat that can go against the current as well as with it."

"How far up we got to navigate that?" asked Baptist. "Preacher, you know?"

"My knowledge don't go on this voyage any further than this," said Preacher Luster. "Oncet I floated downriver to New Orleans. Hain't never been up."

"Nobody told us how far we have to navigate it," said Anson. "All they told us was that, somewhere above this, the Cumberland flows into this river, same as the Tennessee. And it's the Cumberland we got to find."

When the menfolk had tied up the boat, they fought their way through the willow thicket on the bank of the Tennessee to the bank of the Ohio. It was dusk when they came back.

"Supper ready?" asked Anson. "Let's eat and turn in early. In the morning, when we leave the Tennessee and get into the Ohio, we start bushwhacking. Bushwhacking," he said, "will take all hands. Ketty, you can steer. Baptist, you and George can row. Tish, you and Rachel and Lettice and Squire can help Shubeal and me pull the boat along."

"You mean we got to hang on to them willer bushes and pull this here boat up that thar river?" asked Rachel.

"That's bushwhacking," Anson told her.

"Cal," said George, "you can keep a lookout for sawyers. Preacher and Lennie can stand in the bow and look too. That river's sewed thick with them."

"How'll I know a sawyer when I see hit?" asked Cal.

"I'll show you tomorrow," promised George, "as soon as we get into the Ohio."

At daylight the next morning, before the menfolk took up their oars to navigate the last stretch of the Tennessee, Anson and George again lifted Cal to the roof of the cabin. Close to the bank, clear of the current, the *Dragonfly* floated along. As she neared the mouth, where the clear water of the Tennessee merged with the muddy water of the Ohio, Anson called out, "All right, ever'body! Take hold! Pull hard on your oar, Baptist. Got to get closer to the bank. Ketty, come take the steering oar. Don't let the boat slip into the current as we swing round this point. If we do—"

"If we do," echoed Baptist, straining on his oar, "hit's fare-ye-well, French Lick, howdy, New Orleans!"

Ketty took the steering oar from Anson. Cal, sitting near her, watched eagerly. George shifted his broadhorn to the side of the boat opposite the bank and took his place in front of Baptist. Lennie and Preacher Luster stood in the bow. Anson, on deck in the bow of the boat, gathered the others around him.

"Line up along the gunwale," he said. "Grab a limb. Pull and walk. When you get as far as you can go, hurry back and grab another."

Slowly the *Dragonfly* moved around the bend into the Ohio.

George, facing the stern, turned and scanned the muddy water.

"Cal," he called, "look ahead and to your left."

Cal looked. "I don't see nothin' but water," he reported.

"Keep looking. You will."

After a time the black jagged end of a tree trunk, stripped of bark, rose slowly above the surface of the water. Like some man-eating monster drawing its breath, it rose higher and higher until it stood ten feet above the water. For a minute it rested. Then, as slowly as it had risen, it slowly sank into the water again, out of sight.

"Now ain't that a plumb purty critter!" declared Baptist. "The Tennessee ain't got nothin' half as fancy as that."

At a terrapin's pace the *Dragonfly* crawled up the Ohio. Otters and weasels along the bank dived into the water at her approach. Gray-mantled herring gulls skimmed over, looking for fish. The sun beat on the voyagers. Worrisome bluebottle flies buzzed about their heads. Their hands bled. Their backs ached. Their eyes smarted with sweat.

Rachel relaxed long enough for a backward look. "I declare"—she sighed—"I can still see where we rounded that bend."

"Don't look back," advised Baptist.

"Thar's one of them things!" shouted Cal.

Everybody looked upriver.

"That ain't no sawyer!" exclaimed Baptist. "That's a-goin' sideways, see? Not up and down. That's a doe, out for a mornin' swim. And I ain't got but one notion in my head." He swung his broadhorn onto the roof. "Shubeal, you come and help," he said.

Together they slid George's canoe over the side of the boat into the water. As Baptist climbed into the bow of the canoe, Shubeal dropped into the stern, and the two of them, forgetting they were tired, paddled with rapid strokes upriver toward the doe.

The bushwhackers, clinging to branches to keep the boat

from slipping downriver, shouted encouragement to them.

Baptist and Shubeal, stroking mightily with their paddles, closed in on the doe. Baptist, on his knees, raised his paddle. As the canoe came alongside, he swung the paddle hard against the doe's head. Like something possessed, the doe turned and spurted away upriver. A quarter-hour passed before the canoe was again within reach of her. Once more Baptist swung his paddle and struck her on the head. The doe faltered, turned her course toward the bank, and continued swimming, hard-pressed by the canoe. Again Baptist struck her. Stunned, she hesitated. Then, calling up all her waning strength, she started swimming again.

"Hit her, Baptist! Git in thar and hit her!" shouted Preacher Luster.

"Preacher," said Anson, "looks like anybody who can holler that loud is strong enough to do a little bushwhacking."

The doe reached the bank. Bravely she staggered up the slope. But the frantic swimming and the blows from the paddle proved too much for her. She fell among the tangle of willows, and lay panting and spent.

Baptist jumped ashore and plunged his hunting knife into her heart. Then, leaving her dying, he and Shubeal paddled dowriver, pulled the canoe aboard, and took their places on the *Dragonfly*.

When the boat reached the doe, the menfolk tied up. "Reckon we ought to cook her and eat her on the spot?" asked Baptist when they had finished skinning the doe.

"We ought to use all the daylight we have for getting upstream," said Anson.

They carried the meat on the deck and started inching upriver again, Ketty steering, George and Baptist straining against the broadhorns, the bushwhackers pulling with their hands, their arms, their shoulders, their backs, their stout spirits. At sunset they chained the boat and climbed the sandy bank among the willows. Carefully George and Anson carried Cal ashore. While some of the voyagers kindled a fire to cook the meat, others made pallets under the leafing trees.

"I never was so tuckered out in my whole endurin' days," said Preacher Luster. "Jist a-watchin' you folks has nearly broke my back."

George walked away through the trees and underbrush and climbed a sandy hill a short distance from the boat.

"I could walk in twenty minutes, easy," he said when he came back to the fire, "all the way we've come today."

chapter 24

THREE days later the voyagers sighted what they were anxiously looking for—the mouth of a river emptying into the Ohio. The bushwhackers, Preacher Luster among them, hanging on to their willow limbs, feasted their eyes on the sight and sent up, each according to his nature, hoorays, groans of relief, and thanks to a merciful God for His kind providence.

As the menfolks studied the river, however, doubts nagged them. For this river was not what they had expected of the Cumberland, on whose banks, somewhere, was the French Lick. This was a little river, such as a body might throw rocks across. And it was as gentle as a summer night.

"This can't be it," declared Anson, his shoulders, so used to wilting, wilting once more. "It ain't nearly big enough," he declared.

"Then," asked Baptist, "what river is hit? In all the talk I heared around them fireplaces in Wataugy, I never heared tell that any river emptied into the Ohio betwixt the Tennessee and the Cumberland."

"Maybe they thought this river wasn't worth mentioning," said George.

The argument went around and around—this is the Cumberland, this ain't the Cumberland, well, if it ain't the Cumberland, what river is it, then?—until Preacher Luster complained he was plumb frayed from hanging on to bushes, and couldn't they tie up while they argued.

"Why don't we try this river a little way?" suggested George. "The current's so gentle we can row against it. Let the bushwhackers rest a spell. Then, if we decide it isn't the Cumberland—"

"Then what do we do?" Preacher Luster groaned.

"Bushwhack up the Ohio till we find the right river," Anson told him.

They bushwhacked the boat into the mouth of the river. Then, with Anson at the steering oar, and with Shubeal poling, George and Baptist braced their feet, leaned far forward, set their strokes together, dipped their big oars into the water, and pulled. Grudgingly the *Dragonfly* responded, gliding forward with every pull on the oars, but threatening to slip downriver with the current before the oars could propel her forward again.

Until the shadows lengthened, the menfolk toiled, all the while speculating as to whether the river could be the Cumberland or some other stream that plagued them with hope while it wore out their bodies.

"Let's sleep on it," suggested Anson, as the setting sun marked a path of flame on the river. "Come sunup, maybe we'll be clearer in our minds."

The sun rose the next morning in a clear sky. But nobody was clearer in his mind about the river.

276

"It's a toss-up," declared Anson, "whether we go on or whether we turn back."

"Let's toss up, then," said Baptist, picking up a small flat stone that lay at his feet. "Humph!" he said, studying a fossil imprint on the face of it. "What d'ye make of that? A fish. All right. Fish side, we go on. Plain side, we go back to the Ohio and bushwhackin'."

He tossed the stone in the air. As it fell to the ground, the voyagers crowded about it. It lay fish side up.

"Ever'body satisfied?" Baptist asked.

"Ain't hit a mighty little fish to decide so big a matter?" asked Tish. "And hit dead and gone so long ago?"

"In Salem," explained Ketty, "when the Elders couldn't decide a thing, they drew lots."

"All right, then," said Baptist, "we'll draw lots. If the lot and the fish both say this is the Cumberland, why then, this here is the Cumberland."

"But the Elders—the Elders weren't just anybody," explained Ketty. "They had special wisdom."

"Whar'd they get that?" asked Baptist.

"From God," said Ketty. "They always prayed before they drew the lot."

"Then what's wrong with Preacher Luster a-drawin' the lot for us?" Baptist asked. "Hit looks like an act of Providence we got you along, Preacher. Tish, I reckon, killed two cats when she bored them holes in your scalp. One for this here and one for hitchin' up Ketty and George."

He cut two willow twigs from nearby bushes and trimmed them.

"Here," he said, holding them in front of Preacher Luster, their lower ends hidden in the closed palm of his hand. "If you draw the long un, Preacher, we'll bushwhack up the Ohio till we find a river that ain't full of question marks. If you draw the short un, this is the Cumberland, and we're French Lick bound. Git to prayin', Preacher."

The voyagers gathered in a circle. Preacher Luster shut his eyes, clasped his hands, threw back his scalped head, and raised his face and his voice to heaven. He reminded God of the trials and tribulations through which the voyagers had already passed—the Suck and the Whirl and the Boiling Pot and the Shoals, the skulking, scalping red men, the hunger, and the dying, and the misery of heart and soul, and now the uncertainty. Wouldn't God, he begged, be with the weary pilgrims, lost on the way, like the time He went in front of them other folks, a pillar of fire by night and a pillar of cloud by day? Guide his hand, he asked of God, guide it without a waver to the right stick.

A hush followed his "Aman!" All eyes watched as he stepped forward and drew forth a stick.

"Hit's the short un," announced Baptist. "That settles hit. We're on the right track."

"The right river," Shubeal corrected him. "Seems like I never did hear a more satisfyin' prayer than that un, Preacher," he added, blowing his nose. "You shore know how to talk to God."

They went aboard the *Dragonfly* once more and toiled up the gentle river, on whose surface the west wind blew silver wavelets before them.

"Why don't we hoist a sail?" George suggested. "Get the benefit of this wind?"

"What sail?" asked Baptist.

"We could try one of Tish's blankets," suggested Shubeal.

"Too heavy," said Anson. "It'd might' nigh take a hurricane to fill one of them blankets."

Ketty went into the cabin and shut the door. She rummaged among the piled-up bundles until she found her own belongings tied in a roll. In the dim light she untied the string and spread out the garments—the gray peplumed dress, like the one she wore, and the snowy flaxen underthings she was saving for her wedding day. She picked up a petticoat and fingered the stout cloth. Salem would be scandalized, the Elders, and Brother and Sister Meyer, and Sister Oesterlein—no, not Sister Oesterlein—to see her parading a petticoat before the menfolk. But the wilderness, she remembered, kept a stern school. In it a body learned quick enough what comes first and what waits.

She rolled up the other garments, put them where she had found them, and went on deck again, carrying the petticoat.

"Will this do for a sail?" she asked, handing the petticoat to Anson.

"Why, Ketty," said Anson as he fingered the stout, closely woven cloth, "if we'd 'a' gone to a shipbuilding yard looking for a sail, we couldn't have found a better."

He spread the petticoat on the roof.

"All hit needs," said Baptist, looking on, "is to cut that thar band off hit and slit that thar seam, and thar's a good square sail."

"Tie up and we'll find a mast and crosspiece," said Anson.

"I declare," muttered Tish as she watched them go, "not a thought in their noggins 'bout where Ketty's to get herself another petticoat."

"Never mind," said Ketty. "I've got the one I'm wearing. I did tear part of it off to make a bandage for the red man. But some day I'll make myself another, when George plants me a flax patch and makes me a flax brake and a scutching block and a hetchel and a spinning wheel and a loom. I'll wash the one I'm wearing for my wedding."

The menfolk, ranging in the woods, found a tall ash sapling to serve as a mast, and a slimmer sapling for a crosspiece on which to hang the sail.

"This sail was made to order, Ketty," declared George as he ran the crosspiece through the deep hem of the petticoat. "Sewed and ready to hoist."

He tied the crosspiece to the top of the mast.

"Tish," he said, "bring the rest of that pawpaw rope."

"Tish," said Baptist, "them whole two months at Fort Patrick Henry while Anse was gone to Caroliny, I wondered what in creation you was a-plaitin' all that rope for. How did you know we'd be a-needin' hit?"

Tish fetched what remained of the rope. George cut two long lengths from the ball and tied one end of each to the top of the mast. Baptist and Anson lifted the mast into place against the forward wall of the cabin, its base held steady by Tish's loom. Shubeal tied the loose end of each length of rope to a stern corner of the roof. George cut two short lengths of rope and tied one end of each to a lower corner of the sail. Then he seated himself at a forward corner of the cabin roof and caught one of the loose ends of the rope. Baptist, seated at the other forward corner, caught the end of the other rope. Anson took the steering oar. The west wind tugged at the sail and filled it. Slowly the *Dragonfly* sailed upriver against the current.

Shubeal gazed at the top edge of the sail. "I reckon this here river'll never see a fancier sail than ourn," he said. "Look at that thar lace!"

"Cal," said Baptist, "I bet we could prop you up here and you could hold this corner. Me and Shubeal can row and move us along still faster. This wind's a-dryin' up the earth awful fast, and if we aim to plant corn, now ain't no time to dawdle."

Ketty climbed the ladder to the roof. "I'll help Cal if he needs me," she said.

Sun glinted on the water. Meadowlarks sang in the open places along the banks. A woodpecker drummed on a hackberry tree. Off in the woods, serviceberry trees blossomed in clouds of white. Spring was nearing high tide.

But not even the confidence with which the *Dragonfly* sailed upriver toward the French Lick—that Promised Land Baptist had sung about so long ago as they were leaving Fort Patrick Henry—could quite swell the feelings of the voyagers to high tide. Memories were still too clear. And too many days had yet to be marked off the calendar on Cal's splint before the long waiting was over and Anson would have the answer to the question that every day he asked. "You think, Tish, he will walk again?"

"George," said Ketty, her voice low, "I'm beginning to understand Anson. And how much I owe him for bringing me on this voyage. But I don't know how to repay him . . ."

"And live your own life at the same time?" George finished her thoughts.

She nodded her head.

George reached in his pocket and held before her three coins, a Spanish milled dollar, a pistareen, and a Portuguese Half Joe. "See?" he said. "There's more than one kind of coin with which to pay a debt. You can pay your debt to Anson through Tish."

"How?"

"By being the sister Tish deserves, and so very badly wants."

"But we'll be separated by wilderness," said Ketty. "How can I do anything for Tish?"

"To be, Ketty, is as important as to do. If you're a devoted sister to Tish in your heart, no matter how many wildernesses separate you, she'll know. You'll find ways to tell her. Give Tish affection," he added, "and in time she'll make of Anson a man who knows where he's going. Maybe, even, *why* he's going."

Ketty pondered his words. "There's one thing more," she said.

Leaving Cal to manage the sail, she climbed down the ladder and walked to the bow of the boat, where Rachel and Tish, Lettice and Preacher Luster were sunning themselves on the deck.

"Rachel," she said, "I want to ask you for a gift—a wedding gift."

Four pairs of eyes stared at her.

"When George and I are married, and leave you to go to our claim, we'd like—would you, you and Shubeal—"

"You want to take Farrer along. Ain't that what you're a-aimin' to say?" asked Tish.

"Farrer?" Preacher Luster opened his pale blue eyes

wide. "Thought all along he was your young un, way he sticks to you like a cocklebur."

"And leave Shubeal with jist one boy to help him in the fields?" asked Rachel, paying no mind to Preacher Luster.

"Menfolks can help one another, Rachel, come cabin raisin' time and seedin' time and gatherin'-in time," Tish told her, "like they always done. 'Tain't," she added, "as if Farrer's a full-grown man."

"Hit'll be a good long spell before them spindly arms of Farrer's can do a day's work," Preacher Luster told Rachel.

"Your head'll be cured one of these days, Preacher," said Tish. "When you ain't a-preachin' the gospel, you can help Shubeal in the fields."

Preacher Luster turned a feeble look on Tish.

"A body can't stand on a stump in the woods and preach all day ever' day," said Tish. "I noticed from the start how Farrer takes to Ketty," she added.

"We'll be very good to Farrer, Rachel," promised Ketty. "We'll love him like our own firstborn."

"You let Ketty take him, Rachel," put in Lettice. "Hit's whar the young un belongs, with Ketty and George."

"I don't know what my pore dead sister Patsy'd say," said Rachel. "I jist don't know what she'd say."

"She'd say hit's all right," Lettice told her.

"Course she would," added Tish. "She'd be proud."

"Well"—Rachel hesitated—"I reckon so, then."

Ketty hastened back up the ladder.

"Tish and Lettice have settled everything," she said to George. "Farrer's going to be our boy. How soon will we get to the Red River?"

"Not nearly soon enough," said George.

For days they toiled upriver, helped along by the sail when the wind was at their backs, stopping now and then to kill a deer and to pick merrybells, or to catch a mess of fish, finding once in a while a heartening sign that the far-off promised land was closer—a pair of hand millstones, grown over with lichens, set up for grinding; a patch of new-girdled trees, the big chips still smelling sweet of sap. One day they heard voices upriver.

Menfolk on the *Dragonfly* grabbed their rifles.

"Hello!" called a man from the woods. "We're white. Put down your guns!"

"Show yourselves!" called Anson.

Out of the woods came two white men. Like messengers bringing good tidings, they were welcomed aboard and pelted with questions. Who were they? Surveyors, they said, out surveying the line between Virginia and North Carolina so folks back at the Lick would know whose land they were on. How much farther to the Lick? Depended on how much hunting they had to do along the way.

"How far to the mouth of Red River?" asked George.

"Oh, no ways at all," said one man. "One day. Two days at most. The next river flowin' in from the north, that'll be the Red."

John Donelson? Why, John Donelson wasn't more than two-three days ahead of them. Folks at the Lick had about give Donelson up, but he'd get there by and by.

"Did James Robertson go overland to the Shoals," Anson asked, "to see if the folks could get to the Lick easier by land?"

"This turrible winter was so almighty cold, hit never

284

entered Robertson's head the boats'd set out," explained one surveyor. "So he never went to the Shoals. The Cumberland was froze solid. Robertson's folks, they drove their cattle right acrost it. Said a body could hear that ice a-crackin' and a-groanin' for miles."

Did all Donelson's boats get through? Not all. They'd had Indian trouble. One whole boatload killed by red men. Had river trouble, too. Lost some of the boats and a lot of their plunder. One man died of frostbite. How were things at the Lick? Busy as a beehive. Folks buzzing everywhere. Cabins going up. Land being cleared for corn patches. Only trouble was, folks didn't have much to eat. They'd heard corn was being sent overland from the Kentucky settlements. Course, the price of a bushel'd be as high as a popple tree, and nobody could pay it. Maybe they figured just the sight of corn'd help a body.

Two days later, in the early morning, the voyagers came to the mouth of the Red River. Anson ordered the *Dragonfly* tied up, and, if he didn't look glad, neither did he begrudge what he was doing. When the voyagers had landed, he took his rifle and went into the woods in search of game for a wedding feast.

With all the children watching, George slid his canoe over the gunwale of the *Dragonfly* into the Cumberland, rowed it into the mouth of the Red, and tied it up. Then he loaded into it his surveying tools, his ax, his rifle, and such household plunder as Tish could spare.

Tish called Ketty into the cabin. "Oncet," she said, "I heared you a-tellin' Lennie that a woman that's married changes them pink ribbons her dress is laced up with for blue. I don't reckon you brung any blue ribbons with you, seein' as how you didn't arrange that we'd get stuck on them Poor Valley shoals and George Soelle'd happen along and help us off. And I hain't never had no ribbons of any color. But I got this." She held out to Ketty a little ball of blue yarn. "Carded and spun hit myself and dyed hit with indigo broom. I was a-savin' hit to knit somethin' fancy. But—you take hit. Hit'll lace good as a ribbon."

Ketty, struggling against the tears that welled into her eyes and choked her voice, took the ball of yarn. What sister could do more than Tish had done for her? How much—how very much she owed to Tish! Here was a new debt, heaped on top of old debts. And she knew no way to pay them. She buried her face in her hands and let her tears flow.

"A body oughtn't to cry thataway on her weddin' day," Tish said. A minute later she walked out of the cabin and left Ketty alone.

Shortly before noon, when deer meat was broiling before red coals and merrybells were bubbling in a stew kettle, George and Ketty stood on the river bank beneath a red oak tree shyly putting out its pinkish velvety leaves. Ketty wore her clean gray dress, the bodice laced with the blue yarn. George held one of her hands in his. In her other hand Ketty held a spray of serviceberry blossoms George had brought her from the woods—blossoms as white as the purest notion ever entering a body's head, and fragile as love when it goes out smiling to meet life and death. And Preacher Luster married them.

When he had said "Aman!" Ketty walked over to Tish. She plucked one spray of the serviceberry for a keepsake and laid the bouquet in Tish's hands. "This, Pretitia, is for you," she said.

Like a stone image Tish stood, holding the bouquet. Suddenly her eyes filled with tears. Her lips quivered. Ketty, knowing part of her debt was being paid, put her arms about Tish and kissed her.

"We'll be marking off the fifty-six days too, Tish, till Cal's splints are off," she said. "We'll be remembering. And when the corn's laid by, we'll come."

When the wedding feast was over, Ketty took Farrer by one hand, George took him by the other, and the three of them walked to the river's edge, where the canoe *Walk-on-the-Water* waited. They climbed in, Ketty in the bow, George in the stern, Farrer between them, and headed the canoe upriver. As the voyagers watched from the river bank, they paddled out of sight.